MAR 2 9 2011 MV

D0340072

Other Kingdoms

ALSO BY RICHARD MATHESON

The Beardless Warriors
Button, Button (The Box)
Duel
Earthbound
The Gun Fight
Hell House
I Am Legend
The Incredible Shrinking Man
Journal of the Gun Years
The Memoirs of Wild Bill Hickok
Nightmare at 20,000 Feet
Noir
Now You See It . . .
The Path
7 Steps to Midnight
Shadow on the Sun
Somewhere in Time
A Stir of Echoes
What Dreams May Come

Other Kingdoms

Richard Matheson

3 1336 08541 4069

TOR®

A Tom Doherty Associates Book · New York

This is a work of fiction. All of the characters, organizations, and events portrayed in this novel are either products of the author's imagination or are used fictitiously.

OTHER KINGDOMS

Copyright © 2011 by RXR, Inc.

All rights reserved.

A Tor Book
Published by Tom Doherty Associates, LLC
175 Fifth Avenue
New York, NY 10010

www.tor-forge.com

Tor® is a registered trademark of Tom Doherty Associates, LLC.

Library of Congress Cataloging-in-Publication Data

Matheson, Richard, 1926–
  Other kingdoms / Richard Matheson. — 1st ed.
    p. cm.
  ISBN 978-0-7653-2768-0
  1. Americans—England—Fiction. 2. Fairies—Fiction.
3. Magic realism (Literature) 4. Great Britain—History—George V,
1910–1936—Fiction. I. Title.
PS3563.A8355O84 2011
813'.54—dc22

                                                    2010036532

First Edition: March 2011

Printed in the United States of America

0 9 8 7 6 5 4 3 2 1

*With all my love
to Ruth Ann,
the one beautiful princess
in my life*

Acknowledgments

My abundant gratitude and love to Diana Mullen for her end-less assistance in the preparation of this book. She has been a tower of patient help to me.

And to my son Richard for all his loving support and as-sistance.

What a different view of the world dawns upon us when we open ourselves to the soul-life in Nature. . . . To do this deliberately . . . is to experience a quickening that knows no end. It leads through door after door, over threshold after threshold. . . .

—**Marjorie Spock**

Introduction

To begin with, my name is not Arthur Black. My family name is White. My given name is Alexander. The publisher of my twenty-seven novels decided that Alexander White was not an appropriate name for the author of the MIDNIGHT series—choice selections such as *MIDNIGHT BLOOD THIRST* and *MIDNIGHT FLESH HUNGER.* Among twenty-four other tasteful items. Accordingly, he gave me the name of Arthur Black. I went along with it. I needed the money. At three thousand dollars a shot—later three-five—I managed to squeeze by.

Despite the questionable tenor of my thirty-year oeuvre, I hesitated to write this book. Why? Because it's true. No matter the wonders and indescribable terrors (which I have nonetheless attempted to describe, anyway), every incident is factual. You will, undoubtedly, question that statement. Rereading my manuscript, I am tempted to question it myself. Yet my account is true; I swear it. Forget the MIDNIGHT series (assuming you have had the poor judgment and loose change to actually read them). This is not (is *not*, I emphasize) fiction. Bizarre, incredible, bone-chilling though it may be (and I have tried not to overstate the more grotesque elements), there is not a doubt in my mind that they all took place in the year 1918, when I was eighteen years old.

I am eighty-two years old now—which gives you some idea of how long I waited to write this book.

Arthur Black (as you know me)
February 9, 1982

I

Chapter One

I was born in Brooklyn, New York, on February 20, 1900. The son of Captain Bradford Smith White, USN, and Martha Justine Hollenbeck. I had one sister, Veronica, younger than I, who died the same year these strange incidents began.

Captain Bradford Smith White, USN, was a swine. There, I've written it down after all these years. He was a total swine. No, he wasn't. He was a sick man. His brain was gnarled—shadow ridden, you might say.

Veronica and I (especially Veronica) suffered greatly at his hands. His discipline was iron based. The Navy spared him from being institutionalized, I believe. Where else could his near-demented behavior be permitted? Our mother, tender-hearted and emotional, died before she was forty. I should say, "escaped" before she was forty. Her wifehood was an extended sojourn in Hell.

※　※　※

I present a small example:

One day in March 1915, Mother, Veronica, and I received an invitation (an order) to attend a dinner on father's ship (a supply ship, I recall). None of us wanted to go, but there was scant alternative—Daddy's ship for dinner or, for refusing, several weeks (perhaps a month) of indeterminate punishment.

So we donned our respectful bibs and tuckers, and were driven to the Navy Yard, there to discover that Daddy's ship was anchored on the Hudson River, which, with driving winds, was being whipped into minor tsunamis.

Would any husband and father in his right mind have permitted his family to face such a perilous experience? I ask you, would any husband and father in his right mind not have canceled the entire crazy venture and taken his family to a decent restaurant? I answer for you. Of course he would. Did Captain Bradford Smith White, USN, behave as though he was in his right mind? One guess. We were scheduled to have dinner aboard the USS *White*—*Swine*, it should have been named. If we all drowned en route—what is it the ruffian set says today?—*tough titties*. Regrettable but unavoidable.

We stepped, lurchingly, aboard the Captain's gig—his private launch—and departed. The side awnings were lowered, Dad's concession to reality, no doubt. The wind, however, was blowing so tremendously that the awnings kept flapping open at their bottoms, spraying us with Hudson River. Needless to say—I say it regardless—the waves were more than choppy; they were semi-mountainous. The gig shuddered and bounced, tilted and rocked. Mother pleaded with the Captain to turn back, but he remained adamant, lips compressed and bloodless. We would be arriving at the ship "toot-sweet"—he actually used the phrase, or, should I say, butchered it? Mother held a handkerchief to her lips, no doubt to prevent losing any prior meals that day. Veronica wept. I take that back;

attempted (in vain) to keep from weeping, because the Captain loathed her tears, making it abundantly clear that he did with many a dark critical glance.

Somehow, despite my conviction that we were all destined for the bottom of the river, we finally arrived—still alive but damp—at Dad's ship, which, dear reader, was scarcely the conclusion of our mal de mer nightmare. There were, you see, no convenient steps to the deck, only an exterior metal ladder, which, because of the leaping waves, was running with water. Up this slip-and-slide companionway climbed the White clan, totally convinced that death of one variety or another—by falling and/or drowning—was imminent. (Actually falling first, then submersion in the briny deep.)

The spotlight of the gig glared on—increasing our blind ascent—what with the ship's spotlight also on—and Mother went first, assisted (poorly) by a terrified sailor. To my amazement—and disbelieving relief—she neither fell nor submerged, achieving the deck, still damp but unscathed. Veronica went next. At that moment, I summoned a hope for guardian angels. Surrendering completely her effort not to weep and offend the Captain, she labored, assisted, up the puddling ladder, slipping more than once and shedding copious tears and sobs. I followed; gripping the cold ladder railing so rigidly, my hands went numb. No assistance for me. Father either assumed I was strong enough to manage on my own—or else harbored a secret hope that I would tumble to a watery grave and relieve him of an irritating son.

Whatever the case, I climbed alone, clutching the ladder railing with both hands. Above me—I tried not to look up but did, distracted by the wild flapping of Veronica's skirt, catching sight, at one point, of her underpants—a momentary glimpse of wetness. No surprise. I did the same. I wonder if Mother had, also, suffered alike. The weakness could not possibly have come from Father's side of the genes. If he had any weakness, it was a total inability to identify with other human beings.

At one point of the death-defying climb, Veronica slipped off the ladder completely, screaming in terror, the high heel of her left shoe (why didn't she wear mountain-climbing boots?) nicking the top of my head (why didn't I wear a fireman's helmet?), which began to drip blood. A chancy moment. Was Veronica to hurtle to the river? Was I to bleed to death?

Neither. Veronica, sobbing, stricken to the core, poor sweet dear that she was, regained her footing, assisted by the sailor who was with her, and was hauled up onto the deck by another sailor, a burly, redheaded, chuckling lout of a man. I followed, and so, to my chagrin, did Captain Bradford Smith White, USN, a thin smile on his granite lips. He was amused by the entire event. I'm sure Mother could have killed him. Ditto. Twice over.

A few words about my sister. Veronica was a truly gentle soul. Once, in a driving rainstorm, she picked up a bleeding puppy that had been struck (and deserted) by a speeding motorist. She carried it home—five blocks—in her arms. By a stroke of ill fortune, the Captain was not away that afternoon and ordered her to remove "that damned, whining beast" from the premises before it bled all over the handmade Chinese rug.

Only a hysterical, weeping fit by Veronica—and an atypical

temperamental foot-stomping by Mother—not to mention a few choice verbal attacks by me, laced with impulsive profanities (for which I later paid a hefty price; I leave that to your imagination) persuaded the outgunned Captain Bradford Smith White, USN, to—stiffly—allow Veronica to take the shivering, silent—still bleeding—"mutt" to an unused corner of the cellar.

I went down there with her, disobeying the good Captain's injunction to "go to your damned room." (Another dereliction for which I paid hefty price number 2.) There I watched the dear, sweet, bless-her-noble-heart girl—still crying softly, gulping down body-racking sobs—care, with loving gentleness, for the puppy (she was, poor girl, a teenage Florence Nightingale), washing and bandaging, with household bandages, no less. ("Puppy needs them more than *him*." Revealing to me—as if I needed it—her detestation of our father.) Fixing the puppy's cuts and bruises, then kissing its damp head, crying anew when the puppy licked her hand.

Happy ending? You want a happy ending? Skip it. In the early morning, Veronica rushed down to the cellar to see if the puppy was all right. It was gone. She ran to question Captain Bradford Smith White, USN, and Mother told her Father had gone for the day to discharge his naval duties—probably beating some sailor to death with a chain. But I digress.

Crying helplessly, Veronica, suspecting the worst (most logically), hurried outside. To find the puppy on the back porch, curled up in an uncovered cardboard box. Needless to say—I am vengefully pleased to say—it was still raining, and the puppy was shaking uncontrollably and dying. Which it did that afternoon. I would like to describe the burial ceremony conducted by a heart-stricken Veronica, but the memory is too painful to relive in detail.

One more Captain Bradford Smith White, USN, anecdote. One more black star in his *Book of Swinishness*. Its conclusion? He castigated Veronica (severely) for ruining a blanket, using a box of household bandages, and digging an unauthorized grave in the backyard soil and, further, conducting an "un-Christian" funeral ceremony without express permission from the Church. Was he kidding? No.

☙ ☙ ☙

Veronica was never very healthy, much less robust. Mother drove her—a long, inconvenient drive—to a naval hospital for treatment. Captain You Know Who would not permit Veronica—or Mother or me—to be treated by a local physician. He was a naval officer (by God), and treatment for a naval officer's family must (repeat, *must*) by administered by a naval hospital or clinic. (By God.)

Veronica grew weaker by the year. By the time the influenza epidemic landed on the United States, she was primed for the blow, hardly resistant at all. Poor, dear, sweet Veronica. I still miss her and weep for her unhappiness.

The Captain had his brutal effect on me, mostly in my preteen years. A Pisces (it has been labeled "the trash bin of the zodiac"), I, too, cried a lot before I was fifteen. Then my rising sign, whatever it may be (actually, I know), must have risen strongly and declared itself, for I began to shut myself off from Captain B. S., USN. He no longer "got" to me. If I'd been the happy owner of a loaded pistol, I would probably (I do not say "undoubtedly") have shot him many times over. For

Veronica. For Mother. For myself. No guilt involved. I knew that much. More like a sense of grinning justification.

※ ※ ※

I have avoided, long enough, the transmission of my "terrible tale." (Remember, of course, that it is, as well, a wondrous tale.) You know, already, that I have been too emotionally bound up to convey it for more than sixty years. So if I forget myself and allow my Arthur Black commercial overstatement to leak through, kindly take pity on the blind-eyed, money-seeking element in my elderly author persona. I promise you that what I am about to tell you did not ooze from my diseased brain. It *happened.*

※ ※ ※

Return with me to 1918. I was eighteen years of age. World War One was in full swing. Captain Bradford Smith White, USN, wanted me, naturally, to join the Navy; he would see to it that I got a "proper" position. Does it surprise you to read that I demurred? I enlisted in the army. I cannot adequately describe the intense pleasure I experienced when I witnessed the look of utter revulsion on his face when I told him the "good news." (I was going to war for Uncle Sam!)

So there I was, an army enlistee, no doubt destined for a journey to France.

It was not the exact beginning of my nightmare-to-come, but it was certainly a good start.

Chapter Two

On April 16, 1917, the United States declared war on Germany. What a "declaration" of war means, I have no idea. I suppose it means, "We will now fire shells and bullets at you and fully expect reciprocation." Or, "You are no longer our friend, and we hereby declare that we regard you as our enemy." Or some such nonsense.

On June 7, National Draft Day, I enlisted and eventually became a nonentity in the 111th Infantry, Twenty-eighth Division, AEF (American Expeditionary Force). I have already told you about dear old Dad's reaction to my back-turning on the U.S. Navy. After I'd related the news to him, he retired to the bathroom, there to expel at least a two months' supply (probably more) of bile at the displeasing information.

Later, I discovered that conscription applied to any young patriots between the ages of twenty-one and thirty-one. So I could have waited. What, and deprive myself of the pleasure of viewing the Captain's face curl up with disgust? No, I did it at the right moment. So I could have been killed sooner. No matter. Actually, I could have been killed, anyway.

In July, I was shipped by train (I was merely a package to

be shipped from pillar to post) to Camp Kearny in California, where I cut a dashing figure in my rumpled garb and Boy Scout hat, no leggings, three weeks in overalls. For sixteen weeks, I learned the skills of open warfare, part of which was trench warfare. General Pershing did not approve of it—he preferred offense attacks.

I was defined as a "rifleman." Due to supply shortages, our rifles were made of wood; we got real ones only on the shooting range. We were also taught the "operation" of the bayonet. I came to the assumption that the victim of a bayonet insertion would require an operation, Major. We were also instructed in camouflage. As though it would be of value in the trenches.

Captain Bradford Smith White, USN, would have been gratified by the fact that there were no "Nigras" in my company; they served exclusively in a segregated regiment. They were later (Capt. would not have been gratified) completely integrated in the French army, issued French helmets, rifles, and other equipment. Those blacks who remained in the AEF performed such prestigious services as grave digging and onion peeling.

Why were we called "doughboys"? I was told that soldiers marching in Southwest deserts were covered with so much sweat-stained dust that they and their uniforms took on the appearance of adobe coating. "Adobe" was, presently, altered to "doughboy." Probably not true, but as good as any explanation. The soldiers' blouse buttons resembling lumps of fried dough? Dubious.

On December 7, 1917, the United States declared (that word again) war on Austria-Hungary. No way out of it now.

I was shipped overseas on a small British liner. We slept on a lower deck, officers getting upper berths. The food, to be charitable, was god-awful, the smell even worse, the water barely drinkable—there were moments when I almost regretted not taking the Captain's offer to assist me. Almost.

It took thirteen vomitous days to arrive in Brest. There, empty of stomach, we were transported in French "forty and eights." (Box cars—forty *hommes*, eight *chevaux*—horses.) Traveling in said style, we were taken to the British sector and, there, driven in small, old, rattly, drafty trucks to "the Front"—euphemism for Death Zone. There, bolstered by cheap French champagne—seventy cents a quart at that time, five dollars a quart when demand exceeded supply, or when the French discovered that we had more money than we knew what to do with and didn't want to get blown up with currency in our pockets. At any rate, we paid it.

Thus, in late December of 1917, I "entered" the trenches. That was how they expressed it. "Entered" the trenches. As though it was a stage direction. Which, in a way, of course, it was. The problem being that the play was a one-act tragedy-farce starring us. With no hope of a happy ending. And, conceivably, no performers remaining to take final bows. Until the next season, when an all-new cast was called upon to emote—or die.

So, physically, mentally, and militarily unprepared, I entered the trenches.

Chapter Three

How do I describe "life" in the trenches during World War I? Historical-Pastoral? To quote Polonius: Tragical-Historical-Comical? Pastoral-whatever? Who knows? I am not the Bard of Avon. I'm Arthur Black. Perhaps *Hamlet* plus *Macbeth* plus *King Lear* plus any other gory play penned by Shakespeare. Too bad he didn't write *The Inferno*. That would have come closer.

I won't go into many details here. I'll save them for later in my story. Correction: my *account*. All I'll say, at this point, is "By golly, it was fun!" Minus a few small elements. A thousand rats, for instance. We shot them, pounded them with shovels, et cetera. Not too many, mind. They *did* warn us of impending bombardment: They vanished beforehand.

Speaking of bombardments—another element I'll sketch in at this moment. Where we were had been, so I was told, woods and farm fields, which were soon artilleryized (my own word) to a forest of splintered tree trunks.

Shell shock.

Explosions, you see, create a vacuum, and when the air rushes back in, it creates a bit of a stir in the cerebro-spinal fluid,

which has a tendency to—how should I put it discreetly?—
make a fellow grumpy. No problem. Grumpy doughboys were
removed from the line and treated, with gentle loving care, at
one of the many glamorous resorts in the Gallic countryside.
That may be an exaggeration. It is. Bleeding from the ears
and shrieking with pain, they were removed from the lines and
probably never seen again.

Now I'm giving you details. Sorry. One more. Dawn attacks
by representatives of the Triple Alliance—Germany, Austria-
Hungary, Luxembourg. They were admirable opponents, since
they had been preparing for nine years before the rest of us.
Been discussing it since 1888.

No more grisly details until later. You Arthur Black fans,
hold on—you'll have your demented appetites whetted, I
assure you. For now, I will confine myself to more technical
information. (You Arthur Black fans may choose to skip the
next section. Though, if you do, I will summon forth the
Great God Horribilis to suck the marrow from your bones. So
there.)

Moving onward. Life in the trenches was not really fun,
by golly! Less than fun. Two million of us went to France.
Fewer than two hundred thousand came back. Does that give
you a hint? It took a long time for me to escape the distress of
memories.

The trench I lived in was five feet deep with three more
feet of sandbags. I am glad it was a French-British trench. I
was told that the American trenches were only four feet deep,
which could scarcely prevent one's head from being blown
off. We had a fire step, which allowed the bravest of us to fire
at the Huns or hurl hand grenades. We were good at that

because of baseball experience. Strike three, good-bye, Mr. Kraut! At least that was my Arthur Black fancy.

The Brits, knowing better, placed proper emphasis on trench life. Hand grenades, machine guns, and mortars were more their style. Plus, warnings about the Germans' proclivity toward same. Good for them. If it weren't for their cautioning words, you could be looking at a collection of blank pages. *MIDNIGHT NOTHING* by Arthur Black.

✠ ✠ ✠

Walking past Harold Lightfoot that afternoon changed my entire life.

I say "walking." It was closer to slogging, the trench floor being three inches deep in mud. Sunday afternoon. Either the Germans were observing the Sabbath or they were temporarily out of ammunition.

At any rate, I splashed brown viscous goo across the legs and lap of the young man, sitting, unnoticed by me, cleaning some kind of weapon. I say "some kind" because, following its mud immersion, there was no way to distinguish what kind of weapon it was except that it was as long as a rifle and disgustingly splattered. "*'Ey you BF, mind your step!*" were the rotund young man's opening words to me.

"I'm sorry," was my immediate response.

"Well, you *should* ruddy well be," he charged. "Cleaning this shotgun isn't all beer and skittles, y'know!"

I needed subtitles on that one. "*Shotgun?*" I ventured. In a French trench? By a British soldier?

"Yes, shotgun!" he snapped at me. "That blow you up?!"

"No, I—" I was lost in the language again. All I could do

was repeat (with an extra word), "I'm *so* sorry." I tried to smile as best I could. "I didn't realize . . ." I pointed toward the trench floor. "The mud. It's so *deep*."

My renewed apology—and, I assume, my smile—did the trick, broke the ice, assuaged the injured party, whoever he was. "Well, all right," he said. He smiled back, the sweetest smile I'd ever seen since Veronica's. It charmed me. I put out my hand. "Alex White," I told him.

He held out his hand. The smallest hand I'd ever seen since Veronica's. But strong. His grip was steel. "Harold Lightfoot," he said. I almost laughed but managed not to. Lightfoot? The strangest name I'd ever heard since—since what? Captain Bradford Smith White, USN? No, Dad was the strangest *person*. Almost. Hang on.

"So where you off to, Alex?" he inquired. "Perambulating? Catching the sights?"

I laughed, a little. He also spoke a language I understood? "No," I said. "Just stretching my legs, I guess."

"It *is* quiet," he said, as though he understood my comment.

I decided that he must have. "The Germans must be praying," I said.

He chuckled. "That could be," he agreed. "But praying for what?"

"Our destruction, of course," I answered.

He chuckled again, more volubly. "That's for flaming sure," he said. He sniffed aside and gestured toward the wooden soup-supply box he was sitting on. "Care to join me, White-head?"

"White," I corrected. "Thank you." I sat next to him on the box. "Very generous of you."

"Oh, bollocks to that," he said. Language again. (I smiled—wanly—as though I "got" that, too.) "I could use a little company. Don't know a bleedin' word of French. And the Tommies are KBB." Seeing my face, he added, "Sorry. KBB means 'King's bad bargain.' Rotten soldiers. Got it?"

"Got it," I said, smiling.

That returned smile again. Utterly charming. "Glad t'hear it," he said.

"And BF?" I inquired.

He looked embarrassed. "Out of turn," he said.

"Means . . . bloody fool?" I guessed.

"Something like that, Whitehead," he confessed.

"White."

"Oh, yes. Mistake again." That smile. It would likely bring on forgiveness for a capital crime.

Before continuing, let me (partially) explain my opening comment to my introduction of Harold Lightfoot, that he changed my entire life. He did. Mostly for the better. Not entirely, though, as you will—to quote Arthur Black—"presently discover, hopefully to your edification, more likely to your—" Well, let that go. I don't want to spook you so soon. Let's just say that, yes, most definitely, Harold Lightfoot changed my life.

⚔ ⚔ ⚔

"You're a Yank," said Harold Lightfoot. "From where?"

I told him Brooklyn, New York, and he immediately launched into a detailed lecture, informing me that, of course, it was a well-known fact that England had a city named York. The "new" world being established exclusively by English immigrants (according to Harold), they named that city *New* York (emphasis his), followed by a conversion of Jersey into *New* Jersey, Hampshire into *New* Hampshire, and the whole kaboodle into *New* England.

He was just completing his lecture when the Germans, having either completed Sabbath service or received a new shipment of ammunition, deposited a few dozen mortar shells on our trenches, several of which fell on our particular spot. Opting for caution rather than probable dismemberment, Harold Lightfoot (his rapid movement verifying his family name) and I retired posthaste to what we called "the cave" at the rear of the trench, where we slept, cooked our gourmet slumgullion—a stew made of "monkey meat" (bad beef) and any other edible lying around that wasn't deadly poison—ate our hardtack—appropriately named—slept, and dreamed our pointless dreams. There, Harold Lightfoot and I cowered while the world exploded around us.

Chapter Four

From there on, my friendship with Harold Lightfoot consisted of (1) language interpretation and (2) general military
information. A smattering of same below.

One:

a. "And pigs might fly!" meant "Yeah *sure!*" (Sarcasm.)

b. "As near as dammit" meant "That was close." (Used
   quite often with nearby landing mortar shells.)

c. "As easy as kiss your hand" meant "Easy as pie."

Two:

a. We were "relieved" of our 1903 model Springfield, .30-
   caliber rifle with a Mauser action. Replacing it was the
   P17 short magazine Lee-Einfield, .30.06 caliber rifle.
   (How Harold remembered all those details still puzzles
   me.)

b. Hand grenades are activated as follows: (1) Pull out
   the "spoon" (the metal lever). (1a) Hold *in* the spoon
   until prepared to— (2) Throw the grenade (preferably
   at the enemy), which will explode, hurtling grenade
   fragments eighty feet. (Step 1a was essential, Harold
   emphasized.)

c. Bayonets? Forget it. A rifle with a bayonet attached would be overweighted. And .45-caliber handguns? Officers and senior noncoms only. Shotguns? I asked Harold about his. He told me he had gotten it in a trade. The shotgun was called a "trench broom." (Think about it.) The Germans objected to it. It violated the "rules of war." I often wondered what kind of strange person devised those "rules," which should have been "stay home and leave well enough alone."

d. Watch out for "lingering gas" in shell holes. Arsenic poisoning was a by-product of gas-grenade explosions. Lyelike, it devoured the testicles of any man taking refuge in that particular shell hole. Not to mention facial disfigurement.

e. Stay away from brothels. Syphilis and gonorrhea (spelling? never could get them right) might detract from your soldiering skills.

f. Forget about what the army taught you about camouflage. In a trench?

※　※　※

Harold mentioned Gatford one cloudy afternoon prior to another land attack. He was feeling fatalistic, I imagine. Perhaps not. At any rate, he mentioned Gatford, starting with, "I wonder if I'll ever make it home."

"Where's home?" I asked.

"Gatford," he replied.

"Where's that?" I asked.

"Town in Northern England," Harold told me.

"Nice?"

"Gorgeous," Harold said. He'd never used that word before. No, once. In reference to the extreme size of a certain female's breasts. But this was more soulful.

"You miss it, then," I said.

"Who wouldn't? It's *gorgeous.*" Twice now. I gathered that he cared for the place.

"Gatford," I said.

"Gatford," he repeated.

"And you think it's gorgeous."

Harold frowned. "You makin' fun of me?" he said.

"No, not at all," I answered, feeling guilty that he thought so. "I'd never say Brooklyn is gorgeous."

"Awright," said Harold, with that smile. I admired that smile.

"Tell me about it," I said.

Gatford, as he told me, was in the northern part of England, thirty or so miles southeast of—no, I don't believe I'll tell you where it is. It's possible you'd think of going there, and that would be a bad idea—for a number of reasons I'll enumerate presently. For now, let it be that Gatford is thirty or so miles southeast of————. And don't think that knowing its name will make it that much easier to locate it. Not so. If Harold hadn't given me precise instructions, I'd have never found it. Nor would you. And Harold is gone.

What was so gorgeous about Gatford? Harold had little success in telling me. All he could repeat was "gorgeous." The gardens, the cottages, the shops, the—well, the entire *country-side,* all "gorgeous" (if a little "different"). That, he never explained. So I got scant specific information about Harold Lightfoot's hometown except that—as he kept reiterating—

it was "gorgeous." For a short while, before common sense intervened, I had the sensation that Gatford had somehow mesmerized him into describing it with a single word. Then I dropped the feeling. Captain Bradford Smith White, USN, had rooted out all fancy thinking from my psyche. God, how that changed! As you will discover, hopefully to your edification, more likely to your— Well, you've heard that before. Arthur Black style.

Anyway, Gatford established itself in my mind as some unidentified gorgeousness in Northern England. At the time, the lack of determinate location didn't matter to me, since I had no intention of immigrating there.

☆   ☆   ☆

And so as the weeks went by, my friendship with Harold Lightfoot increased steadily.

The afternoon he got killed, we were discussing—spacing our conversation with hasty retreats to the nearest cave enclosure to avoid the dire effects of exploding mortar shells—the subject of shotgun utilization. This time, my curiosity was not directed toward the effects of a shotgun "burst." I'd seen them, been nauseated by the sight, and understood them implicitly. Instead, my prying had to do with trading procedure. Who did Harold get the shotgun from? How did he pay for it?

Harold chose not to reveal the identity of the trench merchant. Not a good idea, he pointed out. If word got out who the merchant was, he could get arrested and, conceivably, court-martialed. It made no matter to me. I was interested only in method of payment. Money? I didn't think Tommies made that much. Unless they were higher ranked. Barter? For what?

Which was when Harold, maybe uncomfortable with the withholding of the shotgun source's name, revealed to me what he'd used to trade for the weapon in question. Gold, he said.

"Where did you get *gold?*" I asked him.

"Sent to me," he said.

"By who?" I asked. Is it whom? I never knew.

He hesitated. *Why?* I wondered. Was there crime involved?

It was as though he read my mind. "I didn't steal it, Alex," he said.

"So? . . ." It still sounded mysterious to me.

"My family sent it to me," he said after another noticeable hesitation.

"No kidding," I said, impressed. Now I was merely curious, no longer suspicious. "They own a gold mine?"

"No." He laughed now, off the hook. "They just—" Another hesitation—as though he was proceeding too far again. "—they know where to get it," he told me.

Which is where? I thought. I decided not to press him any further on that. "What, coins?" I asked.

He laughed again, not forced this time. "No, a lump," he said.

"A lump," I said.

He nodded, smiling. "How big a lump?" I asked.

"As big as your head," he said, straight faced. I knew he was joshing. I let the subject go. It was really none of my business. I would have liked to find out more, but obviously, Harold did not care to discuss it. Why, I found out later.

It was at that moment that hand grenades began to drop into our segment of the trench. The first exploded almost harmlessly, buried, beneath mud. Before the second one went off, Harold and I were hiding in our portion of the cave.

I should have known what it meant when Harold grunted and twitched beside me. It is no defense on my part to say that I was unaware, I could not conceive that either one of us might die. Not me, not Harold. We were invincible.

We were not, of course. I thought the cessation of grenade rain was the end of problems at that moment. How could I—I should say, why *didn't* I know that Harold's wound was mortal?

The first shocking realization of the truth hit me—*hard*—when I saw him lying on his back in the trench, a grimace of agony on his round face—teeth clenched and round cheeks taut, eyes almost shut, staring into nothingness. *"Harold,"* I said. (Was that soprano croak really my voice?) I crawled toward him.

Two of the Tommies tried to sit him up. "No, *don't!*" he gasped; I didn't know why right away. "I'm better this way," he said. At least I think he said, his voice was virtually unintelligible. *"Why?"* I remember asking—stupidly, as it turned out. "Because," he mumbled. Then I think he added, "My insides will fall out." Whether he really said that has been another lasting curiosity in my life. It was the truth, however. A few minutes later, when a medic tried to roll him over, Harold screamed with pain and I caught a momentary (harrowing) view of his wound. All that was visible were shattered bones and torn-up, bloody intestines. The sight of that remains with me to this day.

Harold spoke my name, and I leaned over him, a constant flow of tears blurring my sight of his face.

How he managed to smile in the midst of all that excruciating pain, I didn't know then and still don't know. He
did, though. That utterly charming smile. Even with blood
trickling on his lips.

"Listen," he managed to say, "when you go to Gatford . . ."
Go to Gatford? I'd never brought up a suggestion of that. Still,
I was not about to contradict him when he was on the pin-
point of life, the razor edge of death. "You *are* going there," he
said, as though reading my doubt.

"Okay," I said. I had no intention of doing so. But my
friend Harold was about to die. Should I add mental pain to
his bodily anguish? Never.

"When you do," he mumbled; he gestured with his head
for me to lean over closer. I did and he whispered, "Take my
gold and sell it. Buy a cottage—just avoid the middle—" He
broke off, drowning in a deep, liquid breath that filled his
mouth with blood. Choking, he began to cough. I tried to
call the medic, but his right hand grabbed my sleeve; where
he got the strength from is another mystery beyond solution.
He drew me down to his blood-soaked lips. "In the bottom of
my duffel bag," he said. The last words of his life—but those
perfectly clear.

I had to pry his dead fingers from my sleeve. I cried then,
like a baby, not only tears but sobs; I reminded me of Veronica. I labored to my feet, falling twice, and began to stagger
off from Harold's corpse. I realized then—a true measure of
the humbling impact of Harold's death—that the same grenade explosion that had killed my friend had sliced open my
right thigh and hip, soaking my trousers with blood. I didn't
faint immediately, but soon after—to regain consciousness in

a field hospital. *Well, there goes my lump of gold,* was the first unkind comment my brain emerged with.

Which brings up the initial terra incognita of the following days. I never returned to the trench to look into Harold's duffel bag. But in the bottom of my duffel bag, I found a lump of gold, the size of an orange. As I have reported, I am now eighty-two years old. For the last sixty-four years, I have come up with no solution to this enigma.

Another question (among many) plagued me. Avoid the middle of *what?*

Thus ended my relationship with Harold Lightfoot.

I thought.

I also thought that I was never in the market for (using Harold's word) "peregrinating" to Gatford, either for a visit or to settle down. Being so close to his awful death, I was sure (if I even considered going there) that it would constantly return to memory, the sight of his back ripped open—the white, shattered bones, the mincemeat lacerations of his organs, the puddling of gore over all of it. Visit Gatford with that at risk? Never.

In my life, "never" seems to have been a vanishing aspect of my lexicon. It should have always been, I now recognize, "Well, who the hell knows?" For who the hell knew what 1918 was to alter in the tide of events that controlled my existence? I am no unquestioning devotee of astrological observation, but for a long time, I have surrendered disbelief in what is referred to as fate. Fate seemed determined to transfer my bones to Gatford.

How?

Item One. The 1918 influenza death of my sister. She was, as you know, extremely dear to me. Her absence from the home scene created an unfillable gap.

Item Two. My mother's demise in the same year, creating a further gap. Did it matter that the cause was not influenza? The cause was—

Item Three. Captain Bradford Smith White, USN. Who needed influenza when a marital horrorscape with the good Captain was always available? Knowledge of this infuriating fact was, in that same year, embellished by an invitation from Rasputin, USN. Now that I had "gotten" the AEF "misjudgment" out of my system, he was willing to overlook my "foolishness" and locate me a "noncombatant" position in the navy.

That did it. Gatford suddenly looked most inviting. Hades would have as well. In April 1918, when I was discharged from the hospital and all military service "due to physical impairment," I made arrangements to locate Gatford.

No easy matter. It was not in Northern England but in Middle England—Harold's first concealment of the facts. Did he mean I should "avoid" Middle England—entirely? As I said, who the hell knew? I prevailed, following counterinstructions he had given me pursuant to locating Gatford. It took me three weeks to find it. I almost gave up at several junctures. But recollection—and mental conjuring of my three nay items—kept me going. And on a sunny, breezy morning in

May 1918, I located Harold's hometown. There, having walked some distance from the bus stop, I sat on a grass-thick hillock, partly to relieve my right hip and leg, which still ached from my shrapnel wound—but mostly to take my first look at Gatford.

II

Chapter Five

Harold was right. Gatford *was* gorgeous. I believed it from my first view. I had reached the crest of a hill that overlooked . . . what? A sight no Technicolor image could match, much less surpass. Vivid colors—lustrous green for the carpeting of grass; deep-colored green for the foliage of ancient, warp-limbed trees and distant mountain growth; pale, ethereal violet for the sky. And in the midst of this unearthly scene, an eye-catching gray stone cottage with a sloping roof of slate tiles, a covered chimney, two windows, and what appeared to be an open, welcoming doorway.

Below me was a modest stone enclosure. *For a cow?* I wondered. A sheep, a horse? Behind that was a mini-grove of what looked like pine trees and another tree (or giant bush) with a closely packed bouquet of orange yellow flowers topping it. Through the background of this idyllic landscape was a narrow, gently flowing stream. *Heaven,* I thought. A universe apart from Brooklyn, New York, a triple-cosmos distant from Captain Bradford—what was his last name again? I could not recall. Or chose not to, gazing at this vista of paradise.

Immediate questions vied for my attention. Was this the cottage Harold told me to buy? That was too coincidental to accept. In any case, was the cottage for sale or rent? If so, how would I pay for it? My army discharge pay would give me a few months' rent, I assumed. But purchase? With what, my lump of gold? Hardly. The gold was, likely, worth more than the cottage—if it was for sale, and who would sell and depart from this ambrosial spot? No, the gold had to be sold. But to who? (Whom?) No idea.

And so I stood there wondering, conjecturing, dreaming, for a long time. Until the sunlight had shifted and shadows began to creep across my property. (In my dreaming, I was already its owner.)

※   ※   ※

Realizing, then, that I was much in need of something to eat and a place to sleep for the coming night, I stood, grimacing as I always did when exerting pressure on my hip and leg, and started in the direction I took to be toward the town.

As I have often been, my geographical instinct was completely awry. Not—except for mounting hunger and hip-leg discomfort—that I minded. Why? Because (despite the fact that each ensuing view could not possibly equal the breathless delight of my first vision) I was exposed—or exposed myself, to be strictly accurate—to a virtually endless panorama of exquisite (to me, anyway) properties. A brick cottage in varied shades of pink, its face almost covered by an immense rosebush—with two three-sectioned leaded windows on its first and second floor, a gray wood door on the first, a sloping, dark brown tile roof. In front of the cottage was a panoply of spring flowers in yellow, orange, white, and different shades of red; two great cypress trees stood like sturdy guardians near the front edge of the garden, and the property had (not surprisingly) deep green lawns and dark green trees. No stream here. It wasn't necessary.

A double-chimneyed, slate-roofed cottage made of mottled, textured stone and matrix of chalk and green sand. (I was told this later, lest you think I was an architectural scholar.) The design (I was also later informed) was four-square—windows evenly placed with a central door, this one with a rose-hooded archway; hedges and trees and bright green lawns covered the rest of the property. Another eye-catching masterpiece. In the distance, the stream again. Perfect.

A red brick beauty with a heavily thatched roof that reached almost to the ground, windows on the second floor wearing hoods of straw. Enormous trees behind it, limbs in twisted growth, foliage thick. A long row of hedges in front, beyond that the sea green lawn. Far off, a slight view of the stream. Perfect again.

I might have walked (or rather, limped) the day away if I'd allowed it to happen. As it was, I saw a good many more of cottaged properties than I have described. You get the point, though. If Gatford was a beautiful woman, I had fallen hopelessly in love with her.

※　※　※

My tale grows darker here.

Access to the village—which I finally located in the middle of the afternoon (was that the "middle" Harold warned

me to avoid?) was across a bridge that had none of the charm
I'd seen repeatedly while searching for the village. Instead,
the three-arched stone bridge was dark brown in color, approaching black. Its broadwall was cracked and broken, its
dirt walk overgrown with dying weeds. Its two stream foot-
ings (the stream was wider here) looked on the verge of crum-
bling. The entire appearance of the bridge was one of—how
shall I put it? If the bridge could speak, it would surely say,
"Don't bother crossing me, you aren't wanted on the other
side," the other side conveying two visions, both ominous.
One, an expanse of yellowing lawn on which two blackbirds
sat like miniature statues; were they statues or real, unmov-
ing creatures?

They were real, for they flapped away (sluggishly) as I
started across the bridge. Did I imagine a sensation of physical discomfort as I crossed? Probably—the appearance of the
bridge was certainly enough to put one "off one's game" as
they express it in Blighty. Whatever the reason, I felt undeniably queasy. Which feeling did not abate on the other side,
because of the second vision—what might have been taken
initially for a church, but then as a construction fully as menacing as (or more so than) that of the bridge. Its belfry turret,
churchlike façade, and arched windows were all encased or
framed with lumps of limestone and flint. On each corner
of the thatch-covered roof was a tower. On top of one—it
seemed mockingly to me—stood a stone cross. On top of
the other three were the stone figures of great birds about to
take flight. I could not imagine anyone sitting in that Gothic
structure, seeking God. On the contrary, to me (or to my Arthur Black persona; even at eighteen it was present) it seemed

more like a proper setting for one of my later novels. *MID-NIGHT ABBEY.*

But enough of that. I was not looking for a forbidding first impression. I had loved everything I'd seen until now. Why let Arthur Black's bleak, impending disposition undo my pleasure? I would not. I moved on.

To more Arthur Black versus Lasting Optimism moments. Who can say which was the victor? It was a battle royal. A nasty squabble, at any rate. For the more I saw of the village, the less enchanted I became. Instead of perfection, the cottages seemed slipshod, thrown up with lack of interest, certainly lack of care. Hurriedly, in fact. As though—

No, no, I struggled. *Arthur Black be gone!* I didn't call him by name then; he didn't exist yet.

But I really had to fight the negative reaction. Oh, it was somewhat better as I reached what I suppose, laughingly, could be described as "downtown" Gatford, a gathering of cottages close together, uninviting shops, and narrow alleys. Not much better.

In one of the alleys, I ran across the Golden Coach, a pub. Not a charmer, not inviting, totally belying its romantic name. But nonetheless a pub, and I was both thirsty and hungry. So I entered same in search of respite. Did I find it? Judge for yourself as I describe what happened.

"'Ello, soljer," said the man behind the counter.

The interior was so dimly lit that I didn't see him at first, seeing only dark paneled walls, dark chairs and tables, one small window.

I then caught sight of the barkeep, a bulky bearded man with jet-black hair, wearing an oversize red-stained shirt (not with blood, I trusted), his arms and hands thick with beard-like hair. Despite his apelike appearance, he seemed amiable enough. "Y'new in Gatf'd?" he added to his initial greeting.

"Yes, sir, I am," I responded.

"Just arrived?"

"This morning," I said.

"Ah-*ha*." He nodded as though my reply had some signifi-cance, then said, "Wot's yer name, lad?"

"Alex," I told him. "Alex White."

"Alex White," he repeated. "Good name."

"Thank you," I said.

"I'm Tom," he said, extending his right hand.

"Pleased to *meet* you," I said, the word "meet" emerging like a wheeze as his bone-crushing grip crushed the bones in my hand. Felt like it, anyway.

"So wot's yer pleasure, Mr. Whitehead?" he inquired. *Jesus*, I thought, was getting my last name wrong something in the water? First Harold, now Tom. "Ale," I told him.

He rattled off the names of seven different brands. I replied that any one would do; give me the one he thought was the best. While he drew the brew (good rhyme, that), I stopped and opened my duffel bag to take out the lump of gold.

If I had placed a giant rearing spider on the counter, I doubt I would have evoked more of a recoil on his part—so excessive that he splashed out half my ale. "*Whoa!*" he cried.

I could not disguise my surprise: another good rhyme. "*What?*" I asked.

His next words were equally surprising. "*Take it off,*" he said, actually he ordered.

"What's wrong?" I asked, confused.

"I just . . ." He grimaced as though in anger—or in pain.

A chill ran up my back. He sounded alarmed, almost frightened. I removed the lump of gold from the counter and slipped it into my jacket pocket. "I don't understand," I said. "Why does it bother you?"

"*Where did you get it?*" he asked—again, demanded.

"From a friend," I said.

"A *friend?*" he sounded—at the very least—dubious.

"Yes," I answered. "A British soldier."

"Named Lightfoot?" he said, he didn't ask.

Now I was totally perplexed. "Yes, Harold Lightfoot," I told him, "in France."

"Why did he give it to you?" he wanted to know.

I was becoming irritated by then. "Because he was *dying*," I said coldly.

"Dying."

"That's right, *dying*," I said.

He stared at me, then said, "Harold Lightfoot."

"*Yes*," I said. I was really angry now. "What's the problem anyway? It's just a piece of gold."

"I *know* it's a piece of gold, Whitehead," he said. *Christ!* I thought, *it's White! White!*

"So?" I demanded now, "*What's the problem?*"

His change of manner was as confounding as his obvious dismay had been. He smiled pleasantly. "No problem," he said, "one doesn't see gold lumps that big very often, or ever." He smiled again. "Sorry I railed at you." I knew, somehow, that he was lying. There was more to this than rarely—or ever—seeing lumps of gold that big. A good deal more. But what?

Our conversation after that—if it could be called a conversation—was empty talk. Where was I from? What was it like in France? Was I planning to stay in Gatford? I soon gave up trying for an explanation of his cold behavior re the lump of gold. Taking my glass of ale and duffel bag across the room, I sat at a table by the window—through which precious little daylight penetrated. There I sat, mulling over the peculiar—aggravating—incident. I took the lump of gold from my jacket and examined it. *Mystery on mystery*, I thought. What was the answer?

Chapter Six

"Mr. White," said the quiet voice, making me start.

I looked up. Standing by the table was a shadowy figure.

"Yes?" I said.

"May I sit down?" he asked, sitting down.

Since I did not have to respond to his pointless request, I didn't. I regarded him as he sat across from me. He was elderly, I saw, lean, his expression sedate. Later, I learned that his sedate expression did not denote peace of mind so much as permanent sedation; he lived on drugs.

"My name is Brean," he told me, "Michael Brean." He extended his right hand in a "shake" position. I felt I could not ignore the gesture, so I shook it. "Hello," I said.

"And hello to you, Mr. White," he responded. Just as I was wondering how he knew my correct name, he added, "I overheard your discourse with Tom." *Discourse,* I thought. Is that what it was?

A few moments' silence. Then he said, "About your gold."

Aha! I thought. Suspicion? I suppose.

"May I look at it?" he asked. At that very second, sunset light managed through the grimy window, altering his look of sedation to one of—well, close to it, anyway—menace. "Well, I don't know," I heard myself say. Impulsively—unthinkingly.

"Oh, please," he said, "I'm Gatford's only jeweler."

Does that mean anything? I thought. Then greed o'erwhelmed suspicion, as Shakespeare might have put it. Might he actually purchase the lump of gold? I set it on the table before him. "Let me know what you think," I said.

Did I imagine it, or did he really lick his upper lip, really bare his teeth? It must have been imagined; another early sign of Arthur Black's bugbears. Or else it really happened. In light of future events, it was certainly possible. But let that go for now. I know it was true that Mr. Brean eyed the gold lump with a covetous eye. The breath he drew in was a strained breath. The rapidity with which he unpocketed his spectacles was not imagined.

He must have examined the lump of gold for several minutes (it seemed longer) before he said, in a remarkably calm voice (it occurred to me later), "Yes, it's gold, all right. Pure gold."

"Care to buy it?" I asked quickly—greedily—obviously.

He looked at me with hooded eyes. Was he suspecting me now? Was I a thief? Had I purloined the lump? Or—more likely—found it by some roadside and made no attempt to find its rightful owner? All visible on his sedate but questioning features.

Then he said, "Well, let's discuss it."

A dropping sensation in my stomach. He wasn't going to make an offer. Nothing like it.

"Sure," I said. Then I added, suspicious again, "I know it must be valuable, though."

"Oh, undoubtedly," he said, apparently agreeing.

I felt better then. Part of me cautioned, *Don't let him flummox you now.* But not so strongly as it might have been. I was, fundamentally, ready to do business.

"You got it from—where?" the old man asked.

"A soldier friend in France," I said.

"Lightfoot." He nodded.

"Yes."

"And he got it from?" he asked.

"His family," I answered.

"Ah." He nodded again. "His *family.*" I didn't like the way he said that.

⚔ ⚔ ⚔

The conversation—or, as you may suspect, the interrogation— went on for some time. He asked me if I knew that ancient Egyptians were obsessed by gold. (To vindicate his own obvious inclination?) Pharaohs were buried in gold coffins; they referred to gold as "the flesh of the gods." Although gold had little practical use (he assumed that I knew), it had always possessed a magical enchantment for mankind—and, clearly, him.

Gradually, my suspicions faded. Not about the lump of gold. I grew more curious about its source all the time. No, my suspicion regarding Mr. Brean. It became obvious that he wanted to own the gold, that he regarded it as a highly desirable piece of Nature's handiwork. Simply put, he wanted to purchase it at a price.

Which is what it sold for—a price, that being one hundred pounds. I knew it had to be worth more, and so did he.

Accordingly, in the written contract (I thought I was being very shrewd insisting on it), Mr. Sedate Face agreed that if the lump of gold brought in more return from the city emporium he did business with (never identified), he would share the profit with me. How this worked out—shall I hint horrendously?—I will reveal later. Another mystery on mystery.

So the deal was consummated, as they say in business circles. I accompanied Mr. Brean (against the advice of the barkeep Tom, who told me to throw "the damned lump" into the nearest lake and forget about it) to his office, which was really his home, an obviously expensive "cottage." There, he gave me what cash he had on hand (fifty-seven pounds and change) and filled out an I.O.U. for the remainder. He scoffed repeatedly at Tom's dire warning. "These people are obsessed with superstition," he told me. *Obsession again*, I thought. He seemed obsessed with the word.

※ ※ ※

Which was the end of that. Mr. Brean walked me to the Gateford Inn. (I learned, later, that Gateford was the original name of the community.) There, I acquired a room—I seemed to be the only customer—had a meal in their dining room, empty as I dined, retired to my room, and fell asleep quite rapidly.

To suffer with a dreadful nightmare. In which I attended a double funeral—for my mother and sister. The dreadful element was that the good (bad) Captain met me at the door, took me aside from the other guests, whoever they were (I didn't know any of them), and informed me that it had been decided by the navy "front office" that they would pay only a "limited" amount for the service, and therefore . . . well, I'd see.

I saw, all right. Both my mother and Veronica lay in stained, ragged cardboard boxes, both wearing torn, muddy nightgowns. Worse than that, neither had been made up in any way. Their hair was uncombed and tangled, and their faces looked as they had when they died—gray and twisted, some of their teeth showing behind black, retracted lips.

I screamed at my father, "How the hell could you have it done this way?! Are you insane?!"

Yes, that's right. He *smiled* at me, that damned, cold, superior smile. "What do you know?" he asked.

"This is monstrous!" I yelled. *"Monstrous!"*

Still that maddening smile. "What do you know?" he asked again. (Which is when—sweating and shaking—I woke up in a tangle of sheet and blanket.) *"God damn you!"* I muttered as though it had really happened. I lay there until the shaking had stopped. And I knew, at that moment, that I would never go home. *Home*, I thought with murderous contempt. It wasn't that anymore. I'd stay in Gatford. If I went back to Brooklyn, I'd kill him. No, I'd stay in Gatford.

I didn't know then that it was a mistake.

Chapter Seven

The cottage I rented resembled a Nazi war bunker. I was about to write *"reminded* me of a . . ."* but that would be inaccurate, of course. In no way could it have reminded me of a military structure used in World War Two. You recall that I am writing this in 1982. I can therefore state, with impunity, that it looked like a Nazi cement (or was it concrete?) bunker. Not that it matters a damn. Stay with me. I'm eighty-two years old and have a tendency to ramble. I assure you that the weird stuff will be forthcoming—word of honor, Arthur Black, Esq.

Back to the cottage I rented. It resembled—sorry, just kidding. It was located on the edge of town. Not too attractive, the grounds (limited) overgrown with weeds and huge fern-like bushes, one of which resembled (no, not a Nazi bunker) a rearing lizard. It even had a yellow eye, a bright flower.

As to the rest of it. Not much to brag about. Very little, for that matter. Massive, lumpy granite walls, one recessed window, a shapeless doorway with an ill-hanging door, one story with a plank ceiling forming what I suppose you would call a second floor; it was called a "crogloft," meant for hay. This was reached by a ladder and was dark and devoid of air. To be my bedroom, I realized, although it was not roomy enough for a bed, I'd sleep on a hay-stuffed pallet. I suppose I had little justification to complain, though, since the rent was a pound and a half per month. And at least the steeply pitched tile roof looked sound.

⚒ ⚒ ⚒

The steeply pitched, "sound" roof leaked like a sieve. I woke up in the middle of my first night in Comfort Cottage (named, I am convinced, by some sardonic humorist) near adrift on my pallet, my clothes ready for hanging on a line.

In somewhat of a testy mood, I trudged—deliberately wearing still-soggy apparel—to the farm of my landlord. He expressed deep surprise at my appearance and patiently explaining manner. Remember, I was only eighteen but did not wish to establish my stay in Gatford as a teenage curmudgeon. His reaction, accordingly—I learned a mini-lesson from that—was cordial. He would dispatch a repairman that very day to assess needed repair to my roof. He stated that the cottage had been unrented since 1916 and he hadn't seen to its maintenance since.

That afternoon, the repairman arrived. And my adventure enlarged.

"Afternoon," he said, a wiry man in his—no way of knowing, could be forties, fifties, sixties, seventies, eighties, or more; he looked fit enough to manage any age. He extended his hand and gave me a grip that made me wince and remember Harold's forceful handshake.

"I'm Joe Lightfoot," he told me.

I'm sure I gaped. "Lightfoot?" I murmured.

"That's the name," he said.

I tried to speak but couldn't. I swallowed with effort and regained my voice. At least enough of it to ask, "You're Harold's—relative?" I hesitated before finishing the question, not wanting to name a specific relation—uncle, brother, father.

His answer, as they say, floored me. "Who?" was what he said.

"Harold," I mumbled. "Harold Lightfoot." I could not believe that such a name was commonplace.

But it was. I learned, from him, that Lightfoot *was* a commonplace family name in Gatford, had been for centuries. He had never heard of Harold—although he did know a Harry Lightfoot.

He asked me who Harold Lightfoot was, and I told him. He said it was known that several young men from Gatford had enlisted in the British Army; at least one of whom he knew of had been killed. His mother still lived in Gatford. Somewhere in the woods. He'd never heard of Harold's death.

And that was that. (For the moment) the rest was tile roof and leakage. He retrieved the ladder from inside the cottage, leaned it against an outside wall, and scrambled up to the roof. There, he seemed to know exactly where the worst leak was (above my pallet) and repaired it with some dark concoction he'd brought with him in a pail; he had the "spreading tool" (I don't know what else to call it) inserted beneath his belt like a leak-combating weapon. He also pulled the soggy pallet outside and placed it in the one—miraculous, I thought—patch of sunlight available. He'd replace the pallet the following day, he said; continue his repairs. He suggested that, for the night, I sleep on my army overcoat.

Which I did. And although it rained again, I remained dry, slept well and dreamless (I was grateful for that) until early morning. Joe was already at work on the roof. I had brought, from the village, a loaf of rye bread, a thick wedge of cheddar cheese, and a bottle of milk. This I had for breakfast, offering some to Joe, who thanked me but said he'd "already supped" on oatmeal and coffee.

I thought, since there was nothing for me to do, that I'd go for a walk through the countryside. As I started away from the cottage, Joe called down, "Stay on the path, young man!" I made nothing of the remark. I should have.

The path leading into Gatford woods was distinct enough. In its early stages, it had flat granite rocks lining its direction. Only as it led into the woods did the stone lining discontinue. Still, the path was clearly visible. It seemed (only *seemed*, I told myself, not wishing to succumb to negative fancy) to become more quiet as I entered a thickening section of the woods—more trees, more bushes, more grass and flowers—a little farther in, the sound of the "babbling brook" commenced that way. As I neared the stream. Or the stream neared me. I later wondered.

Why I made my mistake so soon, ascribe to carelessness— or, more likely, to paying no attention to Joe's words. At any rate, I left the path and walked over a carpeting of leaves toward the luring sound of the stream. A minute (or less or more) in, I reached the bank of the stream and found there, as though waiting for me (avast with negative fancies! I ordered myself), a fallen birch trunk on which I perched myself and gazed at the smoothly running water. It was a hypnotic sight. The water, in a shaft of sunlight, looked silvery. I remember sighing with pleasure at the sight. At that moment, I felt inspired, not angry as I'd been before; determined not to return to Brooklyn. This was so much more peaceful and comforting. All the new elements in my life seemed attractive now, so reassuring. Even Comfort Cottage was attractive in its own lumpy, shapeless, leaking fashion—no, it wouldn't leak now with Joe repairing the roof. The rye bread was delicious, the yellow cheese, the creamy milk. All was pleasing.

In this billow of appreciation, I picked up a small rounded stone and tossed it into the stream. It plopped delightfully.

At which I thought (or thought I thought), *Don't do that, boy.*

Strange, I was sure I thought. Why did such a reaction occur to me? *Boy?* I'd never conceived of myself as *boy.* Why now? I picked up another stone.

I said no, the thought immediately came to me. I started. Then, as though in reprisal, the foliage of the trees I sat beneath began to shake. And I recalled—as though I actually heard his voice again, Joe calling down from the roof, *"Don't leave the path, young man!"*

I pushed to my feet. The pain in my hip and leg—which had not been more than mildly annoying for months—suddenly flared, and I would have fallen had I not thrown down my right hand, jarring its palm on the birch trunk. I cried out, *faire la move* (grimacing in French) in pain; it felt as though I'd come in contact with an electric shock. Rearing up, as best

I could—very clumsily, in fact—I lurched back toward the path. I thought.

I couldn't find it. *The damn thing's vanished!* I reacted. *Where the hell is it?* I knew I hadn't walked that far from it. *A minute? Less! God damn it!* I felt genuine fury at my inability to regain the path. *No, God damn it, not inability!* Something was playing a trick on me! A God damn, vicious trick! *Why?* What had I done to offend that "something"? Tossed a God damn stone into the God damn stream? I ran and ran.

Sense took hold of me at that point. A voice inside my head that said, *Calm down, you idiot. You're letting your imagination run away with you.* It was your own mind—enjoying that state of inner pleasure—that told you not to disrupt the perfection of the streamside loveliness by throwing a stone in the water. Then a follow-up thought on the same subject, a dumb reaction to the trembling foliage, an ungainly stand due to your still-healing wound causing a loss of balance and a palm-down fall on the birch trunk, the "electric shock" no more than a tender nerve's response to the impact. A moronic, lurching run followed. *Stupid,* I told myself. Totally stupid.

Looking around, I saw the path; waiting, I thought at first. No, *not waiting.* I scolded myself. Just *there.* I reached it and turned back toward my cottage. As I did, I saw another path I hadn't noticed earlier. I stopped for a few moments to look at it. The path disappeared into tree-filled thickness. *I suggest you don't enter it,* I said to myself. *No need to suggest it,* my mind replied. *You've had enough for one day.*

Which is when I saw the feather. It was white—startlingly

white—lying at the foot of the new path. I leaned over and picked it up. As I did, a wind began to blow through the overhead tree foliage. I shuddered, my skin erupting into gooseflesh. Instantly, I dropped the feather; I'd had barely a moment to look at its delicate beauty. *Enough!*—cried my mind. Reason was abolished. Primeval fear swept over me, and I ran again. Imagining—or not—that I heard a faint voice calling out to me from the woods inside the previously unnoticed path. *No!* (The thought was both enraged and terrified.) I ran until I saw my cottage in the distance. I slowed down then but walked rapidly until I reached it.

"I wondered how soon you'd be back," Joe said. He was still at work on the roof. It seemed a bit late to me, and it was. I hadn't been gone that long, had I? I let the question lapse. After what I'd been through.

"You left the path, didn't you?" Joe said, telling me.

I drew in a rasping breath. "How do you know?" I asked.

"You're flushed," said Joe. "Your cheeks are red."

Damn, I thought. I hadn't mulled it over, but I believe I didn't intend to tell him what happened. But I did, the words spilling quickly.

"Wait a second," Joe told me. He came down the ladder and stood before me. Listening patiently to my semi-breathless account, then finally smiling. "I told you not to leave the path," he said.

"You think that . . . *something* really happened?" I could only call it "something"; it was the best I could manage.

"Of course it did," he said without hesitation.

"*What?*" I think I demanded.

"It was the wee folk," he said. "You're lucky they let you escape."

I gaped at him in wordless disbelief. "The *wee folk?*" I said.

"*Yes.*" He nodded, still smiling. "The little people."

"*Little people,*" I said, completely dumbfounded now.

"Yes, little people," he repeated. "Those who live in Middle Earth."

Chapter Eight

Captain Bradford Smith White, USN, was, if anything, a stark realist. Neither Veronica nor I—nor Mother, for that matter—were encouraged (say, rather, "permitted") to express an opinion unless—and even then—we could "back it up" with factual information. This was the attitude I was raised with. Facts first, then opinions. Verify all statements. Especially those with any "outré" element. Father loved that word.

You can deduce then with what incredulous doubt I stared at Joe. Inbred from birth, my cynicism reigned supreme. Oh, I was frightened enough by what happened to me when I was sitting by the stream and when I picked up that white feather. But those were nerve-affected incidents. Explaining them as Joe did? "Persiflage." Another of *Dad's* favorite words, however badly defined. "Poppycock." Another favorite, perhaps more accurately used. Were Joe's words poppycock? I thought they probably were.

"You don't believe me," Joe said, as though reading my mind.

"Well . . . Mr. Lightfoot," I began, politely if dubiously.

"Joe," he corrected.

"Joe," I said. "You're . . . well, you're asking me—*expecting me*—" I added quickly, still in the thought (prejudice) realm of Captain You Know Who. "—to swallow [was that too harsh?]—to accept what you're telling me."

"Why?" he asked. "It's the truth."

"*Wee folk?*" I said—not too scornfully, I hope. "*Little people?*" I made a scoffing sound. "Why not *invisible* people?"

"They're that, too," Joe answered. "You didn't see them, did you?"

He sounded so gullible to me. Not *me;* the Captain's well-disciplined son. I could only speak his name. My tone was clear enough, though—disbelieving, almost pitying—that I could see him tensing, face and body.

"Very well," he said, his voice stiffened. "Believe what you will. But don't go off the path again if you value your life."

The way he said it made me shiver. And realize, in an instant, that he only meant me well.

"I'm sorry," I told him. I meant it sincerely. "I didn't mean to be insulting. It's just—" I was on the verge of telling him about the Captain's influence, then decided against it. "I'm sorry," I repeated, even more sincerely this time. He was a good soul who meant no harm. Who was I to be so insulting to him? And I *had* been insulting, no doubt of that.

The Joe I'd accepted him to be from our meeting—genial and helpful—returned with my apology. He smiled and I smiled back; I tried to make it genuine. "All right," he said.

I hoped I was not reverting to insult when I chuckled. "It *is* quite a lot for me to—buy, though." Was "buy" the wrong word? I wondered.

Not for Joe. He chuckled back at me. "Well, yes, it is," he agreed. "I should have given it to you slower."

There it is, I thought. Nothing but goodwill toward me, that was Joe.

"I was just relieved to see you back in one piece," he said. I tried to maintain my feeling of camaraderie with him, but I must confess, those three words jarred me. *In one piece?*

I said them aloud, trying to sound amused.

"Well, just a joke," he said. "Although—"

My smile and positive feeling vanished as he let the last word hang. I couldn't help it. "Although—!" I challenged.

"Nothing," he said. "I spoke out of turn."

Yes, you did, God damn it! My mind ranted. Fortunately, I didn't vocalize the complaint. Instead, I said, "You shook me up a bit."

"I'm sorry," he apologized now. "I was trying to warn you. I like you, Alex."

"I like you, too," I managed to say, trying to recoup some semblance of amiability.

Trying too hard, I said, "So tell me about—"

"The faeries?" he asked. Testing me, I'm now sure.

Oh, *Christ!* I acted most adversely. *"Fairies?"* (I spelled them wrong at the time.)

"That's one of their names," he said.

I could not prevent my tongue from forming the (yes, very insulting) words, "Tiny, little ladies in silk gowns, flitting about with their tiny, little wings?"

He tensed again but then controlled it. "Some of them," he said patiently.

Oh, persiflage, poppycock, shit! I thought. "Come on, Joe," I pleaded irritably. "Enough!"

"You don't believe me," he said.

"I don't believe that," I told him.

"Any of it?" he asked.

I had to let that sit for the moment. Finally, I answered, "I'm not sure."

"What part?" he said.

I had to think that over, too. "I believe that . . . *something* happened out there," I said. "As for the rest . . ."

"Well, let it go," he said.

"No!" I shook my head determinedly. "Let me have it. *All of it.*"

⚥ ⚥ ⚥

Their realms are Neverland, Eden, Emhain, Middle Earth, and much more. (Joe told me; I believe it was Joe, maybe not.)

They move through the woods, usually unseen.

They are solitary, rarely meeting with humans.

They can shape-shift, often appearing as animals. I had a big problem with that one.

They can make grass move and leaves rustle without a breeze. (That got to me.)

They can intrude on thoughts. (As did that.)

They can appear to you if you keep an open mind.

They are intrigued by people though avoiding them.

They are generally distrustful and disgusted by human behavior. (That I could believe even if I couldn't believe in faeries, whatever the hell they were.)

How could I detect them? (1) A sudden trembling of leaves. (2) Sudden gooseflesh. (3) Loss of time. All three made me think. Those things *occurred.*

🐈 🐈 🐈

"I know you'd rather not," Joe finished. "But if you want to see them, spend a lot of time sitting in nature, meditating." I was surprised he knew that word. "Do something creative." (*Where did that come from?* I wondered.) "Stay clean. Sing a lot."

Stay clean? I thought. In Comfort Cottage? And *sing a lot?* I had little voice. If I *did* believe these things, my singing would scare the hell out of any little people within listening range.

"All right," I said, still not giving up. "What do I look for? What do they look like?"

A mistaken query. They could look like *anything,* he told me. *Great,* I thought, *here it comes.* It depends on their whims. A tree? Why not? A firefly? Of course. A dwarf or a mermaid? Sure. A flower, a plant? Indeed. *Jesus God in downtown Pandemonium!* I raged within. How could I possibly believe what Joe was saying? He'd gone too far. His explanations were ridiculous. *Ridiculous!*

Only one thing bothered me. *"Avoid middle—,"* Harold had said before he died. I'd been trying to guess "the middle of *what."* Had he meant *Middle Earth?* Was that it, after all? If so, why?

🐈 🐈 🐈

I tried to keep myself as clean as possible. Not because of what Joe said, but simply because I'd been raised that way. Mother always looked immaculate. Veronica always smelled as sweet as a rose. The Captain? Obviously adhering to naval regulations—clean as a damn whistle. So it was my training—by example, not regulation. The average teenage boy sloppiness did not exist in me. The average teenage boy *anything* was missing, I regret to say. Which is why I was so cool and critical about everything. But especially about Joe's admonitions.

I did not sit around a lot, meditating. God knows I did not sing a lot. If Joe's words had rung true to me, I might have vocalized night and day on the premise that my froglike tenor would keep the wee folk far away from me in droves. What I did—and I swear it was not for fairy-precaution—was consider the creative suggestion. I had for some years—since I was fifteen, as I remember—harbored the secret notion of trying to become a novelist. When I was twelve, maybe thirteen, I launched from said harbor a vessel of poetry authorship. A vessel completely unseaworthy, I hasten to add. No verser, living or dead, had a thing to worry about. A sample? *When Columbus sailed, he said, "At least—I'll find a short route to the East."* Beyond that, it got really atrocious. Not to me, of course. I was a cocky twelve-year-old. Nothing got through to me. Especially when Mother praised my attempt. Veronica, more honestly, wasn't sure that I was treading on the heels of Robert Browning—or Jim Browning, who, at the time, murdered his mother and wife, and prior to his hanging, wrote a poem that began, *Mother, mother, why did I smother—you and Geraldine?—That was mean.* In brief, I gave up poetry (I never showed anything to Father) and retreated to reading Gothic novels. Odd, I never before attributed Arthur Black's subject matter to that.

So there I was, eighteen, with a hidden agenda in mind. An agenda for which Joe had inadvertently stirred the coals, igniting flames. I say "inadvertently" because I know that Joe was unaware of my undeclared ambition; he meant only to advise—and warn—me of the mystical world "out there."

So—fool that I was—I commenced to write a novel. I blush to reveal the title: *Terror in the Trenches*. That was the best one. I refuse to tell you what the others were. It had to do with a young man—odd choice?—who, assigned to the Gallic trenches, proceeded—personally—to decimate the entire Boche Army. I *did* manage to include some of the more graphic truths about trench life—rats devouring dead bodies, for instance—but fundamentally, the story was one of unabated heroics and finally, graphic demise on the bayonet of a chortling German. The book was fifty-seven pages long, and that was too much. Review? One word. Godawful. I planned— eighteen and brainless—to submit it to the primo publishers in New York—I'd show the damned Captain!—or, if necessary (most unlikely, I truly believed) London. Fortunately—thank God for the literary world—I never sent it anywhere. Rats (I'm not sure, now, it *was* rats) chewed up the manuscript. Breaking my author's heart, but now, at eighty-two, a source of profound gratitude. I will say that the wheels *did* begin to turn, later installed on the Arthur Black hearse. The rats— *was* it rats?—did me a favor.

※　※　※

The next peculiar incident took place a week or so after I had surrendered the notion of becoming a world-renowned

novelist. My life, in those days, seemed peculiar in every respect. Certainly, this one was.

It was late night. I was asleep on my pallet—by then I was
accustomed to it. *Suddenly*, (to quote Arthur Black at his worst)
there was a pounding on the door below. I woke up with a jar.
Who in the hell? I thought. Did fairies knock? Didn't they just
come gliding through the walls? In a state of groggy amusement, I struggled to my feet, managed to descend the ladder
without falling to my death, and approached the door,
which—did I tell you?—Joe had rehung. All this time, the
pounding persisted, accompanied by a faint voice command-
ing me to "*Open up!*"

I did as commanded, to see a sight I treasure to this moment: A sweaty, wild-eyed Mr. Sedate Face, whose face, far
from sedate, was twisted with fury, teeth bared. "Mr. *Brean*," I
muttered.

"*Don't 'Mr. Brean' me!*" he shouted.

"What?" I asked, unable to think of anything else.

"*Don't 'what' me, you thieving bastard!*" screamed Mr.
Brean. That's right. Screamed. So loud, I jerked back as if
from a blow to my solar plexus. (What my father called the
stomach.)

"What the hell?" I asked. Not him, probably the universe.

"*As if you didn't know!*" he yelled.

Now *I* was getting peeved. Though "peeved" would hardly
be the word for Mr. Brean's apoplectic rage. "Know *what?!*" I
cried, demanded.

"*I suppose you just don't know,*" he bellowed.

"*No, I don't!*" I bellowed back. "*Why the fuck don't you tell me?!*" I was not inclined to use bad language, but his behavior maddened me.

A heavy stillness fell on Comfort Cottage. *I could use a fucking fairy!* I thought, thoroughly incensed.

"I'm not sure you *do* know." Mr. Brean's voice was close to human now. Then his features distended again. "No, you *do* know," he recanted. "You're trying to trick me again!"

"*And how am I doing that?*" I asked, *very* angry now.

He stood motionless and sweaty for a number of seconds. Then he bared his teeth again, reached into his overcoat pocket—*must be cold outside,* my mind commented irrelevantly—and drew out a small cloth packet, tied with a knot. It took him near to a minute to unknot it and part two edges of the cloth. I looked down at the contents.

Then looked up at him. *He's gone insane,* was my conclusion.

"*Well?*" he said in a cracking voice.

"Well *what?*" I retorted, "*What?!*"

"I suppose you don't know what it is," he said; his voice was cracking again. I was beginning to feel sorry for him, he was so pitifully overwrought.

"Damn you!" he erupted then. "Don't tell me you don't know what it is!"

I no longer felt sorry for him now. I felt abrupt concern for my existence. "I don't know what it is," I told him, as controlled as I could.

"*I want my money back,*" he said in a trembling, threatening mutter.

"Your *money?*" I had no idea where that remark came from.

Then it hit me. "Are you telling me that *this* is—?" I began.

"*Yes!*" He didn't let me finish. "It *is!*" He overturned the cloth.

Drizzling to the floor was a cloud of gray dust.

I stared down, not seeing much, because there was no light in the room. I could not comprehend what I'd seen. Was Brean serious? "You're telling me—?" I started.

Again, he interrupted. Rabidly. "I'm *telling* you! You sold me *gold!* All that's left is *dust!*"

"I don't understand," I told him weakly.

It seemed as though he shuddered in the darkness. "I think you do," he said, "and I want my money back or I'll see you behind bars for the rest of your life."

I could only stare at him.

Dust? Gray dust?

There was no further conversation. (Had it been a conversation?) Without another word, Mr. Brean whirled and vanished into the night. Leaving one pathetic would-be novelist in a state of absolute confusion. In the morning light—not that I slept a wink from Mr. Brean's departure to the arrival of the sun—I examined the layer of dust on the downstairs floor. "Examined" is an overstatement. My inspection was tentative, gingerly. For the life of me, I was unable to fathom how a lump of gold (hadn't Brean—a *jeweler*—identified it as such?) could be reduced to a pile of dust. Gray, at that.

My confusion was not undone by a visit from Joe that a.m. Mr. Sedate Face was dead, the victim—apparently—of a heart attack. I was spared the prospect of a long gaol sentence. (That's how they spelled "jail" in those days.) An uncharitable reaction, I concede. But Brean was really nasty to me. Furthermore, I was innocent of any wrongdoing, fully as thunderstruck by the incredible transformation of gold to dust.

So I swept up what was left of my lump of gold and fed it to the lizard fern.

Chapter Nine

Next peculiar incident; onward with my wacko tale. Wacko but, I assert once more, completely true. I had decided, by then, that Mr. Sedate Face had either gone completely mad, or was already mad. Would I have noticed in the pub that afternoon if I hadn't been intent on selling him the gold? More plausibly, of course, he had devised a plan to get his money back and keep the gold as well. Precious metal into powdery dirt? Nonsense. Brothers Grimm stuff.

Where was I? Yes. I decided to take a walk. No, not sidestepping into the woods—although, by then, I had deduced a "rational" explanation for that incident as well. But better safe than superstitious. As per Joe's advice, I'd remain on the path. Okay. Well done. A walk on the path, no more.

That was my plan, at any rate. Which I observed in the beginning, not even pausing by the other path to see if the white feather was still there. Idiotic if I had, my mind declared without hesitation. Why would a feather remain in place? A *feather*, for God's sake? Subject to any random breeze? That was—

Before my mind could present the word "ridiculous," I heard a voice calling to me. "Young man!"

I confess to several moments of good sense reversal, several moments of pure primitive dread. *It's a fay*-erie! cried my momentarily disabled brain, awareness clobbered. That's how I thought it was pronounced.

To my credit, I fought it off. *Don't be* absurd, I ordered myself; it was not a damn fay-*erie!* And, with that, I abruptly recalled what I imagined (or thought I imagined) my last day on the path; again, a voice calling me, the words indistinct.

I forced myself to turn. Another moment of temporary trepidation (good phrase, that). Then, once more, bathing my mind with satisfaction, rationality returned. (Not so good a phrase.) It was a woman standing near the foot of the path. A tall red-haired woman dressed in most un-fay-*erie*like clothes, such as might be worn by any female resident of Gatford. Not a tiny, winged, transparently gowned fay-*erie*. Well, Joe *did* say they could shape-shift, my maddening brain insisted on recalling. *Oh, shut up!* I told my maddening brain.

"Come over here," the woman said, her voice and smile inviting.

Oh, damn, I thought. *Isn't that the sort of invitation one would expect from the "wee folk"?* I had to fight that off as well. I didn't move, however. I remained fixed in place.

Amazing how a few well-spoken words can totally undo the superstitious angst of any given moment. That was the exact result of what the woman said to me. "Don't worry, I'm not a faerie. I'm a real person."

Something was released in me, like an unblocked flow of water, fresh, invigorating water. Returning the woman's kind

smile, I approached her. "There, that's better," she said, sounding relieved.

"I'm sorry, I apologize," I felt obligated to say.

"Not at all," she said, excusing my dubious behavior. "I
don't know how long you've been in Gatford, but if any time at
all, you've undoubtedly been exposed to local old wives' tales."

Or old roofers' tales, I thought. I returned her renewed
smile—it was a lovely smile (on her part, I mean, I don't know
about mine) and said, "I have. A lot of them."

"Too bad," she responded. "They *can* be overdone."

Indeed, I thought. "They can," I agreed.

Another smile—completely lovely—as she extended her
hand for shaking. "I'm Magda Variel," she said.

"Alex White," I told her. Her grip was comforting, her palm
warm against mine.

"I'm very pleased to meet you, Alex," she said.

I nodded. "Thank you," I repeated. *Why did you say that?* I
questioned myself. *Not very gracious.* Immediately, I added,
"I'm glad to meet you." *Glad?* I questioned my brain again. *You
mean "pleased," don't you?* Well, what the hell; I let it go. How
old was she, anyway?

"Would you like to see where I live?" she asked.

Again, my provoking brain came up with several vexing
ideas: The witch inviting Hansel and Gretel into her ginger-
bread house. A shape-shifted faerie luring me to Middle Earth.
A crazy woman asking me to visit in order to dissect me? *In
one piece,* Joe had said.

God, it was hard to fight that off! Near impossible. But I
did it, more power to my teenage strength of character—or
denseness. I wouldn't do it now. I *was* uncomfortable.

Through all this, Magda, the lovely (she *was* lovely, I realized), tall, red-haired woman, waited patiently, saying finally, "Still uneasy?"

"No," I lied.

"Come, let me take your arm, then," she said, taking my arm. I positively shuddered. "Lord, you *are* afraid," she said. "I'm sorry. Would you rather not do this?"

"No, I'm sorry," I lied again, "I *have* been exposed to too many old wives' tales." ("To too"—Arthur Black would have shuddered at that ugly combination; but I was only eighteen, what did I know?)

"Yes, you have," Magda Variel responded. "Far too many."

"Onward, then," I said bravely (at least sensibly).

We walked together into the woods. If A. Black had written that sentence in one of his shock boilers, it would have presaged ghastly events. As it was, our entrance into the silent woods presaged nothing. I thought.

"So tell me," I said, "these old wives' tales. Are they all nonsense?"

"Not all," she answered casually. Evoking another involuntary shudder by her very vulnerable (not too bad a phrase, not too outstanding either) teenage companion. "You're still afraid," she said.

"I guess I am, a little," I admitted. "This has been a most *unusual* month. I'm trying to deal with it. But it hasn't been easy."

"I understand," she said. "My first year here was very trying—all the stories people told me—that they swore were true."

"But you said they aren't all nonsense," I reminded her.

"That's right, they're not," she told me, "but nothing to be alarmed about."

"Fay-*eries*," I said, "the way I say it. *Faeries*, then. *Do they really exist?*"

"Oh, they exist," said Magda, not realizing that she chilled my bones with the reply. "Not so plentiful as many Gatfordites would have you believe. But some of them are real hooligans mostly. Fooligans."

"*Fooligans?*" Despite my uneasiness, the word amused me.

"Hooligans who like to fool you," Magda said. "I made up the word."

That evoked a snicker from me. "How do they fool you?" I asked.

"Oh, many ways," she answered. "Taking things away from you. Bringing unexpected things to you. Making trees or bushes shake. Oh, now you're frightened again," she said, reacting to my reflex shudder.

I told her about my experience by the stream that past afternoon. She agreed with me that I had probably misinterpreted the abruptly rustling foliage. On the other hand, it might have been a faerie-induced stir. "If so," she said, "you're fortunate they teased you no more than that. They could have done you harm. They probably liked you, though, for some reason."

"Well, I'm very likable," I said, the thin waver of my voice revealing my actual emotion—minor terror at her words.

She smiled, knowing what I felt. "You *are* likeable," she said, tightening her grip on my arm. I felt a warmth of gratitude for her sympathy. Like a mother, I thought. A beautiful mother.

"Just remember one thing," she went on, "they cannot—*will* not harm you if you treat them with respect. If you want, I'll give you several means of protecting yourself against possible intrusions."

"Thank you," I murmured. I was not exactly grateful to her. I would have preferred her to agree with my original estimation, that the entire subject was—sorry—bullshit. Or, as a later spokesman called it, *bull pucky*. But it wasn't; if I were to accept Magda Variel's words—and there was little reason at the moment not to do so.

In that moment, we emerged from the silent, uneasy-making woods.

"There's my house," said Magda.

I confess to being startled by the sight. Not so much by the house itself as by the sweeping expanse of lawn leading up to it. I had never seen such a wide, open lawn extending to a cottage. Not that Magda's house struck me as being a cottage. It was, in fact, more like a Victorian mansion. Backed up against a tree-thick woods that stretched to the stream (I later learned). The house—I can't, in conscience, describe it as a cottage—was a mix of brick and timbering, the upper floor supported by iron brackets, the roof made of red tiles, the two brick chimneys tall and ornamental. The front door entrance was obscured by an archway on each side of which were hedges shaped like baby carriages—or "prams," as I suppose they were called back then. A dirt path led to the archway, a narrow stream of water flowing across it.

"Very nice," I said. "Did you have it built?"

"No, no." She smiled in amusement. "It was built in 1857. I purchased it six years ago. That is, my husband purchased it." She paused. "He died some years ago." Was that addendum meant for me? Probably not; I let the idea go.

❆ ❆ ❆

There were dried leaves fastened to the door. "What are they for?" I asked. Naïvely.

"For protection," she said, opening the door.

I knew immediately—without seeing more than the hint of a smile on her lips—that she was teasing me. "From the fay-*eries?*" I said, trying (and failing) to sound serious.

She laughed softly. "I thought you'd believe that," she said.

"Not quite," I said. "Almost."

"Come in, my dear," she told me in a deliberately creaking voice.

Plump and ready for the oven, I thought of replying. I didn't say it, though. The joke had gone beyond the pale. For me, anyway.

It had for Magda, too. "Oh, do come in, Mr. White," she said in her normal (warm) voice. "I may end up kissing you discreetly, but I won't be roasting you for dinner."

"Glad to hear it," I replied. I wasn't really mollified. (Is that the word?) Kissing me discreetly? Was that appropriate flirtation? She was old enough to be my mother. And Mother would never flirt with a teenage boy. Would she?

At any rate, regardless of my frame of mind, I entered the cottage of Magda Variel.

My first reaction was as follows: *Jesus, it's so* gloomy! It was. So much so that, initially, I could not see anything. Then my vision focused and I saw—not clearly, but barely— shelves of books, crammed with dark leather volumes, several chairs, a sofa (I'm not sure what they called it back then), and a large round table.

What I did see—very visibly—was a painting, above the mantel of an oversize fireplace. I saw it so visibly because on each side of it was a glass-encased candle, burning and illuminating the painting.

It was the portrait of a young man—about my age, I guessed, delicately handsome—I can't think of a better way to describe him. It was as though some fastidious Renaissance artist had chosen to describe an angel on Earth—innocent and beautiful. That was Edward. He was attired in (how perfect) Edwardian finery, looking very elegant, indeed. And smiling. A most pleasant smile that—predictably, I later realized—reminded me of Magda's pleasing smile. I knew, in an instant, who it was—her son who had (as Joe had told me) died in the war.

"You're looking at Edward," Magda said, breaking into what had been a noticeable silence on my part.

"Yes," I said. "He died in the war, didn't he?" I winced at the temerity of my remark. What if I was wrong?

But I wasn't. Magda's questioning took on an edge. "How did you know that?" she asked. Close to demanded.

"Well"—I felt compelled to lie; I don't know exactly why— "I was in France. And the portrait hanging there is like a . . ." The word eluded me.

"A *shrine?*" said Magda. I felt that I had truly offended her. There was only one solution: the truth. I told her that the man who repaired the roof tiles on my cottage said that there "was a woman" who had lost her son in France.

I must have said it convincingly, a gift (or a failing) I have when speaking the truth; Magda relaxed quickly—I could see as she lit an oil lamp on the table. "I'm sorry," she said, as though she had done something objectionable. "It's still a painful subject to me. Edward *did* die in France, in 1917. He was about your age. It came close to breaking my heart."

"I'm sorry, too," I said. "I spoke too abruptly. It was rude of me."

Her hand grasped mine. She *was* strong, I could tell. Before, her grip had been restrained. Now, it almost hurt.

I must have winced—or made a sound of distress—because, immediately, the grip of her hand relaxed. "I'm sorry, did I hurt you?" she asked in concern.

"You're strong," was my deflected answer.

"I was disturbed," she told me. "It won't happen again."

It won't, because I doubt I'll be coming here again, came the immediate thought. Too many discomforting distractions (not a bad combination). She was beautiful, all right. That was one of the distractions. Kiss me discreetly? Would discreetly be enough for a healthy (healing wound aside) eighteen-year-old male whose physical experience in France had amounted to nothing other than occasional solo gratifications?

At any rate, with that (unaware of my decision), Magda gave me a conducted tour of the house. I have already indicated what I saw of the main room. In improved lamplight, I saw them all more clearly, notably the floor-to-ceiling bookshelves packed with bound leather volumes; black leather, as I said. Window-covering drapes in scarlet linen, a pair of red-upholstered antique chairs on each side of the fireplace, the sofa (or whatever it was called back then), odd-looking objects (d'art?) across the fireplace mantel. The rest was nothing special to my eye, except, of course, the portrait of Magda's son, hanging over the fireplace mantel, framed, I could now see, in what appeared to be decorated gold. I had an instant impression (precursor to my Arthur Black conceits) perhaps that Mr. Brean's vanishing gold had, somehow, been magically whisked to Magda's house and converted to a picture frame. I dismissed the notion, irritated at myself. Foolish idea.

The tour was conducted on; nothing special. A voluminous kitchen; I'll describe later. A library. I got the impression that it was, for some reason, off-limits to visitors. A bathroom with the obvious equipment: a commode plus a sink and bathtub, the tub sitting on what appeared to be four pterodactyl claws. The room smelled very sweet; again, for obvious reasons, I assumed. A far cry from the trench smell. You could slice that. A study—more floor-to-ceiling shelves of books, black leather bound, of course, a most roomy desk and antique chair.

"Nothing special," I said? Until we reached the bedroom, Magda's bedroom. Dimly lit; she made no move to light the candles—two of them, one hanging overhead, one on a table to the left of the bed.

The bed. That was special, reader. In the faintness of visibility, it looked, to me, like the brothel of a queen—or empress. Though I doubt queens or empresses converted their sleeping quarters into brothels. (I'm not positive.)

How to describe the bed? First of all, it had a canopy of silk plush. Next, the bedcover looked to be the same material, its surface embroidered with arcane symbols I could not make out and was hesitant to ask about. Finally—I mention it last—

the bed surface was immense enough to sleep at least three hefty figures, assuming that they ever slept on such evocative acreage.

Let me add that the carpeting in the room—what I could see of it—was nineteenth-century gros point, Magda later told me; I was hardly an expert on English carpeting. In a corner of the room was a red-upholstered chair, next to it, a six-sided table. On which sat a crystal bottle half filled with some dark red liquid, several crystal glasses, and a small pile of books, bound in you know what by now. I must admit that I did not catch sight of all these things at the time. I saw them later.

"So?" said Magda.

"Yes?" was all I could think of in response.

"You like my house?" she asked.

"Yes, I do." I managed to pretend.

"And this room?" Her tone was definitely suggestive, conclusion jumped.

I swallowed. Tried, anyway. My throat was bone dry. "Exotic," I answered. It came out as a throat-clogged mutter.

"What did you say?" she asked.

I cleared my throat, trying—hard—to think of a better word. I couldn't. "Exotic," I repeated. This time audibly.

"Good," she said. "That was Edward's notion."

Edward's notion? I didn't—or didn't care to—understand.

"He was very artistic." Magda explained, "He decorated much of the house. Come." She moved to the bed and sat down, patting the mattress.

Brainless hesitation on my part. I *was* a standard-model teenage male. I should have jumped (or something) at the

chance. I didn't, though. Did my subconscious (or supercon-
scious) pick up something that alerted me? No idea. But I
didn't move. I couldn't. For some reason, I didn't dare. I know
it sounds dumb, but it's true.

"Oh, Alex, *please*," she said. She sounded genuinely hurt.
"You're *still* afraid? I'm old enough to be your mother. I'm not
about to ravish you. *Or* hurt you in any way. I just want you
to see how comfortable the mattress is."

"I'm sorry," I said. Not sure what I was sorry for.

"Well, never mind." She stood. "You'll want to go."

Oh, God, I thought. *I've really offended her this time.* "I'm
sorry," I said again. Uncertain, it came out flat as a board.

She took my right arm with a gentle grasp. (A workable
combination? No.) "I'll take you to the door."

By then, I felt really stricken with guilt. She'd been so
cordial. Who was I—?

The thought evaporated with her next words; they made
me feel even worse. "I was going to offer you some tea and
cakes," she said, "but I know you'd prefer to leave."

Words tangled in my brain. *My apology, Magda, I've been
thoughtless. Please forgive me.* Even worst of all—*I'd love to
try the mattress!* Thank God the jumble of abject apologies
stifled that one. I still felt lousy but remained mute (blessedly
so) as she led me to the front door and released my arm. "It's
been lovely meeting you," she said. It sounded less. "Come
again when you feel safe about it," she finished. She kissed me
lightly on the cheek. "There—was that discreet enough?" she
said. With that, she closed the door on me.

I trudged back to the main path, immersed in gloom. What
had I done? I kept remonstrating myself. *Stupid idiot. Just*

because she patted the damn bed? I knew it was more than that but ignored the more. I knew something had prevented me from staying but had no idea what that something was. I felt uncomfortable moving through the silent woods. *Go ahead,* I thought irrationally. *Rustle all you want, who cares?*

Reaching the main path, I turned toward my cottage. If my way had been blocked by a quartet of leering wee folk, I'd have angrily booted them in the ass and told them to get lost. Fortunately, nothing blocked my way and I walked, unimpeded, to my cottage.

Chapter Ten

As if my anger and depression were not sufficient, I received an additional jolt upon arriving at the cottage. I was about to open the door when, startling me, it opened by itself, or seemed to. I jumped back with a hollow cry as a figure appeared from the shadowy interior. Before I could stop my heart from pounding, I saw that it was Joe. *"Whoa!"* he said, surprised to see me. He smiled involuntarily. "It's you," he went on. "You startled me."

I blew out heated breath. *What the hell are you doing here?* my brain demanded. *The roof is done. Looking for more work?*

"I brought you some food," Joe said. "Thought you might be out. Got you bread and cheese, a bottle of milk, some ham."

It didn't help my frame of mind to add a measure of guilt to it. The man had done something nice for me, and here I was mentally lambasting him. "Thank you," I muttered. It came out totally unconvincing.

He changed the subject after saying, "Welcome," and gestured toward the path. "Been out walking again?" he said. I sensed that he was merely being polite.

I nodded; barely. "Yes."

"Didn't go into the woods, I hope," he said.

"No." I shook my head, barely. Then—perversity be my name—I decided, on impulse, to tell him all. "I *did* go into the woods. To Magda Variel's house." *There*, I thought. *Make of that what you will.*

What he made of it came as a total shock. "Magda Variel's house," he said.

"*Yes*," I said, mentally daring him to criticize.

"Not a good idea," he said.

I couldn't hold in my resentment. "*Why?*" I believe I ordered.

"Because she's a witch," said Joe.

For several moments—an eternity, it seemed—I stood frozen, staring at him. Then blank reaction deepened to fierce rancor, to fury, to absolute wrath. "Oh, that's too much," I told him in a clotted voice.

"You don't believe me," he observed. It wasn't difficult to see.

"I do *not*," I responded, using, without realizing, one of Father's oft-repeated phrases.

"You should," he said.

Ire mounted in me. First, little people in the woods. Now, a witch? What next? A dragon in downtown Gatford?

"Young man, listen to me," Joe began.

"*No*," I interrupted vehemently. "*You listen to me.*" (Another of the Captain's incessant phrases.) "I just spent close to an hour in Magda Variel's house, and a nicer woman I haven't known since my mother. And she's old enough to *be* my mother! She showed me her house and was charming—

absolutely *charming*. She was going to give me tea and cakes, then I said something that hurt her feelings and she sent me home—" I grimaced. "—to my cottage, I mean."

"Young man," Joe started again.

I broke in on him once more. "You might be interested to know that she said the same thing about *faeries* that you did. I'm still not sure about them. But *listen*, Joe. She's a lovely woman with a lovely personality. Don't tell me she's a witch! That's ridiculous!"

"All right," he said in a quiet voice. "Find out for yourself."

His confidence unhinged me, I admit. "Why do you say this?" I asked.

"Listen," he said. That it sounded neither angry nor flustered bothered me. I admit again. "She wasn't always this way. She and her husband and their little boy were much liked in the village. They had people to their house for dinner. They visited other people. She was a substitute teacher at the children's school."

He paused. The silence wracked me. It was *so silent*.

"Then her husband died. An accident. The horse he was riding fell, its neck was broken. Her husband lingered for a week. Then he died."

Another silence, heavy and discomforting.

"She lived in seclusion [God, he *did* know words] with her son. Then, on his eighteenth birthday, he enlisted in the army. His mother tried to talk him out of it, but he was adamant. [Another unexpected word from a simple farmer.] He left Gatford, went to France. In a month, he was killed. Mrs. Variel fell apart. She stayed alone in her house. And became a witch."

Now he lost me again. "*Became* a witch?" I contested, "How does one *become* a witch?"

"Maybe she'll tell you," he said. Now his voice was edged with resistance. I'd injured Magda's feelings. Now I'd injured Joe's. Perfect day. I watched him walk away.

I still didn't believe it, though. In memory, I retraced each step of my afternoon with Magda from the moment I met her at the path to her house until the moment she'd put me out. Had she said or done anything . . . well, *witchlike*? I simply could not visualize her wearing a coned black hat, riding a broom, and conversing with an indigo cat. She was *lovely*. I was an idiot not to sit on that mattress beside her. Who knows what fervid moments might have ensued? But a *witch*? It was—to quote myself—ridiculous!

※　※　※

The resentful disbelief of later afternoon led to the bizarre event of the evening. Still feeling cranky and charged with righteous anger, I walked to the Golden Coach, taking into no consideration the fact that I would have to find my way home (*Home*—ha!) in the dark. I wanted—needed—a drink to wash away my guilt and aggravation. I was *mad*. And madness in a young man—this one, anyway—can be prodigious. And detrimental.

So there was I, in company with barkeep Tom and several other Gatford worthies, when the trio of louts came in. I call them louts, but that is probably unjust. I would have estimated any three young men as louts because of my stretched-thin temperament that evening. It was, therefore, with the best of intention, I'm sure, that one of the three approached and said (politely—I'm also sure), "We hear that you participated in The Great War."

I confess that laid me low. "Great—War?" I murmured. Instantly prepared to hurl him through the window. At least.

"My chums and I are planning to enlist," he told me.

"You are" was all I could say. *Great War?* Jesus!

"We want to help put the filthy Boche in their place."

Yes, I thought. *The filthy Boche. In their place.* I considered tossing my ale in his smiling face. Punching out his sparkling lights (eyes).

But he was so polite, so GD polite. Also, he was twice my size, a bulky, overmuscled farm lad. And he did say "help" put the filthy Boche in their place. At least he wasn't planning to put them in their place all by himself. Or with his two companions. Generous of them.

So I chose to speak with them. Not kindly or sincerely. Speak, however, when the young "lad" (as Joe would, doubtless, have called him) asked for information re their intention to "confront the bloody Triple Alliance." Not quite so colorful as "filthy Boche," but a deal more accurate.

"Let's see, now," I began. "First of all, it seems to rain a lot. I've heard it said that the explosions do something to the clouds. Maybe, maybe not. It *does* rain a lot, though. The trenches get muddy. Not so nice. The food is pretty awful, too. Slumgullion is the worst. You'll find out. And the explosions? Caused by mortar shells or hand grenades. They can do some harm."

I'd saved the best for next. Should say "for the best," because the word is replete with sarcasm.

"The mortar shells and hand grenades can do a number of

uncomfortable things. Remove an arm or a leg. Blow off your head, in fact. During one attack—which didn't work—I had to crouch in a shell hole with an officer who'd lost his head. I mean, *lost* it. All that were left were bloody shreds of his neck. Not too pretty a sight. Shrapnel can also blow out your guts." I thought of Harold when I said that.

Then I hit them. "Mostly, of course, dead bodies are buried in a spot behind the trench. All the rain uncovers bodies, so they rot. The smell of that—well, lads, I'll leave that for you to imagine. Not very nice. Can't say I liked it much. You know who liked it, though? I mean *what* like it?"

I paused for emphasis.

"The *rats*," I told them. "Big ones. Big as cats. Why were they so big? Because they ate the dead soldiers. I mean *ate* them. *Gorged* on them. They were especially fond of eyeballs and livers. Smacked their furry little lips as they devoured those goodies." I may have exaggerated a little there. But I was pissed off at that threesome of rustic dumbbells. And I wanted to sicken them. Maybe I'd talk them out of enlistment. It wasn't my intention. Still . . .

"You'll enjoy shooting the rats; they explode nicely. Just don't shoot them all—they warn you about attacks the filthy Boche are planning to launch." I probably didn't use that last word, memory diffused by eighty-two-year-old cloudiness.

But I went on. Deeply pleased (what a mean compulsion) by their obvious reactions—mouths agape, eyes staring and unblinking, bodies rigid.

"When I say 'warn,' I don't mean the rats can talk," I continued. "I mean they run away before the attacks begin. Little bastards must be psychic. You can have fun with them, however. Rat war. Throw the dead bodies at each other, watch them splat against faces if your aim is good."

Another pause for dramatic emphasis. There definitely was a hint of Arthur Black–to-come in me.

"I don't mean to tell you that the only unpleasant smell was that of rotting corpses. Not at all. There was also the odor of the cesspools—or as we called them, the shit pits. That's rather unpleasant, too. Not to mention the lingering odor of poison gases—rotting sandbags—cigar and cigarette smoke— cooking food. All combined into one ghastly perfume of war." I *did* say that; not bad for eighteen.

"Is that it? Not exactly." I went on, "Mustn't forget the lice. They lay eggs in the seams of your uniforms. Nasty buggers. Cause *trench fever.* Severe pain and fatal fever. Then, of course, the muddy trenches and the cold cause *trench foot.* Feet get blue and swollen, have to be amputated sometimes. Anything else? No, that's all, lads. Best of luck. Slugs and Frogs, you can worry about on your own."

I never found out whether they had enlisted or not. I only knew that I felt justified in my rant. Not that I felt any better about Magda—even Joe. But a percentage of the steam had been released.

Is that enough description of trench warfare? I told you I'd get around to it. Satisfied?

Chapter Eleven

It rained for three days straight afterwards. Straight? It never rained straight, either vertical or horizontal. It always seemed to fall at an angle, mostly right. And hard. Damned hard. I couldn't sleep upstairs in the cottage because of the pounding on the roof tiles. I tried to sleep there, then after one restless night, tossed my straw-filled mattress (damp, of course) down to the first floor. The pounding on the roof was slightly more endurable there—especially with half a torn handkerchief stuffed into each ear.

Trouble was, with that arrangement, I thought I heard a distant party taking place, voices, laughter, banging noises, faint music. After a second night of that, I slept, exhausted, through the party. *Enjoy yourself, I'm sleeping,* I informed the far-off celebrants, whoever—or whatever—they were. It never crossed my mind that it was fay-*eries.* I'm not sure I believe it was. It was probably me.

At any rate, three days of constant rain. In the sky and in my brain. I was depressed. I attempted to convince myself that it was the dismal weather and the emotional hangover from my harsh rant to the three farmer boys. That failed to

wash, however. I knew exactly what it was. Joe's probably im-
provident warning added to my already strong-enough guilt
regarding my behavior to Magda. How had I offended her? By
simply hesitating to share that mattress with her? Was it that
bad a gaffe? Well, it was. Otherwise, why would she have
changed her tune so abruptly? *Rats!* I finally concluded. *You
did her wrong, however unintentionally.* Was all lost? Likely. Her
offense meter was too easily activated.

⚹   ⚹   ⚹

My excessive guilt resulted in a vision. Or, more conceivably,
a hallucination. I knew a soldier who had experienced one,
catching clear sight of his mother. So clear that he clambered
out of the trench to embrace her, telling us, with a happy
laugh, what he was about to do. Only to embrace a sniper's
bullet in his brain, poor foolish kid. (He was seventeen, had
lied about his age in order to enlist in the service.) Could it
have been Edward? I wondered. Had he seen Magda out in
No Man's Land, smiling, arms extended?

Because that was what I saw one night, waking from a
heavy sleep. Standing downstairs in No Man's Land (the cottage), smiling at me, arms extended, gesturing for me to go to
her. I suppose I might have been chilled by the sight. I wasn't.
Even when she simply wasn't there and I realized that she
had, doubtless, been hallucinated. I felt warmed by the remembrance. She hadn't really appeared to me, of course. I was
certain of that. Nonetheless, the vision comforted me and
made me vow to visit her again.

Three more days, now of sunshine, drying up the countryside. I decided that the time had come. I donned as passable an outfit as I could manage in the still-humid air of the cottage and started up the path once more. Anticipating, with intense pleasure, the prospect of seeing that lovely woman again.

By the time I'd reached the foot of the path to Magda's house, my pleasure had degenerated to a state of intense disgust with myself. I'd let an obvious hallucination urge me to this foolish plan? *Disgusting.* Absolutely so. Naïve and disgusting. Almost as naïve and disgusting as letting Joe's words affect me. A *witch?* An ancient crone, bad teeth and all, incessant cackling and cat conversing, wearing dark cerements, coned cap, and perched on a flying broom, eating little children? Sure. Made a lot of sense.

A lot of non-sense. She was a sensitive woman who had no desire whatever to see me again. Why would I even permit myself to consider such a stupid action? I'd insulted her. She did not care to let me in her house. I was a numskull for thinking it.

So what did I elect to do? My only excuse is this: I was eighteen. What more could be expected from my limited awareness? Nothing intelligent. Far from it. Irritated at myself, lamebrained to a fault, I decided to confront the faeries and spit in their wee folk eyes, defy their damned Middle Kingdom. Remember this—I really didn't buy any of it. Joe's words? Foolish. Magda's words? Sincere but illogical. Oh, listen, folks. I knew I was being stupid, but I chose, with true teenage stubbornness, to ignore my calculated stupidity and "press on," as the Brits like to say. So I did.

Almost to my end.

⚹ ⚹ ⚹

As I entered the woods, it was with a combination of bravado and trepidation. Over and over, I repeated my subconscious mantra: *It's nonsense, all nonsense.* Although, down in the cellar of my brain, that little chump of an unsophisticate pestered me, or always, with the invariable query: *How do you know?* I didn't. That was the trouble. So when there seemed to be an odd trembling of the tree leaves, I reacted with instant trembling myself. *Oh, stop it!* I fought back. *It's a damn breeze in a damn tree!*

Explaining a bending of grass blades directly in front of me? *Yes!* I insisted mulishly. Natural explanation; nothing more. I walked on, trying to ignore the sudden chill I felt. Was that goose flesh rising on my arms? *No!* Well, yes. It was getting a little chilly. May. Northern England. Spring climate unpredictable. *Yes. Good.* Everything explained. A desire to laugh at all the silliness of superstition. I giggled, picking at an insect crawling on my hair. Which wasn't there. Then a second bug. Not there. Simple nervousness, I told myself. The body obviously connected to the—what, the skull? Well, to the nervous system. Right you are. What time was it? I should buy a watch. I might have been inside here for hours. Was I?

There was a sudden flash of movement to my right. I looked so quickly in that direction that I felt a painful crackling in my neck. Nothing there. *A faerie running? Don't be stupid. A squirrel, maybe. A rabbit. Calm down, White.*

A flickering of light around me. Real? Or nervousness again? Couldn't be hallucination, could it? *Why not?* I shivered. Someone was watching me. The woods were watching me. *No, Alex, don't be ridiculous. Woods do not have eyes. Calm* down.

Then I thought I heard those party celebrants in the distance. Same sounds. Talking, singing, banging noises. Now *that* was disturbing. *No, God damn it! I heard nothing but the inflaming of my brain. Don't let it bother you, White old White!*

Ah. Another person. An old woman carrying a basket, a dark shawl over her shoulders. "Hello!" I called, "Do you—?"

The words congealed in my mouth. The old lady was gone. I don't mean stepped behind a tree or anything. I mean *gone.* Vanished.

Time to leave, I "calmly" instructed myself. I started to turn. But couldn't. My legs were glue. I couldn't move. Overhead, the foliage of the trees began to shake. Violently. And there was no wind. None at all. The tree leaves, twigs, even the branches were whipping loudly in the non-wind.

Which is when, giving up to dread, I sobbed. Aloud.

Then cried out, shocked and terrified, as a powerful hand grasped my left arm and jerked me around.

Magda.

"*Come,*" was all she said.

And, abruptly, she had turned me and was running me back through the woods, her hand so tight on my arm that it pained. While she ran, wordless, she took something from her coat pocket and, reaching around me, dropped it into the right-hand pocket of my jacket; I had no idea what it was. "What *is* that?" I asked. Breathless by now.

"*Keep running,*" was all she said.

I felt a mixture of relief and gratitude suffusing me. I was with her again, and she was saving me. From what? I no longer doubted, my mantra shattered. Whatever it was, there was definitely *something* in the woods. Something dangerous. And Magda was rescuing me from it, bless her. A witch? She could be Satan's sister, for all I cared.

Now she was doing something else as we ran. And ran and ran and ran—the damned wee folk seemed to have lured me a football-field distance from the path. To my perplexed surprise, I saw that with each long stride, she was throwing white flowers to each side of our rush. I didn't ask her why she was doing it. I was sure she had a reason.

Now I was beginning to notice (I'd have had to be deaf not to notice it) an increasingly thunderous noise like that of a herd of stampeding elephants crashing through a bamboo forest. I had an urge to look back and see what it was, but common sense dissuaded me. She wouldn't want me to, I thought. That alone was enough to dissuade me. So, horrified, gasping for breath, a terrible aching in my hip and a stabbing pain in my side (I didn't know about stitches in those days), I sprinted on, partly of my own volition, largely by the powerful yanking of my racing savior.

⚡ ⚡ ⚡

When we finally reached the path, I collapsed, both legs devoid of strength. Magda made a soft sound of alarm, trying to prevent my fall. No use. I dropped to one knee, then the next, and in a moment, I was sitting on the ground, palms down in an attempt to keep from totally sprawling. I looked up, blinking dizzily. "Whoa," I muttered.

"You feel strange," she said, she didn't ask.

"Very strange." I nodded, sure that my head would topple off if I nodded too energetically. "Never felt like this before."

"I know," she said. *How do you know?* I wondered.

I tried to stand but couldn't. I remained recumbent. "What happened?" I asked, looking for a simple answer to drive away the darkness of my senses.

I didn't get it. "You did a foolish thing," she told me.

There it was. Introductory verification of what I didn't want to accept. "Oh?" I murmured, sounding utterly stupid.

"You know what you did," she said. "Did you think you could defy them?"

Them, I thought. The very word made me shudder. I drew in a shaking breath. "They're really there, then," I acknowledged, changing my life—not knowing it.

"Of course they are," said Magda. "Didn't that man—the one who repaired your roof—warn you?"

I had to admit it. "Yes."

"But you ignored him. *Why?*" she said.

I couldn't tell her. *Well, you see, he said that you're a witch, and that made me angry.* Right. Perfect answer. If she demanded further explanation, I'd tell her that I was so upset by what I'd told the three farmer boys that I wasn't thinking straight. Not that much of an excuse either, but better than the witch revelation.

So all I said was, "I don't know. I just wasn't thinking."

She was so quiet that I felt the need to speak. "I saw an old woman," I told her.

"She wasn't real," Magda replied. "She was one of their tricks, I warned you about that." (Had she? I couldn't remember.)

Her tone was parental and, in spite of everything, old bells were jangled and I could sense myself bristling. She could see it, too.

She gazed down at me in further silence, and I felt a dreadful sense of guilt. I didn't speak, however. No reasonable comment had occurred to me. *Don't look at me like that,* I thought. I felt certain that she knew I was lying about why I went into the woods. Or, at least, withholding the truth.

At last (it seemed such a long time) she asked, "Do you think you can make the house?"

Make the house? I must still have been semi-groggy from the frightening incident because the phrase made no sense to me. I stared at her. Then made another blundering remark as her question suddenly made sense to me. Well, almost. "I'm not sure," I said. "It's pretty far away."

"No, it's not," she countered. "You can make it." *Make* it? *Reach* it! Yes, of course. *But it* is *far away,* I thought.

"Come along," she said gently. "It's only up the path."

Which is when I realized that the house she was referring to was hers. A burst of further gratitude laved through my bones. She was not expecting me to "make it" to my cottage. Generously, she was inviting me back to her house. God bless us, every one! As Tiny Tim exulted. Or said, anyway.

Chapter Twelve

By then, the wave of dizziness had subsided, and I decided I could stand. Magda helped me to my feet. As I put weight down on my right leg, I hissed with pain. "What is it, dear?" she asked. The anxiety in her voice was music to my ears.

"My *war* wound," I told her, trying to sound comically melodramatic and failing completely.

"What *happened?*" she asked worriedly. I told her about the grenade explosion in the trench, not mentioning the even more horrendous wound incurred by Harold Lightfoot. I let her believe my wound was solo, relishing the look of sympathetic concern it brought to her face. "You poor darling, it must have been terribly painful. I wish I could carry you to the house."

She held my left arm again and placed her right arm around my waist as we headed for the path to her house. I confess (to my shame) that I probably limped more exaggeratedly than needed. But I was eighteen, folks. I'd just been through a ghastly experience. And my companion was a beautiful scarlet-haired woman who was redolent with sympathy. So I milked it, kid that I was.

"What really made you enter the woods?" she asked. Was she already suspicious of my initial explanation?

I gave her answer number two—the Farmer Boy Triplet account. All right, they weren't triplets. I said they were, immediately dreading the possibility that she'd find out it was a pathetic fib. But I went on, once more, milking the moment. Not that it needed that much lactose-evoking. My account to the three had been accurate. Cruelly stated but accurate. Magda's reaction was strong. "Oh, no more," she said, pleading. I realized, as she spoke, that my words had probably brought to the surface traumatic memories of her son and what he may have suffered in the trenches.

To change the subject, I reached into the right-hand pocket of my jacket—my hand rubbing hers as I did—and felt around. My fingers touched the object, soft and seemed to be round. I drew it out and looked at it. A flower, white. "What's this?" I asked. It was mere curiosity.

Magda stopped so abruptly, it almost made me stumble. The expression on her face was indecipherable. (Good word, that.) Had I gone amiss again, said something that I shouldn't have? How was that possible?

"I found it in my pocket," I thought I explained. "You put it there when we were running." That didn't explain my question, but it was the best I could do.

"And why do you think I did that?" she asked. Now I guessed at her reaction. She assumed that I was, somehow, mocking her. *Mocking?* No way. She'd saved me, probably my life, why would I dream of—? No, impossible.

"Well," I answered, sensing what she wanted me to say. "Some kind of protection."

That loosened her expression. "Yes," she said. "That's exactly right." I felt such relief that I scarcely heard the words of what else she said. Something about primrose—what the flower was. Something about faeries (that damned word again) being so fond of primrose that she thought it might delay their pursuit. Which, apparently, it had. "That's all it takes?" I remember asking. Subconsciously, I already accepted the explanation. She saved me from . . . *what?* I didn't dare to consider the possibilities.

"There are various plants and flowers that they're very fond of and drawn to," Magda told me as we continued toward her house, me limping quite a bit, not to exaggerate my condition but because it hurt like hell. Magda broke into her explanation to commiserate. "Poor dear," she murmured. "It's your wound, isn't it?"

"Yes," I said.

I felt another surge of warm relief as Magda kissed me on the cheek and said, "We'll fix you up when we reach the house." I almost wished the lawn was wider, I felt so comforted by her arm around my waist, her warm hand on my arm, her very presence. "What other plants and flowers?" I asked, wanting the moments to last.

"Mistletoe, foxglove, and poinsettia are popular among the faeries," she went on. I had to chuckle at the word "mistletoe." Magda looked at me suspiciously until I explained about Christmas kisses. She smiled and continued to enumerate various trees also "popular" among Middle Kingdom citizens—birch, willow, oak, and rowan being most "popular."

She was starting to tell me what shiny stones the faeries favored (another passable combo), their most "sacred" stone, the green emerald. "Naturally, I wouldn't dispose of them to slow down pursuit," she said, a smile of suppressed amusement on her lips—which I, suddenly (why had it taken that long?), noticed how full—and kissable—they looked, although I doubt the notion of kissing Magda actually occurred to me at that instant, just the general (I think) observation.

At any rate—I've asided enough; we reached the house and Magda helped me in. Before we entered, though, I asked, "What about the water? Also protection?" Now I was fully aware of catering to her. I wondered if she knew it (probably), but she only smiled. "That's right," she said.

"And the dry leaves on the door?" I asked.

"Now you're overdoing it," she told me.

I winced. She knew, of course. "I'm sorry," I said. I really was.

She closed the door, and for a moment, the gloom of the interior gave me a sense of uneasiness. I had to—quickly— remind myself that Magda had just—I might as well admit it—saved me "at the crunch," as Mr. Churchill would have put it.

My vision focused then, and I made out the familiar room, most notably the candlelit portrait of Edward smiling serenely above the fireplace mantel.

My leg and hip were really bothering me now, and Magda, without another word, helped me across the room, past the ceiling-high bookcases. *Not into the bedroom*, I thought. I sim-ply wasn't ready for that, although, it seemed that she might do that, having me lie on her bed to rest.

Instead, she aided me into the kitchen.

I was charmed—but not surprised—by the appearance of

the room. It was as warm in invitation as Magda was, mostly light-textured wood paneling and a ceiling painted pale yellow. Against the wall, farthest from me, was the cast-iron stove, dark utensils hanging from overhead bars, three on the left, two on the right. The stove itself, recessed in a black brick wall (black, I assumed, from the heat and flames of the fire underneath). At the moment, only a footing of red coals glowed across the bottom. On the left side of the stove was an oven door, a black cloth hanging from its handle—or its knob, I couldn't tell which.

In the center of the room was what looked like—and was—a heavy oak table, one (oak) chair pushed under it, a large candlelit lantern hanging above it, so close to the ceiling that the candle smoke had left a black patch on the ceiling.

Magda led me to a voluminous oak armchair standing to the right of the stove. Magda told me later that it was an antique, deliberately voluminous to accommodate hoopskirts. She helped me to sit down. As I did, the pain in my hip and leg flared sharply, and I uttered a soft involuntary groan. "Oh, *darling,*" Magda said, obviously concerned.

"I'll be all right," I said. Already the pain was lessening.

"You're very brave," she told me. "I hope Edward was able to control pain as you are."

What if he was killed in a moment? The cruel thought jumped into my brain. Thank God I didn't voice it. All I managed to say was, "I'm sure he was."

She stood gazing at me for what seemed to be a long time, her expression, again, indecipherable. (I *do* like that word.) "You look like him," she said. Then, turning so quickly that her long skirt rustled, she moved to a small wall-hung cabinet and opened it, removing several earthenware containers, two cups and saucers, and a covered cracker box. She looked, at that moment, so domestic, reminding me of my too-soon-lost mother that I had to know—I *had* to. "Mrs. Variel," I began.

"Magda, please," she corrected me pleasantly, now checking an oversize pot on the stove, satisfied, at the pot's water level.

I braced myself; you might say I girded my mental loins.

"Yes?" she said, turning from the stove.

I drew in a fitful breath.

"What is it, Alex?" she asked. I'd have preferred that she called me "dear" or "darling"—but there was no time for such an irrelevant disappointment.

"Magda," I said.

"Yes, dear, what is it?"

I had to ask, as awkward as it was. "My roofer," I said.

"Joe, yes, I remember," she replied.

She waited then. *Oh, god, I wish I'd never started this!* my brain lamented.

"What is it, darling?" Magda said. She'd called me "darling" now. That only made it worse.

Tongue-tied is a legitimate description. My tongue was double knotted. I could only stare at her.

"What about Joe?" she asked. So God damn understandingly that I would have welcomed a giant crack in the kitchen floor, swallowing me whole.

"Alex, *what?*" she asked. She sounded worried now.

The words came tumbling out. *"He said you were a witch."*

❊   ❊   ❊

Magda stood before my chair and gazed at me with what I can only describe as a fixed expression. Anger? Disappointment? I wasn't sure. Finally, she spoke. "Would you say that again?" she asked. Or *was* she asking? Maybe she wanted to hear me speak the words again. But why? If she *was* a witch, was she going to zap me (1982 slang) with a bolt of lightning?

I knew I had to repeat what I'd said. I did so, but so softly, I could tell she couldn't hear my voice. I tensed myself. The action made my hip-leg pain amplify again, making me wince. I hoped she wouldn't think I was sympathy seeking (another possible phrase: A.B. circa 1982) as I repeated the words again, slowly and distinctly. No point in trying to obscure them. They were what they were. "He said you were a witch."

More fixed gazing. Then Magda turned and moved to another armless oak chair to the left of the fireplace. The grating noise the chair feet made as she drew it over to mine made me wince again. (I was definitely wince prone that afternoon.)

Placing the chair across from me, she seated herself. *She even sits gracefully,* it came to me—true but not exactly the point.

"Alex," she began.

Oh, Christ, don't lecture me! My brain rebelled instantly. Captain Bradford Smith White, USN, commenced too many lectures with my name, in that exact tone.

"*What?*" I heard myself reply, responding not to her but to my father.

"Let's not be truculent," she said.

At least the Captain had never used that word. I doubt he knew it.

I controlled my unthinking reaction, reminding myself that she had, in all probability, saved my life. "Sorry," I muttered. I was but didn't sound it.

"That's all right," she said. "I suppose I am what your roofer said, at least as he interprets it. To him, I'm a witch. That's true. I *am*."

I shivered so violently in my voluminous chair (my shiver more voluminous by far) that it creaked beneath me.

Magda was amused by my reaction. "Alex, Alex," she said, "what on earth do you think a witch is? And I must tell you, I dislike the word, it rouses such grotesque images. Isn't that what's been making your behavior so guarded since your roofer told you what he did?"

I had to admit the truth of that. Crones with cone-shaped hats addressing black cats? Her words rang true. But not enough.

"You aren't sure yet, are you?" Magda said, "You still believe I'm something to be frightened of. As you're now, I'm *glad*, frightened by the little people. They *are* something to be frightened by. I'm not. Can't you see that?"

Her words—and voice—were so persuasive that I almost lost my apprehension about her. Not quite, though. There was still a lot about her I had no comprehension of. (Apprehension, comprehension. If Black had written poetry, he might have rhymed those two.)

"Let me tell you what a witch—as you refer to it—really is," Magda said.

She went on to explain that so-called witchcraft was a

religion—"and it *is* a religion," she emphasized—called Wicca, a feminine form of the Old English word *wicce*, meaning "witch." A sizable cult, its membership was extensive. (Although, as far as she knew, she was the only one in Gatford.) In common with more orthodox religions, Wicca has worship as its main goal. The cult is primarily matriarchal, its high priestess "not me, a far greater person," Magda emphasized, though not identifying her. "She's respected as the Queen of Heaven, her symbols the moon and stars."

Wicca recognized responsibility toward nature and sought to live in harmony with the environment. They did not accept the concept of *supernatural*, believing that true power was naturally available. They recognized both outer and inner worlds and interaction between them. There was more, which I fail to recall. Wicca was (is?) basically a fertility cult, its festivals geared to the seasons.

"Most memberships meet at certain dates," Magda told me. "The spring equinox, the summer solstice, the autumn equinox. I attend them when I can. Mostly, I worship alone. I tried to start a coven once [a "working unit," she later explained], but it didn't work—the others were dismayed by my proximity to the Middle Kingdom. They thought it was damaging to the religion."

"And is it?" I asked, trying to involve myself in the moment.

Magda smiled. "I don't think so. But I'm what you'd call a dilettante *wicce*. I go my own way."

I started to cough, clearing my throat. "And magic?" I asked.

She looked at me, a curious expression on her face. "Magic?" she said. "Why do you ask that?"

Already I felt awkward and embarrassed. Why had I asked such a question? Was I psychic? Or just stupid? No way of knowing. Then.

"Well," I said, voice trembling. "I just assumed—"

"That witches performed magic?" she asked, but said, "I don't. Hardly ever. On occasion, I perform a ritual during which what you assume to be magic occurs. But nothing more. Any other questions?"

I knew she was becoming impatient with me, but there *was* another question preying at my mind (my brain). "Why did you become a witch?" I asked, adding quickly, "I mean a *wicce*." I hoped I pronounced it right.

She gazed at me silently, and I wondered if she was going to answer. Or had I asked another offending question?

"I was a Lutheran," she said. "Most Scandinavians are." *Scandinavian?* I thought. She didn't look it. "My parents half were, my mother English," she explained. "They came to Northern England when I was three—I never knew why. Faithfully, I went to church with my husband and Edward. Then my husband was killed and then Edward was killed. I was completely devastated. The religion didn't comfort me. I left the church and lived awhile without religion. During that time, I turned to nature for comfort. And when I accepted that Wicca was a nature-oriented faith, I turned to it—four years ago. Now are you appeased? Or am I still a menacing creature in your eyes?"

I was bereft of words. I felt only shame that I'd doubted what was so clearly the kindness of her nature. All I could murmur, humbly, was, "Forgive me."

"*Oh, my dear.*" All impatience vanished from her voice

and posture. How it happened, I do not recall, but suddenly she was on her knees in front of me, arms around my body, clasping tightly. "Thank you, darling. *Thank* you," she whispered.

I guess that was the moment I fell in love with Magda Variel, my beautiful red-haired witch.

Mistake.

Chapter Thirteen

Let me alter this to chapter fourteen. Thirteen being a proven problem (I like that combination) of a number. Look it up yourself; it won't be difficult. For instance—in tall buildings, there are no thirteenth floors.

So I do the same for my written building—not, too bad, my written skyscraper. There will be no thirteenth story.

Chapter Fourteen

I moved in with Magda soon after our flight from the faeries. No lovemaking involved. That surprised (frankly, disappointed) me. But I could not romantically approach my new mother. It seemed as though she had assumed that role.

I had to hold on to Comfort Cottage (what a joke) for three months. I'd paid that much in advance, and my landlord balked at returning money. So I had a rented residence in addition to my residence with Magda. An entrepreneur at eighteen. Not bad.

The first accommodation Magda provided was to perform a ritual titled Drawing Down the Moon.

I wasn't sure why she did this. To reassure me how benign Wicca was? To give me a demonstration of genuine Wicca magic? To acclimate me to her way of life?

No. She had something far more memorable to "exemplify"—as they say in Northern England. An easier word? Something far more "remarkable," then. To demonstrate—to *prove*.

It took place on a night when the moon was full. Build-up of power, Magda explained, was more achievable when all participants are unclothed. Since we were so newly acquainted, however, she would forgo this element of the ritual. She would, rather, attempt to "charge the atmosphere" by garbing herself in a thin silk robe, electing modesty for "dynamism." She also chose to dance alone, since being a novice, I would, doubtless, foul up the procedure. She didn't say "foul up," of course; she suggested only "possible mitigation" of the ritual. No help for it, however. I remember disappointment on my part. Even beneath her usual impervious outfits (not, I swear, that I made any attempt to perviate them—is there such a word? I doubt it), I could tell that her figure was sumptuous. No other word is accurate.

The ritual began. Low illumination—several candles only. Incense and burning herbs suffusing the air with an exotic, fragrant haze. Fireplace warmth heating the room to tropical sultriness.

Magda twisting and turning in a ritual dance. I tried, very determinedly, not to look at her body. My mind succeeded generally. My eyes and groin had less success. Her figure was (by gods in Heaven or Hell) totally sumptuous, her breasts (I confess I absolutely gaped at them) close to immense. Her stomach ovoid and milk white. Except for the ebony triangle between her long, moving legs, which, I swear to you, I did not attempt (other than sporadically) to look at.

Did I mention (no, I didn't) that throughout her dance, the succulent Magda (she actually seemed to become more beautiful with every second) chanted softly. The melody was catchy, but the lyrics, if I may call them that, were in Latin—I believe they were in Latin. I got totally caught up by, lost in increasing entrancement. Maybe it was the dim, flickering light, perhaps the sinuous sweep (good combo) of her body, the lung-filling intoxication of the combined incense.

Whatever it was, the miracle began.

※   ※   ※

I'm sure you're all familiar with the word "electrify." Of course you are. In this day and age, it has no more significance than the flicking up of a wall switch to turn on bulbs.

In 1918, things were different. Electricity meant less than gas stoves to an Eskimo. I knew it existed; *Tom Swift and His Electric Dog.* (Just made that up.) I'd read about electric lights on the *Titanic.* I knew what electric power was supposed to be, but it had never affected me personally; that's the point I'm trying to make. And even on that evening, I was not aware of what was taking place. Even now, I'm not quite sure. I know only that it had to be electric. Had to be.

Initially, a tingling. I can come up with no more accurate description. Have you experienced acupuncture? If so, you know how thin wires are often attached to the needles, then fastened to some electric source—my guess, a battery of some sort. The feeling—I had it in my leg and hip—was a small intermittent electric shock—or *tingling*, to return to that more authentic word. It was not what one would term exactly pleasant. Neither was it painful. Especially since it was all located in the area of my shrapnel wound. I sensed—I *know*—it was deliberate. Clearly, Magda's ritual was a healing one.

Did I tell you?—probably not, it's been a long time since I've written a coherent book—*MIDNIGHT EROS*, if I recall correctly. Anyway, in case I haven't mentioned it—Magda bathed for a full hour before the ritual began. The candles she lit were thick and purple—five of them. She wore a heavy scarlet robe before she doffed it, revealing the near-transparent gown. Her hair was tightly bound around her head. There was no makeup on her face, not even lip rouge. Purity? I couldn't tell you, but it seems a logical explanation.

Back to the miracle. Next, my leg and hip were seized by numbness. Then, within this numb sensation, I felt what seemed to be tiny fingers manipulating nerves and tendons, altering an artery, pressing bone in place. Because of the numbness, I felt no pain. It was, instead, a weird experience, I tell you, unlike, to the slightest degree, anything I'd ever known before. It lasted, I would estimate, less than five minutes. During that time, Magda stood motionless, arms extended toward me, pointing a hazel wand at me. I knew what was happening but had no conception of how it was happening.

Then a return of sensation in my hip and leg, a minute or

so of new pain (slight). Was it cosmic recuperation? Once more, look not to me for clarification. I have none. All I remember is that brief period of new pain ending and the incredible realization that my shrapnel wound no longer plagued me. On the contrary, I felt no indication of the wound whatever—later, when I looked at my hip and leg, although there were faintly visible scars, there was no other evidence that my flesh had been torn apart by the grenade burst.

How do I describe the emotion I felt toward Magda? Looking at her through a veil of tears, I watched as she extinguished the incense and purple candles, the herbs. She redonned her scarlet robe. I do not recall so much as a physical tremor as, in pulling on the robe, she momentarily revealed the voluptuousness of her body. I was beyond mere sensation, suffused, instead, with such loving gratitude that I began to cry. Helplessly, joyfully. "Thank you," I managed to say before my voice was lost beneath a torrent of sobs.

"Oh, my dear," she murmured, coming over to where I was sitting. I did my best to stand and meet her, but my legs were simply not up to it. Not because of pain but because impassioned gratitude had taken all the starch out of every part of me except—I can use only the one word—my heart.

Magda caught me falling and held me up. I wrapped both arms around her, clutching at her soft warmth. "Thank you, thank you," I was able to repeat before uncontrollable weeping beset me again.

"My darling, I'm so glad," she murmured, kissing my cheeks and, once, my lips. I made nothing of that, so emotionally bound that only grateful love was in charge.

Then she laughed. She actually laughed. "Is that enough magic for you?" she asked.

I laughed, too, through the tears.

⚡ ⚡ ⚡

Life with Magda continued harmoniously after my healing. I transferred my belongings from the Nazi bunker (I've explained that) and moved them to her house. We became good friends, prior to somewhat other.

I remember one of the early evenings after I became her houseguest. (I didn't know, then, that in her eyes I was considerably more.) We were having dinner in her kitchen. She had made—she was a superlative cook—a delicious stew, chunks of tender beef, gravy immersed with vegetables including carrots, onions, zucchini, turnips, and the like. Small red potatoes also. She had a garden behind the house where grew (most successfully) all these items. If there were any bugs or other vermin to be dealt with, she was not required to deal with them. Some kind of protective "armor" to prevent such incursion? I never knew, but I suspected. Wicca had to be valuable for something in excess of religion. (An unkind remark. Scratch it.)

At any rate, dinner in her kitchen. And pleasant conversation. At one point of which I made the innocent suggestion that perhaps my healing was, at least partially, due to me, my mind in a state of hypnosis. I didn't even know the word I used in place of it. I knew nada about Freud's activities.

Anyway, however I expressed it, Magda didn't care for it at all. At first, her features hardened, chilling me. Then her customary expression of kind affection returned, and she said, patient as always, "No, Alex, that's not true. It had nothing to do with you. The ritual summoned outside forces. Without that summons being responded to, nothing would or could have taken place."

Immediately, I expressed apology. Whatever had taken place—and I accepted every word of her explanation—to me, it was a total miracle. I mentioned the long walk along the path we'd taken that afternoon. There hadn't been so much as a hint of pain in my hip and leg. "Forgive me, please forgive me. I wasn't trying to take credit for my healing. I was talking out of turn," is what I said.

Magda reached across the table and took my hand in hers. She understood completely. All she meant to convey to me was the truth that, as humans, we had no individual control of our welfare. If we needed help, it was available—from external powers. Wicca knew this, respected it, and utilized it as needed. "Remember that, Alex," she said. "Keep it in your mind always."

"I will," I promised. I had no idea how wrong she was. Well, not exactly wrong. Say, rather, limited. But I was not to learn that for some time.

꙰ ꙰ ꙰

We became lovers soon after. If I do not exceed myself, to describe my teenage bedroom abilities (crude at best) as worthy of the word "lover." Magda, yes. She excelled at every aspect of the word. How she endured my clumsy—but honest, I protest—approach to lovemaking, I have no idea. She never found fault with it, God bless her. There was little but love in her lovemaking. Whatever negative responses she must have had (remember, I am eighty-two now and see with clearer, at least mental, eyes), she never voiced discouragement in my undeveloped (though, understandably youthful) crudity at bedroom tactics.

It began like this. I had just bathed and was headed for my (Edward's) bedroom, when Magda came out of her library. Her smile of greeting was, as always, warmly welcoming, as though she hadn't seen me for a day or so. "Are you all clean now?" she asked.

"As much as possible," I said, returning her smile.

"Good," she said. She moved toward me.

Now, I will admit that, more than once, I had admired (a polite word for "stared at") her figure. Numerous times when she leaned over (a table, a chair, me) I'd regarded her outstanding cleavage with more than casual appraisal. Once, my groin had reacted so equally outstandingly that I had to try hiding the obvious protuberance, although I knew full well that she noticed it.

I remember thinking that the room—the main one—had suddenly grown overheated, affecting, mostly, my cheeks. I also remember trying to initiate some pointless conversation regarding turnips—or potatoes—or some equally absurd growth, which she kindly responded to, although I know she understood what I was seeking to obscure—the obviously thrusting bulge in my trousers.

On this occasion, unlike others of similar proximity, she didn't stop but kept approaching until she'd reached me and pressed herself against me. I started as she drew the towel from my body and dropped it on the floor. "I think we've waited long enough," she murmured. What had it been, a week, two weeks? It no longer mattered. Her lips were engaged with mine, so soft and warm, they turned my flesh to fire. I gained in rigid size with amazing (I thought) speed. I felt her warm, strong fingers wrap around it, tightly. I couldn't help it. I groaned with excited desire, reached up both hands, and grasped her breasts. Had they also swelled in size? I had no idea, but the fantasy I'd yielded to for some time now came true. Amazingly, her lips continuing to caress mine, somehow she'd opened up her dress and both her breasts were in my hands, their nipples as large as I'd imagined them to be, as rigid as me.

How much further can I go on? Despite my elderly, less than working-order condition, the recounting of that afternoon's enterprise, shall I call it, has even stirred a far-off echo in my trousers that, testosterone deprived, I am hard-put (wrong words) hesitant to acknowledge much less conform to; God forbid, the consequences doubtless would be inconsequential if not humiliating.

At any rate, she finished kissing me and led me to her bedroom (that incredible bedroom) by hand, now gripping mine and not my nether region—which, unaided by her, did not abate rigidity for a second. What am I saying? Of course it was aided by her, by her very presence, which became entirely present by the second as she removed all her clothing. By the illumination of the one candle she wick-flamed into light, I saw, not through the veiling of the gown she'd worn during the healing ritual, her beautiful body. Which she used to draw me down onto her amazing bed and in several moments, guided my member deep inside her body. Into which, in a very brief time—seconds, I expect—I cannon-shot the full volume of my boyhood juices. I hoped—in vain, it turned out—that Magda experienced some measure of the vivid ecstasy I'd felt. Not so, I soon discovered. Still, after I'd achieved my virtually instantaneous gratification, she smiled and kissed me tenderly. "I'm glad we did it," she whispered in my ear. "We'll do it again."

And do it again we did—repeatedly, night and day. On her bed, then, later, on the main room sofa (or whatever it was called), even in the kitchen, me spread open on the voluminous chair, Magda straddling me, her lovely face contorted by what I must call lust, her breasts in my face. "My *darling*," she repeated again and again, pulling back my head to kiss me with passionate ardor. *What teenage boy ever had it so good?* I thought. I didn't *know*.

The number of times we made love seems countless. Magda seemed insatiable. If that's what Wicca did, I decided at first, bully and good show!—as the Brits say. Sex became a habit. In Magda's case, I would say, rather, an addiction. As insane as it sounds, after a while I became worn out and even inured it. At eighteen? I seemed to be taking on the demeanor of the old coot I've become. Why I didn't know—when I considered the problem at all, which wasn't much. I know now. Or at least, I believe I know. It wasn't that I was inured, wasn't physical fatigue.

It was fear.

Chapter Fifteen

Fear is a strange, insidious phenomenon. Especially when there seems to be no reason for it.

Take my case. Why was that rat crouched in my stomach, gnawing on my innards? I kept visualizing the trench rats chewing—with great relish—the eyeballs and livers of dead soldiers. Why should that grisly image keep recurring to me? But it did, day by day, worse by night when I was trying to sleep—either by myself in Edward's room or in bed with Magda, our nude bodies pressed together. I simply could not rid myself of the terrible vision. I actually felt teeth nibbling on my stomach, cold ones. I did my best to will the images away. In vain. I even allowed myself—my belief system affected by my forced acceptance of the Middle Kingdom as a frightening reality—that Edward's spirit, resenting my presence in his room (in his *house*) was haunting me. I seriously considered asking Magda to perform some kind of exorcism ritual to compel Edward to leave me be. I realized then that the request would offend—and, more likely, hurt Magda, since it was so obvious, by everything she said, not too often but often enough, that she still grieved for her lost son. How deeply she grieved for him became—alarmingly—evident one night when we were in the throes of physical arousal and Magda whispered, frenziedly it seemed to me, "Fuck Mama! *Fuck* her!" In that moment it, somehow, excited me. Later, it dismayed me. What exactly was my position in her life? Was I only substituting for her dead son?

Which left me where? In a state of greater fear. Uneasy fear. Discomforting fear. I wasn't sure it was legitimate fear, but as time went by, I began to think that it was something like that. Which made no sense at all. Magda, on a daily basis, was as kind to me as anyone could be. Our sex life continued unabated—conditioned, of course, by my mounting disengagement from it. That, alone, was senseless. I was 18, not 180.

She made chefworthy meals for me, washed—and ironed—my clothes, conversed with me whenever I felt inclined to do so, was constantly affectionate, never mentioned my poorly disguised lack of involvement with our lovemaking, though I knew she was aware of it. Often, when neither of us had achieved fruition (is that the proper word—you know what I mean), she only kissed me warmly and permitted me to sleep. Which, as I have indicated, was scarcely achievable by me anymore.

Accordingly when, one evening at supper, she told me that she had to leave for three days—the Wicca celebration of the summer solstice—I didn't feel the pang of abject anxiety I know I would have suffered at the outset of our relationship. I felt, instead, almost a feeling of blessed relief—for which I inwardly—if dishonestly—castigated myself. I hoped there was no outward evidence of my spurious emotion. "Do

you have to leave?" was what I said. Did it sound insincere? I
didn't intend it to. "Yes, dear," Magda replied. "It's something
I never miss." *Good,* I thought, hoping my reaction was not
evident on my face.

❊　❊　❊

So she left and I was alone in her house. Which, at first, rather
unnerved me. Did she have it "booby-trapped" with arcane
witch protections? Was Edward's spirit, now untrammeled
because his mother had departed, going to pounce on me? I
slept on the main room sofa the first two nights. Then, little
by little, the rat gave up its chewing residence in my gut and I
began to feel free of anxiety. I realized that the freedom had
to do with Magda's absence but attributed the distressing emotion to imagination brought on by my being so stunned by
the magic of her healing ritual.

　　Why I felt that way, I couldn't tell you. The magic accomplished nothing but good. So powerful, however, what would
prevent it from being equally as powerful in the service of
evil? Which thinking plunged me into an abyss of dark imag-
inings about faerie evil combined with Magda's magic power,
all intermixed to reduce me to a rat-devoured distress once
more. I fought away the horrid blend of superstitions, but it
took me time. Days, in fact.

　　It all came back, full force, one morning when I went—
let's be honest—*intruded* into Magda's library. There I found
what was, in the beginning, no more than a tastefully fur-
nished, bookcase-laden room that would encourage reading,
bring on studying.

　　Then I found the manuscript. Perhaps I should write the

word in capital letters. MANUSCRIPT. That does seem more appropriate. To me, at least. The manuscript was centuries old, brown at the edges. Yet somehow clearly readable.

I wondered why in God's name (His presence nowhere evident in the MS.) Magda had not hidden the manuscript more judiciously. It was in one of the bottom desk drawers, easily visible. The thought did not occur to me that Magda assumed I would respect the privacy of her library. I was too shocked by what I saw to consider that.

What did I see? I'll describe it briefly as I can. To me, it ran a close second, if that, to the horrors of trench warfare. What were they? I hesitate to describe them at all. I'll try.

A potion prepared (apparently) in a caldron to induce invisibility. Not too shocking that, though totally incredible. Read on.

Shape changing (I believe it's called "shifting"), the ability—or power to alter form to whatever different form one chooses to achieve. In the illustration, a young woman was changing her form to that of a wolf. The vivid depiction showed, in disgusting, graphic manner, her body opened up, her bone structure being cracked and reshaped, her head distorting to the vulpine appearance of a wolf—with every gruesome step of the transformation totally diagramed. Ending with her congruence to that of a red-eyed, slavering wolf. That was the initial shock I underwent.

Shock number two, even worse. I will not (I refuse to) describe every loathsome detail of it. Perhaps the very words will tell you enough. *Self-aborting of unwanted chimera* (monsters). Illustrated in realistic minutiae. Enough said about that. I came close to losing breakfast as I viewed it.

I could go on, but taste prevents me. I will do no more than sketch a few more of the manuscript's abominations. *Sexual attacks from a distance. Summoning of chosen demon. Restoration of the dead.* Et cetera and God help us all. I cannot go on. The illustrations were virtually pornographic in their unmistakable detail. That held my attention for a while. But, even at eighteen, I was so sickened that I had to turn away, restore the manuscript to its drawer, and leave the study as I would a satanic temple—or some such. I could not allow my-self to believe that Magda approved—much less, God forbid, *practiced* these profanities. Wicca permitting such dreadful disciplines? (Now *there's* a worthy A. Black combination!) Impossible. The manuscript had to be used as a research tool, nothing more. I made myself believe it—although that damned oversized rodent returned to nibbling at my insides. It wasn't Wicca, I kept telling myself; it couldn't be. It was more like black magic. Magda practicing black magic.

❋   ❋   ❋

I did no more unwonted investigation of Magda's home. I acted like a well-behaved houseguest from that point on. I'd already had more than my share of freakish incidents, enough to last a lifetime. How about my term of service in the trenches? Weird enough. Add the lump of gold proffered to me by Harold Lightfoot. On top of that, the unexplainable appearance (A. Black combo—*good*) of the gold lump in my duffel bag. The almost unlocatable existence of Gatford. The bizarre behav-ior (I'm getting A. Black combos, head over heel now!) of the barkeep in the Golden Coach. The odd behavior of Gatford's jeweler, Mr. Brean, including his eager purchase of the gold lump, his guidance of me to the absurdly named Comfort Cottage. Joe Lightfoot (his name another anomaly—A. Black again!) warning me about entry into the woods. My first experience there, strange if not fatal. Joe informing me that Magda was a witch. Strange again. Her rescue of me from my second experience in the woods, strange and almost fatal. Her explanation of her particular witchdom. The commencement of our sex life. The onset of the nibbling rat. Finally, the terrible manuscript. I've overlooked Mr. Brean's agitated entry into my cottage with his handful of gray dust, claiming that it was all that was left of the gold. Dear God, hadn't I already lived through enough strange ordeals? More than enough. I'd had it. Give me respite.

At which, the strangest incident of all occurred.

It happened on a lovely sunlit afternoon. So lovely, in fact, that the house seemed stifling (not a workable combo) to me, giving me a desire to go outdoors, maybe for a walk along the path—avoiding the woods, of course. So I sallied forth into the inviting afternoon, ambling along the path. I felt certain I was safe from faerie intrusion so long as I remained on the path. It really was an enjoyable day, warm with a slight breeze, the sky blue and cloudless, the woods beautifully—though, I sensed, threateningly—lush with greenery.

Then I heard the singing.

I call it "singing," but that is too elemental a word. Call it angel singing, if you will. For surely, if angels do sing, that is precisely what they sound like, what I heard. I stopped in my tracks and listened, entranced, as the singing went on. What never struck me as foolhardy was that, after a brief hesitation—probably less than a minute—I had entered the woods, absolutely spellbound, unafraid, drawn by the heavenly singing. It did not occur to me for an instant that I might be being hypnotically drawn to my doom. (Not an A. Black combination, but a most acceptable phrase—"drawn to my doom." I love it; A. Black, that is.) I moved on, heedlessly enraptured by that angel voice. Now I thought I heard the sound of water splashing from a height. A waterfall! I couldn't tell. But I was sure I heard it as well as the singing. On and on through the completely unmenacing woods, through a grove of birch trees, constantly drawn by the angelic singing.

Finally, I saw her.

She had just stepped out from underneath the sparkling waterfall. She was nude. I cannot use the word "naked"; it seems too crudely explicit. Never have I seen nudity as so completely innocent. She was obviously a young woman, yet conveyed the presence of a child. She was no more than three feet tall, almost doll-like in her exquisite beauty. Her hair was golden; not blond but golden, it's the only way I can describe it. Her skin was as white as cream; her figure slight but clear. Nor did she seem at all disturbed at her nudity when she saw me looking at her, made no move to conceal her female parts. Even that sounds gross to me. What I mean to say is that her modesty was evident despite her unclothed state. She actually smiled at me. "Hello," she said. It was spoken in a welcoming manner. Then she added, dumbfounding me, "You're Alex."

I had no voice. It was paralyzed by wonder. She smiled again, knowing that, somehow. "You wonder how I know your name," she said.

"I do," was all I could manage. How do I describe what I was going through? Amazement, yes. Incredulity at the entire

moment. Physical attraction to her captivating body. Embar-
rassment that I even felt such a thing, her innocence was so
apparent.

"I know a lot about you," she said. She moved close to me.
(I felt like a lumbering giant in her presence.) Standing on
her toes, she kissed me lightly on the cheek. "I'm glad to have
you back," she told me.

For a moment, old caution beset me. *Have me back?* Hadn't
she made my two visits to the woods—especially the second
one—terrifying to me? I didn't want to darken the magic of
this moment by confronting her with doubt. I had no choice,
however. I had to know.

"Why did you—" I was going to say, *try to kill me?* but I
couldn't, simply couldn't. If she was luring me to destruction,
I would have to go along with it. And she was gazing at me so
sweetly, so guilessly, that I could only complete my question
with, "—chase me the last time?"

Her laugh was musical delicacy. "That wasn't me," she
said. "That was my brother, Gilly. He despises human beings.
His father was shot by a hunter. Gilly never recovered from
that."

"I don't blame him," I heard myself responding, "He did
scare the . . . insides out of me, though." I couldn't say "hell"
to that innocent face.

"Oh, he meant to harm you, no doubt of that. I'm glad the
witch from across the way threw down primrose flowers. It
infuriated Gilly that he had to stop and pick them up—but he
had no choice. We have that weakness, I'm sorry to say. You
have none in your pocket, do you?" Again, that burst of caution. Was she trying to discover whether she was vulnerable

to me? It seemed ridiculous to consider, since I'd come all this distance without incurring any harm. But I was compelled to say, "I don't know, I haven't checked my pockets lately."

"Oh, that's all right," she said. "I'm not going to chase you. I brought you here, didn't I?"

Yes, you did, I thought. Who was I to doubt this innocent child, anyway? *Child?* I was mistaking her height and manner for age. Her round, smooth breasts, though far less expansive than Magda's, and flowery cilia disproved. "Cilia" is the nicest way I can express it. I wouldn't, for the world, cheapen my description of her. She was too priceless, too . . . I must say it, too angelic. It wasn't just her singing. It was everything about her, head to toe. How could any creature be so perfect? I have no way of analyzing her incomparable pureness. Don't try me. Can't do it. Need I add that I became immediately enamored of her? Had I been three feet tall, I would have told her, on the spot, that I was totally in love with her. But I was six feet two inches tall, an ungainly colossus before her. I would have been ashamed to mention love to such a divinely perfect, diminutive creature. My opinion about faerie folk had altered utterly. If she was a sample, the Middle Kingdom was one of magic. Harold had been out of his mind to warn me about it, if that's what he'd actually done.

"*Are you afraid of me?*" she asked. So sweetly that it made my eyes begin to tear.

"*No*," I assured her. "Although—," I added without thought.

"Although—?" she asked; anxiously it seemed to me.

"It was a little . . . scary," I said.

"Scary? I don't know that word," she replied.

"I mean it—startled me." *Be honest!* commanded my brain. "Frightened me," I said.

"Oh, I'm sorry," she told me. "I didn't mean to frighten you." She smiled, that totally beguiling smile. "Well, maybe a little," she confessed—pleasantly, I thought. "I wasn't sure about you. Now I am. That's why I brought you here unharmed. I could have—" She didn't finish, but I got the point. She had abilities I knew nothing about. And wasn't sure I wanted to.

"Well, I'm glad you brought me here," I said. "It was with the singing, wasn't it?"

"That's right." She smiled again. I was absolutely charmed by that smile. Magda had a nice smile, too, but nothing like—

"What's your name?" I asked, needing to know.

"Ruthana," she answered, pronouncing *ana* as "anya."

"That's a lovely name," I told her. "You already know mine."

"Yes, I do," she said. "Now let me put my clothes on, and we'll talk some more." I'd forgotten (so help me God!) that she was nude throughout our conversation to that point. Her artless nudity dissuaded physical response.

I watched as she dressed. Her garb was certainly atypical, more a gossamer mantle that she wrapped around her body from the waist down and draped across her left shoulder, leaving her right breast uncovered. I noticed that the nipple was erect and wondered, for a foolish instant, if she was attracted to me. I knew, in the following instant, that such a possibility was . . . well, impossible. She was too virtuous for that.

She pointed toward a large flat rock I had not noticed. (I hadn't noticed anything but her since first we met.) "Shall we sit and talk?" she asked. So appealingly that I would not have demurred for all the gold in the world. I moved to the stone—it was really a boulder—and sat beside her. I wanted to take her hand but found it unnecessary, as she took mine, with that irresistible smile again. *"There,"* she said, as though an unspoken rule had been observed. "Now let's talk."

"Yes, let's," I said, feeling stupid at the lack of meaning (to me) in the words.

"You live with the witch across the way," she said.

"Is she a witch?" I asked. I knew the answer. Did I want an explanation? Who knows?

"Oh, she *is*," said Ruthana. "We know she is."

All I could respond was, "Oh." God, I felt stupid.

"Is she cruel to you?" she asked.

"No, she isn't," I said. Despite that gnawing rat of uneasiness, I felt a need to defend Magda. "I guess she *is* a witch," I started my defense lamely. "But she's never been cruel to me, she's always been—" How far could I go? "—kind and . . . thoughtful." I knew I wasn't going to mention the manuscript; that would really blacken the conversation. I wouldn't even bring up the healing ritual. Too much witchlike emphasis in that.

"Well, I'm glad," Ruthana said. "I was worried about it."

Worried about it? How come? Did that mean she was truly concerned about me? Why? Wasn't I one of the human beings that they loathed?

"I thought—," I began.

"Oh, no." She cut me off.

"What?" I asked her, anxiously.

"Gilly is coming," she told me.

The words chilled me. Within that moment, I was back in the woods being chased by him, that thundering pursuit by elephants through a bamboo forest. Ruthana's words seared my mind. *He despises human beings.*

"*Come,*" she said. She was on her feet in a flash (no better way to describe it), pulling me to mine so sharply that it caused a wrenching of pain in my arm. "This way," she said, beginning to run. Yanked off my stance by her unexpected strength, I could only dash beside her, filled with dread. How awful *was* her brother? What did he know about me being there? He must have known, it came to me in a cold rush. Why else was his sister running me through the woods, a look of panic on her lovely face. Not so lovely now, her beauty obliterated by fear. *My god, this Gilly must be monstrous!* I thought, stunned by dread. We ran and ran. Ruthana never said a word. I heard no heavy breathing from her; it all came from me. I didn't dare to say *I* was already getting a stitch in my side. I had to keep running, impelled by terror. *I mustn't let Gilly catch up to me. I mustn't!*

Miraculously, we were at the path, and Ruthana pushed me toward it. "*Wait,*" she said then. Raising on her toes, her small hands gripping my arms, she kissed me on the lips, I realized (incredulous despite my lingering fear), passionately.

"I love you, Alex," she whispered.

Then she was gone, swallowed by the woods. I never caught sight of Gilly. He must have noted my escape and given up pursuit. Was he chasing Ruthana now? How much animosity did he bear her? Could he hurt her? I wanted desperately to know. Was she lost already? How was I to know? I trudged back to Magda's house with only one thing resounding over and over in my brain. Ruthana's final, incredible words. *I love you, Alex.*

God! I thought. *I love you, too!* Meaningless, of course. I was a human; she, a faerie. She had to know it was impossible for us to love each other. Totally impossible.

I reached the house and went inside.

Magda was waiting for me.

Chapter Sixteen

I prepared myself for a scolding. Magda had obviously, only then, returned. She was still dressed up, her suitcase on the floor. She'd just removed her hat and was holding it in her hands. *Now what?* I thought. I tensed myself for the worst.

She threw me off balance with her smile. "Been out for a stroll?" she asked.

What should I say? I wondered. *How much should I tell her?* "Yes," I answered. "It's such a nice day."

"Good," she said. "Have you been all right?"

"Oh, yes," I lied. "I've been fine." It would be anxiety-making enough to keep it all a secret. But I would. The alternative was unacceptable.

She came over to me and gave me a lingering kiss. "I missed you, darling," she said.

I missed you, too. I knew I should have responded but held it in, unable to speak. All I could think was how (*terrible* word) hefty Magda was compared to Ruthana. I knew, even at that moment, that it was an illogical comparison, yet there it was. I tried to tell myself that Magda, like myself, was a

human being, Ruthana a faerie. (Interesting how fully I accepted their existence now.)

My thoughts were cut away as Magda said—almost wist-
fully, I thought, "Didn't you miss your Magda?" She *was* a
beautiful woman. We were (or had been) lovers. Why did I
feel so disturbingly estranged from her? Was I that frightened
of her?

I chose to lie again. "Of course I did," I answered. Then I
overdid it. My excuse? Eighteen and dense. I kissed her neck
and caressed her left breast. (How *large* they were compared
to Ruthana's.) "I missed everything," I lied; again a lie, I *was* a
dolt. *Stop it!* I told myself.

Either I convinced her or she convinced herself. She pressed
herself against me (she was so *fleshy!*) and took my lips for her
own. Her warm, wet tongue slipped in between my lips and
searched my mouth. She picked up my hands and pressed them
to her swelling breasts. "Soon," she whispered, "very soon, my
love. Take me any way you want. Any way at all."

Oh, God, I thought. This wasn't what I wanted. Far from
it. My loins might be in preparation, but my mind was not
engaged. *I loved Ruthana.* The realization came as a shock to
me. Here I was, my beautiful, voluptuous lover thrusting herself against me, yet, even responding physically, my devotion
was elsewhere. Part of me, logical even at eighteen, seemed to
know that I was being stupidly unrealistic. I wished to heaven
that Ruthana had not said what she did. It only confused my
teenage lack of intellect. I had no right to deceive Magda this
way. I knew that much. Accordingly, I made a spontaneous—
utterly stupid—decision.

"I went into the woods today," I said. Honesty is the best policy? Not always.

Magda's reaction was galvanic. She pulled away from me so rapidly, a trace of saliva descended her lower lip. She brushed it away, irritably, looking at me with demanding eyes. Witch eyes, it (wrongfully, no doubt) occurred to me. Would she now reveal her dark powers to me?

Instead, she only gazed at me remorsefully. I knew she'd been offended. Even hurt? I wasn't sure. Even as she said, "You didn't tell me."

"I know," I answered. "I should have. I'm sorry."

Silence from her. Then, "And did the little people chase you out?" I knew that she could not imagine what had really happened.

"No," I said. "It wasn't like that."

"What *was* it like?" Now her tone had stiffened, and I knew I was in for it.

I swallowed dryly. I was very nervous. Surely she could see that. "The girl I met—," I started.

"*Girl?*" she interrupted. Was that anger in her voice? Sarcasm?

"Young woman," I corrected.

"Young woman," she repeated. Stiffly.

"All right, *faerie*," I said, slightly aggravated by then. "She was a *little person*. Maybe three feet tall."

"And what did she do?" Magda asked. Demanded, I sensed.

"Nothing," I said. "We talked."

She gazed at me reproachfully. "*Talked?*" she said; not a question.

I answered it as one, however. *"Yes,"* I said. My youthful ire was rising; I had little control of it in those days. "We *talked."*

"And that was it?" she asked. Was that a hint of genuine curiosity now?

"That's all," I said.

"And then you left," she said. I knew she didn't believe a word of it.

"That's right," I said. "Then I left. *Without harm."* I would not, I vowed at that moment, tell her about Gilly's pursuit and, God knew, about Ruthana telling me she loved me.

"Alex," Magda said then. *"Darling."* I reacted in surprise. Her tone had changed completely. *Now what?* I thought, confused.

"Did you *really* believe that nothing happened to you but a harmless conversation with a faerie?" Her question was given without rancor, but I knew it was intended as criticism. Mild, perhaps, but criticism nonetheless. I knew, for sure, that I would not reveal the rest of it.

"And then you left. *Without harm?"* she repeated my words.

"Yes," I said. I was really getting riled now. Witch or no witch, what right did she have—?

She broke the mood (her mood) in an instant. "You're not telling me the truth, my dear," she said. The last part of her accusation perplexed me. Was she being understanding—or derisive? I wished I knew but didn't. The best I could say was, "What do you mean?" I used to say that to the Captain, delaying the necessity to respond to any given question. I knew I was doing the same delaying ploy but hadn't the wit to deter it.

"I *mean*," she said—as though my question deserved a reply. "A lot more happened to you. Did the young woman *escort* you from the woods?"

"*Yes*," I said. Then felt the compulsion to add, "We were being chased. The same way you and I were."

"Chased by—?" she asked—okay, demanded.

I sighed—audibly. The cat was out of the bag. Partly, anyway. "Her brother," I told her.

"Brother," she said.

Damn it, stop repeating me! My mind exploded. I had the good sense not to articulate it.

"Yes, *brother*," was all I said.

"His name?" she demanded; she was making no attempt to conceal her interrogative irritation (good, damn it, combo!) now.

"Gilly," I answered, pronouncing his name clearly.

"*Gilly*," she repeated.

"*Magda*," I protested.

She relented; a little. "And was it he who chased us?" she inquired.

"I don't know," I said. "It may have been."

"But this young woman—this *faerie*—led you from the woods, unharmed."

"*Exactly*," I said, refusing to back down from her persistence.

"Oh, Alex," she said. Now her voice was devoid of vexation. If anything, it was no more than a form of gentle exasperation. "Don't you understand at all?"

I could feel my lips bearing down on each other. "Understand what?" I demanded.

"You remember what I called them?" she asked.

"Called them?" For the moment, I didn't know what she was referring to.

"I called them fooligans," she reminded me. "You remember?"

I did. "And you're saying—?" I began.

"Yes," she said, not letting me finish. "You've been *fooled*."

"*Why?*" I insisted.

"Because you *were*," she said.

"*That's no answer*," I retorted, angry again.

Magda stiffened—it was not difficult to notice. For a second or two, I stiffened myself, a tinge of fear in me. Then, as visibly, she softened her expression and said, "Alex, I don't know why; the faeries are, very often, beyond understanding. To be frank, I've never heard of anyone being treated as you were. The young woman must have been attracted to you, that's all I can think of." It was said so casually that I'm certain she saw the look on my face, an expression of astonishment that she had, so effortlessly, divined the actual occurrence. If that *was* the actual occurrence.

"I'll only say one thing, then we'd better let the subject go," Magda said. She looked into my eyes for several moments, then completed her remark. "The young woman—a faerie, if that's what she was, and I'm not so certain—placed her mark on you. You must be careful, Alex. You must look to me for protection. Now, let's be done with it. You're safe here; that's all that matters."

Questions flooded over me. She wasn't certain Ruthana was a faerie?! *Why?* And if not a faerie, what? An image flashed across my mind. That delicate creature. What else could she be but some preterhuman being? A missing citizen of Gatford? Beyond belief. What, then? And, further, "placed her mark on me"? What was that? Witch talk? If Ruthana was not some preternatural entity, how could she place a "mark" on me, anyway? All these questions flushing through my beleaguered head at once. Poor Alex White. Eighteen and non compos mentis.

At any rate, I didn't have a clue as to what was going on.

☿ ☿ ☿

Dinner did not help. We had an early supper because Magda was hungry. Her bus trip was a long one, without food. There was not enough time to prepare a meal.

So we shared a cold ham and salad. But I deviate.

I had been mulling over what had been said between Magda and me. Moreover, I had been reenacting, in my mystified skull, my meeting with Ruthana. And, for the life of me, I could not recall a single instance of her behavior conveying menace, much less *evil*, to me. In my mind, I heard her gentle, musical voice. I saw again (visualizing it distinctly) her running me through the woods, gripping my hand so tightly. I relived, in thought, the magical moment in which, standing on her toes, she'd kissed me (yes, passionately!) on the lips and whispered, "*I love you, Alex.*" If, indeed, she had "marked" me, that was the moment when it happened. Again—and again—I reheard that wonderful whisper too soft for A. Black, too romantic. What? *MIDNIGHT WHISPER?* That would never sell. No horror whatsoever. A. Black would get a summarily instant rejection. But I deviate once more. Shame on the storyteller.

"Magda," I said at dinner, girding my loins in advance; I hoped.

"Yes, Alex?"

"What did you mean, Ruthana placed her mark on me?"

"Who?" she asked, immediately adding, "Oh, is that her name?"

"*Yes,*" I said, a tinge of bristle in my immature voice. (I must cease this, harping on my age! So I was eighteen, so what? I should have been more acute? Yes, I should have.)

"And something else," I went on. "You said you weren't sure she was—*is*—a faerie. What else could she be? If not a faerie, how could she place a *mark* on me? What *is* a mark, anyway?"

Her amused smile aggravated me. "Which question shall I answer first?" she asked.

I let the faint sarcasm in her question pass me by. "What else could she *be?*" I asked. Not too politely.

"I don't know," she said. "I think she probably *is* a faerie. From the way you described her."

Had I done that? There was no memory of it. "*Did I describe her?*" I asked—or, rather, challenged.

"Yes, you did," she answered. "I saw it in your mind. Three feet tall, golden hair, slender, naked. Were there wings?"

Was she taunting me? I wasn't smart enough to know. I couldn't dwell on the possibility, anyhow. My mind fell over itself, trying to analyze how she could describe Ruthana at all. Was she psychic? Were all witches psychic? *Wings?* Had there been wings? I hadn't noticed. It seemed unlikely—but the entire incident seemed unlikely. Had it really happened?

Had it been only a hypnotic dream, an unaware hallucination? No! My brain rebelled against that explanation. *It happened! Just as I remember it, God damn it!* Who was Magda to tell me otherwise? The fact that I knew full well it was my own mental confusion seeking an answer, I did not allow.

"No, there weren't wings," I finally managed to say. "I would have seen them." *Irrelevant!* screamed my mind. *We're losing direction here!* "All right, she's a faerie," I said. "We agree on that. Why didn't she harm me? Why take me out of the woods? Why defy her brother that way?"

"You're so sure it was her brother?" she asked. "This *Gilly?*"

A whole new kettle of fish. "What do you mean?" I asked; all I could say.

"Did you *see* him?" she probed.

I thought I had her there. "Did we see him when you were . . . rescuing [I had difficulty mouthing the word] me that day?"

"No, I didn't," Magda said. "Neither one of us did."

The significance of her reply didn't strike me for a few seconds' time. Then it did. "You're saying—?"

"I'm *saying,* dear boy, [*Don't* call *me that!* my mind resisted] that, on both occasions, you didn't *see* this Gilly. You accepted this—Ruthana's word that it was her brother chasing you."

"And who was it?" I opposed her. "Ruthana?" I grimaced at using her name so callously. "The *girl?* The *young woman?*"

"*Can you deny the possibility?*" demanded Magda. Like, I imagined, a court lawyer challenging her opponent with an unanswerable challenge.

"Yes, I deny it!" I cried, too loud, way too loud. "If you'd *spoken* to her . . ." But I knew I'd lost the *point*. I hadn't seen Gilly, not once. I'd accepted Ruthana's words. Never questioned them a single time, I was so enraptured by her presence. Cold teenage cynicism swept across me. Had Ruthana lied about her brother? *Did Gilly even* exist? *Oh, Christ!* I thought. Magda was right. I hated her for being right but had no way of conflicting with her. She'd lived in this house a long time. She had known about the Faerie Folk a long time; she was right across the way from them! How could I contradict (or *dare* to contradict) her?

Dear God, was Ruthana really a "fooligan"? Had she tricked me?

Why?

☒   ☒   ☒

Why plagued me into the night. I slept (didn't sleep) in Edward's bed. Magda wanted me to sleep with her—undoubtedly to couple. I demurred. Not too graciously, at that. Magda seemed to accept my unwillingness. She seemed (again, "seemed") to understand my temporizing, only smiling, kissing me, and murmuring, "Tomorrow, then. You know how much I've missed your love." *That's right, make me feel guilty about that as well!* I thought, at least having the good sense not to express it aloud.

So I went into Edward's bed and spent a few plagued hours trying—in vain, of course—to get some sleep. I was surprised how much my body ached. Had the run in the woods taken that much out of me?

Repeatedly, I dredged up the recollection of my time with

Ruthana. The more I did, the less able was I to go along with Magda's words, however logical they were. I could simply not be convinced that Ruthana had some dark purpose in mind. If so, she surely would have enacted that purpose while I was with her. That was the time to "mark" me, if that was what she'd planned. Why try to trick me, telling me that her brother was coming, that he hated human beings? Was that scenario reasonable? What could she gain from it? How could she be sure I would even return to the woods so she could complete her malefic purpose? What was that purpose, anyway? It was all ridiculous. All that mattered was that final moment, and that passionate kiss, and her whispered words, "I love you, Alex." That was *it*. Case solved. Court adjourned. She *had* "made her mark" on me.

I was hopelessly in love with her.

"I love you, Ruthana," I whispered back to her.

Then twitched in sudden suspense. Something had dropped on the bed beside me.

For a moment—wildly, panic stricken—I imagined some horrific witch-driven creature, sent by a resentful Magda to attack me. I actually visualized, in that dread-filled instant, what that creature resembled, some sort of slime-enveloped growth, unrecognizable by any human standard, with yellow glaring eyes—all six of them—and a panoply of multicolored tentacles—plus numerous pointed teeth. (No wonder I accepted the publisher's spawning of Arthur Black. He already lived partially inside my all-too-accessible brain.)

Then Magda murmured, "Did I wake you?"

For another instant, I imagined the monster addressing

me. Then I knew it was her and knew, immediately, why she was there. "No," I said after considering, for a moment, making snoring noises.

I felt her hands on my shoulders. The sleeve of her heavy robe touched me, and I knew instinctively that she was naked underneath. Verified as she stood for a second, then threw off the robe and pushed her way beneath the covers, pressing herself against me. Her body felt hot; it probably was. *No, don't*, I thought, feeling immediate guilt. I had virtually rioted on her salacious body—encouraged by her to allow myself any uninhibited carnality I chose to indulge in. She had always responded in kind, reflecting each erotic impulse I evoked. Now, how could I—despite the face of Ruthana in my consciousness—rebuff her? But, surprising to say, I did not want to relish Magda's fulsome body now. Worse, she could easily tell that I was not to be aroused by her. Even when, with sudden movement, she pushed down beneath the covers and plunged my organ (which, as usual, made no recognition whatsoever of my indecision and was fully prepared for action) deep into her burning mouth and ground down her teeth. Too hard. I gasped and muttered, *"Don't!"*

She released me and stood, snatching up her robe. "Never mind," she told me, sounding breathless, and peeved.

"I'm sorry," I began. *I'm just a little tired*, I was going to add. There wasn't time. She left before I could speak. *Oh, God, what have I done?* I thought in total dismay. I had the damned erection, why didn't I just allow it to achieve its obvious goal albeit nonattached to my brain? I hadn't done that, though. I'd blown it. In contrast to what Magda was trying to do. (Or was she, impulsively, preparing to bite it off? I had definite indentations on the topic under discussion.)

When I came into the kitchen the following morning, Magda was sitting at the table, an untouched cup in front of her. Leaning over, I kissed her on the cheek. "Good morning," I said, as pleasantly as possible.

"You'd better leave," was all she replied.

Chapter Seventeen

I stared at her, my heartbeat pulsing harder than it had been. *"Leave?"* I asked. I sounded, I thought, exactly like the little boy spoken to harshly by the Captain. "Why?" I managed.

"I think you know," she said.

"Because of last night?" I asked, weakly again.

"Because of what it meant," she said.

"Meant?" I really didn't know the answer.

"Come on, Alex," she told me, "use your brain."

"I'm *sorry*," I said, resisting her sarcastic tenor. "I don't know what you mean."

"I *mean*, dear boy"—*here we go again*, I thought—"whatever happened to you in the woods changed your entire attitude toward me."

"How?" I asked, although I knew exactly what she was talking about. "Because of last night? I was *tired*, Magda. It had been a hard day."

I was relieved that she didn't comment on the fact that I had little excuse for claiming weariness. What had I been doing, chopping firewood all day? Mowing the lawn? Hardly. I'd been in the woods with Ruthana, was that why I was tired?

If so, I could scarcely claim it as an explanation. Above all, I must not reveal, to Magda, what happened when I was with Ruthana. It didn't tire me, anyway. It left me exhilarated. That, God knew, I couldn't tell Magda.

While all this confused peregrination was taking place in my brain, Magda only gazed at me in silence. An expression on her face I was unable to read. Doubt? Sadness? Irritation? I couldn't tell. Probably a combination of multiple reactions to my lame excuse. I waited in anxious diffidence, my heart still beating overtime. No matter I had come to mistrust Magda after finding the awful manuscript. No matter that she seemed, to me, to be ponderous in size compared to Ruthana. No matter all of that. I had no desire to be put from her home. Forced to retreat to the even more ponderous Comfort Cottage.

In vain. When she finally spoke, it was with a shake of her head. "No," she said, "I don't believe you. I want you out of my house."

"Oh, for God's sake, Magda," I protested. "Because of *one night?*" I said it knowing that her words were justified and mine weren't.

"I'm old enough to be your mother," she said. "Would you fuck your mother?"

I was startled by her crude remark. I had no idea how to respond.

She reached out a hand and took mine, smiling. For a moment of intense consolation, I thought that she'd changed her mind. Her words soon dashed that hope. "I'm sorry, dear, but you have to leave this morning."

So I left. Not too happily, but I left. I took my clothes with me; she gave me a duffel bag to put them in, said it belonged to Edward. I trudged down the path, the duffel bag across my right shoulder. If I'd had a full white beard and two hundred extra pounds, I'd have resembled a morose Santa, I looked so ridden with gloom. I passed a man and didn't even look at him.

And I took up residence once more in that awful structure inanely titled Comfort Cottage.

Where the nightmares began.

⚰   ⚰   ⚰

Maybe "nightmares" is the wrong word if you think it refers exclusively to frightening dreams; not so. What happened to me was more, much more. Check your dictionary. Nightmares can also refer to frightening incidents. Check your *Synonym Finder* (much better than the *Thesaurus*, so says Arthur Black). Typical similar-meaning words are *torture, suffering, horror, terror-fraught, appalling, creepy, petrifying,* et cetera. That'll do. You get the point. A good deal (bad deal, actually) more than scary dreams. As you will see.

It all began the second night I was home—I mean back in "Comfort" (bah!) Cottage. Why not the first night? I don't know. Perhaps the Initiator—as, I believe, the Sender (my word) is called, chose to give me one night's grace before commencing the assault.

The assault, in the beginning, was inordinately subtle. I was lying on my bed, thinking—brooding, actually—about the sorry turn of events. My enchanting visit with Ruthana turned upside down and splattered with bile by Magda, followed by our dreadful evening in Edward's bed and expulsion from the house the next morning, painful alienation from Magda. It was especially painful to consider the loss of—loss of—what was her name? How could I forget it already? That was maddening. I saw—*or thought I saw*—her standing in the woods. No, did I? I was wrong. I couldn't remember what she looked like. Not at all. Now that was really maddening. Infuriating. How could I forget what . . . forget *what*? I wondered. Did I forget something? I couldn't remember. Damn it! What would Mag . . . Mag . . . Now what was *her* name? Her? Was it a woman I couldn't remember? No, that wasn't it. I couldn't remember *anything*. Where was I now? I could not recall. I was adrift in total memory loss. My brain had been washed of all remembrance.

The realization stunned me. No terror at first, just absolute confusion. All I could think of was knowing that I couldn't remember anything. *Nothing at all!* And I knew it. At that moment, I had my first glimpse of the nightmare that had, somehow, been inflicted on me.

Next came the awareness (thinking was slower, too) that I felt as though, suddenly, I'd just undergone a week of heavy labor: utterly fatigued, completely drained. What's more, an icy coating over my entire body. You don't think that sounds nightmarish? Try it sometime. No, don't, it's too emotionally engulfing. Lying there, immobile, convulsed by shivering, unable to budge, something else began.

Voices.

I tried to determine whether they were male or female, but without success. If there was a way to differentiate, it was beyond my comprehension. For that matter, *everything* was beyond my comprehension. I was aware only of intense discomfort—both with my body's ice-sheathed paralysis and my (inexplicable) dread now of the room it was in. What room it was and where that room was, I had no idea; I simply couldn't remember. And the voices . . . what were they saying? They did not wish me well. *Au contraire*, their voices were laden with animosity. In the mental fog I was trapped in, I could pick out only disconnected phrases such as "darkness fill you," "punish you," and "suffer torment." There were others, but I missed them in my physical and mental misery. (I know it's inappropriate here, but that *is* a worthy Blackian combo.)

All right. Visualize my plight. Loss of memory, even of identity. Did I mention that? It was part of the nightmare assault. Why I remember so much of it now . . . Well, I am, at present, in control of my faculties. Then, I wasn't.

Where was I? Loss of memory and identity. Check. Utter fatigue and frigidity. Check. *Frigid fatigue.* (No, I won't say it.) The conviction that *someone* was watching me. The voices chilling me more than I was already chilled. I forgot to mention the someone looking at me. Well, I'm eighty-two, I don't remember things in perfect order. I *do* remember that, however. Basically. And I was terrified, let me tell you. I will add only one fact, and that is God's truth.

All this really happened. It was in 1918, and I was the age of the century, the "18" part, I mean. Pardon me for my poetic levity. I'm simply trying to emphasize that all this *did* occur as I describe it. Well, far more vividly than I was able to portray the nightmare I endured that initial night in Comfort Cottage.

※   ※   ※

In the morning, I felt sick. Nothing specific. Just *sick*; all over. The exhaustion and frigidity had abated, but that was all. I ached. My head felt clogged, as did my nose. My eyes burned.

The downstairs room felt oppressively airless, and I had to get outside. I moved to the door and opened it. Another shock. *Good God, an apparition!* cried my mind. It wasn't. It was Joe with a large bag in his arms. "Jesus, Joe, you keep on scaring me," I told him irritably.

He didn't reply. Then he said, "You don't look well."

"I'm *not*," I snapped, "I'm *sick*."

"You look it," Joe observed. *Thanks for agreeing with me,* my mind retorted nastily. "Thanks," was all I said. It came out just as nastily.

"What's wrong?" he asked. Before I could respond, Joe added, "Can I bring this bag inside? I brought you some food."

"I *had* some," I replied, ungraciously.

"It was spoiled," Joe said. He brushed past me and carried the bag to the icebox. "I brought you more milk and bread," he told me. "Ham, apples."

"Let me pay you," I grumped. *You're trying to make me feel guilty,* my brain accused.

"Never mind that now," Joe said. "Close the door and let's talk."

"I was just going outside," I informed him. "I need some fresh air."

"No wonder," he said.

I'd been about to thank him for the groceries, my better self aware of his kindness, but his remark closed that door. *No wonder?* What the bloody hell did that mean?

We went outside and, as if to verify my words, I took in several deep breaths.

"Well, what brings you here?" I asked, not pleasantly. "Outside of bringing me food. And speaking of that, how did you know I was back?" Harsh interrogation. I should have known better.

"Bill Bantry passed you a couple days ago," Joe told me. "He said you were tugging a heavy bag. So I assumed you were back."

He answered my questions in such a patient manner that I felt a pang of genuine guilt and managed a halfhearted smile. "Oh," I said.

"So what is it that's making you sick?" he asked. So much as a real father (as opposed to the Captain) would ask in concern that my guilt was multiplied.

"I wish I knew, Joe." I answered, "I was attacked, I guess is the word, last night when I was trying to sleep."

"What happened?" he asked. I could tell, from his expression, that he really was concerned for me; the reaction warmed me. Didn't alleviate the feeling of sickness but helped immeasurably my state of mind. I had an ally, it occurred to me, warming me further.

So I told him everything, from the memory loss, to the deep cold exhaustion, to the voices, to the sensation that I was being watched.

"You couldn't remember things," Joe said when I had finished my account.

"Not only couldn't remember anything, I couldn't even *think*; my mind was blank."

Joe regarded me in studied silence (good combo; sorry), then said, quietly, "Sounds like faeries to me."

"Oh, come on, Joe," I said. "All that?"

"Yes," was his simple reply.

"But she couldn't—," I commenced, then stopped. Could I tell him about Ruthana?

"*She?*" he asked, reminding me of Magda's query.

I hesitated, then had to remind myself that Joe was my ally, wanted only to help.

So I told him about my meeting with Ruthana.

"She led me from the woods, Joe." I semi-protested, "She said she loves me."

"Did you go back?" he asked.

"There wasn't time," I said.

"Did she expect you to?"

"Joe, how should *I* know?" I was demanding now.

"Alex," he said (it was the first time he had called me that), "who else would know?"

Magda, my mind replied. But I didn't want to drag her into this. I already had suspicions, which my conscious mind would not permit to enter. "All right, maybe I *should* know, but I don't. Why do you bring it up?"

"Because the fact that you haven't gone back could have angered her," Joe said.

"*And make her attack me like that?*" I charged.

"She's a faerie, Alex, not a human being. It isn't possible to know how they think or act. And they *do* have powers. *At a distance.*" His last, emphatic words cut off my protest.

"But she was so *sweet,* Joe," I said, adding hurriedly, "and she saved my life from her brother."

"What brother?" Joe inquired.

"His name is Gilly," I told him.

"Have you ever seen him?" Joe asked. Now he was saying

the same thing as Magda. And it was true. I'd never seen Gilly; his existence was only a description by Ruthana. Now I was really confused. And deeply disturbed. (You know, A.B.) It had become more and more evident that the attack came not from Magda (my unadmitted suspicion) but that beautiful, ethereal creature Ruthana. I felt even sicker admitting it, but now I had no choice.

"Faeries don't think the same way we do," Joe told me. "We never can tell what they think. Or what they'll do."

"*Joe,*" I said; I was pleading now. "If she meant to do me harm, why didn't she do it when I was *with* her? Why do it the way she did?"

"Alex," first name again, warming but disturbing me further. "She could have made a mistake, or she did it as a game. We just don't know how they're likely to behave. That's why we stay away from them. Why we avoid the woods. Didn't I tell you not to go in the woods?" Now his parental concern had edged into scolding, and it made me horripilate. (Oh, *there's* a word lifted from *The Synonym Finder,* not my brain.)

"Yes, you did," I admitted despite the bristling (the word I should have used). I stared at him. "Now what?" I asked.

Chapter Eighteen

Now what? consisted of suggestions by Joe Lightfoot re methods by which to ward off faerie night attacks.

Suggestion 1: Prepare a bowl—four to five inches in diameter—by covering its bottom with a few inches of sand. On top of that, place several white sage leaves and set fire to their ends or edges. Once the flame has caught, blow them out and leave the leaves (bad prose—A. Black) to smoke. This smoke, said Joe, is what's referred to as *smudging.* Pass the smoke around your head and body a number of times, then around the room in question.

The only drawback—when I asked Joe where we get white sage leaves, he didn't know. "You could grow some," he said.

"*Great,* Joe!" I cried, "Think I can grow some by tonight?"

He winced; the only time I'd ever seen him wince. "Maybe . . . mother of essence," he suggested, "black tourmaline."

"I'll run right out and get some," I snarled. I was losing all patience. This was serious business. I'd been terrified. I needed help here. The thought raced across my mind that

Magda would be of more assistance. I chose not to follow that path.

"All right, let's see what else there is." Joe said, "I'm sorry about the white sage; that was stupid of me."

He sounded so honestly repentant that immediate guilt took hold. He was only trying to help.

"You might try burning ragwort, but the smell would knock you out."

"Anything *else*, Joe?" I inquired, bristling again.

"Well, yes, spoiled milk will sicken them. They love fresh milk, but *spoiled*—you have lots of that."

"Now we're getting somewhere," I responded. I thought we were.

"No," said Joe, demolishing that. "You'll need something better. You want to consider a spell?"

"What's that?" It sounded more promising than spoiled milk, anyway.

"It's a little complicated," Joe explained. "First of all, you have to know exactly what your goal is. Well, you do. To protect yourself against attacks. Isn't that right?"

"Well, of course," I agreed testily. "What else are we talking about?"

"*Right*," said Joe. "That's for sure, then. Next, you gather candles, stones, or whatever else you need. I can run into town and get those for you. Next decide what words you want to use. Write down whatever key ones you want to repeat, you know what they are."

I do? My mind conjectured. Well, yes, without a doubt, I knew. Stop the damn attacks. *Oh, Magda,* I thought, *I could really use some Wicca magic right now. No,* my mind resisted. Not yet. I sensed that the realization was more tolerantly inclined but let it slide. The healing ritual had truly been impressive to me. It lingered in my memory.

These thoughts disabled my brain to Joe's instructions as he rambled on. Step 5: If I desired the help of a special deity, I should decide on Him—or Her. I may need to write out special prayers and memorize them. Step 6: Be sure you clearly visualize your goal. If you want to make use of a particular faerie, decide which one it will be. *Ruthana?* I thought. Absurd if she was directing the attacks in the first place. *Gilly?* Yeah, that was a super idea. Step 7: Decide where you want to cast the spell. *When* is not considered, of course. The attacks must be averted tonight.

When it suddenly swept over me what this entire suggestion was, I threw up my hands in grated submission. "Joe! Enough!" I cried, "I can't remember all that!"

He succumbed to silence and stared at me. (A *triple* combo! Arthur Black would go nuts.) Finally, with a faint submissive smile (*another* one God damn it!), he said, "Well, yes, I guess it is too much on such short notice. We'll have to come up with something simple." (*Something simple,* Arthur Black would be nonplussed.) "You can try hand clapping or whistling—faeries hate sharp noises."

"Yes?" I said, "What else?"

"You can throw primrose blossoms around your bed," Joe said.

"That's *right,*" I enthused. "Magda did that, and it stopped Gilly's chase."

"You still believe there really is a Gilly," Joe said.

"*Yes, I do.*" I had to affirm myself somewhere along the line. "Anything else?" I persisted.

"You have a cast-iron skillet," Joe reminded me. "Put it near your bed. Or *in* your bed. And here—" He felt around in his right pocket and took out something, which he handed to me. An iron nail. "Stay dressed and keep it in your *right* pocket as I did; only the right. It makes a barrier around you. If you had a scythe, you could hang it over your doorway. Iron is the faeries' worst enemy."

Now we were really getting somewhere, my mind gloried. Why didn't he start out this way? Why with the ridiculous white sage, spell suggestions? (I'll ignore the *triple* [!] combo.)

"*Thank* you, Joe," I said. "I really appreciate this."

"Glad to help," Joe replied. "Oh, yes, you can also put ashes—you have a fireplace [I did but had never used it] into bottles or small bags and place them in the windows. Faeries don't like the smell of ashes. If you have a mirror, put it near your bed. Faeries hate mirrors. They prefer to see their reflections in pools of water. Too bad you haven't got a cat. They chase away faeries."

Good God, I thought. Joe Lightfoot was a regular font of knowledge regarding faerie dissuasion. God bless the man. What would I have done without him?

Was it my fault that I didn't realize he was completely wrong?

☙   ☙   ☙

I spent the afternoon preparing.

First of all, the primrose blossoms. I'd seen how well they

worked. Unfortunately, I had no such blossoms. I'd thrown away what I had. Magda had a garden of them, but I was hardly going to knock on her door and ask if I could borrow some. I had a few scraps in my jacket, and these I distributed around my pallet, feeling an utter fool as I did. How could these pathetic scraps of blossoms turn away an attack? Looking down at them on the floor, I scowled. Darkly.

I tried the iron skillet next. I was going to nail it to the wall above my pallet, actually the underside of the roof. I had no hammer, though. Joe hadn't offered to leave one. Whether he didn't think I'd need one or never thought of it, I don't know. At any rate, all I had in the way of nails was the one Joe had given me. I don't think I could have nailed the damn thing up, anyway. The surface of the "ceiling" was more tile than wood. So I put the skillet on top of the pallet. It looked ridiculous there. How in God's name could I sleep on that? I couldn't. I put it on the floor next to the pallet. It looked absurd sitting on the floor, amidst those primrose scraps. I felt an utter fool again.

I'd decided to sleep fully dressed with my jacket on, the nail in the right side pocket as Joe had suggested. It would have been a lot more practical to rent a room at the Gateford House. Why didn't I? To save money? No, that would be dumb. The reason I didn't was more far-fetched but seemed a stronger idea. If and when the attack began (as I was sure it would), I'd appeal aloud to Ruthana. At that point, I pretty well believed what Joe had said. That it was a definite faerie attack. If so, who would be more likely the cause of it? Hard to accept, of course, she was so unbelievably sweet. Still . . . Someone was behind it. Gilly? Not hard to accept. Magda?

That alarming possibility in my brain again. She'd put me from her house. She loved me, then felt betrayed when I told her about Ruthana. She had the means. But so did Ruthana. I remembered thinking that, in fact, I had no concept of just how powerful she really was. And she'd said she loved me. Did she also feel betrayed because I hadn't gone back to her immediately? My brain was in turmoil. Ruthana? Gilly? Magda? Yoiks!

I had no idea, so continued with my preparations—which seemed, to me, increasingly insane. I was a Brooklyn boy, after all. I'd seen action in the trenches. I'd done well in school—the only reason Captain You Know Who endured my presence in his house. Wherever that happened to be, he was transferred on occasion. What I'm trying to say is that I had (I believe) a level head. So all this lunatic stuff was anathema to my common sense–oriented brain. It was not reality but insanity. Yet I could not deny that all of it was happening. It *was* and I had to accept it. Throw that in a mix in a logical brain, and what do you get? Immense confusion. Which is precisely the state I was in.

But, regardless of this—a jumble of aggravation, reluctant belief, and, undeniably, dread, I continued with the preparations. Putting ashes from the fireplace into empty jars Joe left me. Installation of same in the windows and air opening in the attic. I thought of searching for a cat, but there wasn't time; it was already getting to be late afternoon. Soon it would be dark.

What then?

　　　　　※　　※　　※

It was not fatigue but a sudden cessation of energy; somehow, I could tell the difference. The sensation of fatigue the previous night was not abrupt. It came on gradually. This was quick. In an instant. I was drained of strength. Almost numb with weakness. Was that someone touching me? Or was it bumping? I sensed the presence of *someone* nearby. Or some-thing.

Watching me.

I began to see—or imagine I saw—shapes of dreadful shadows on the wall. Monsters of all variety. Formless creatures. Giant bugs.

I tried to clap my hands or whistle, but I couldn't summon the ability to do either. I just lay there "like a bump on a log," as my mother used to say. Why was I recalling that now? *Ruthana!* My mind cried, *please stop!*

It didn't stop. It got worse. Now I wasn't a bump on a log. I was a log. Useless, hopeless, weighing a ton, only my eyes— and terrified brain—still mobile. Shadows on the wall. Awful shadows. Menacing shadows. Ghastly shadows.

Then the voices began again.

A chorus of them. Rasping, rattling voices a cappella. "*Die now! Suffer! Flesh be gone! Eyeballs eaten!*" (For a stupid moment, I imagined all the war rats gathered together, wearing church robes, hosanna-caroling about their diets in the trenches.) Then good sense—actually, I was closer to being senseless at that moment—prevailed and I knew, again, that I was under psychic siege. *Ruthana!* I pleaded. *Stop!*

Instead of stopping, something much more hideous occurred.

A bloodcurdling scream seemed to gouge the air. My jumping eyes beheld a sight that, to this day, remains branded on my memory.

An ancient crone—a *hag*, I later learned—was rushing
across the room at me, a look of maniacal glee on her face—
which was half bone, half rotting flesh. Her dress was shred-
ded rags, reveling her scrawny, sagging breasts, which flapped
as she ran. Endlessly, from her mouth—she had no percep-
tible lips—the shrieking howl continued. Now I saw that her
skin and—God Almighty!—her *teeth* were green! Not the
green of plants or tree leaves. More the green of fungus—or
of pond slime. In spite of my frozen state, I felt my stomach
rumble and the taste of bile in my throat.

Then the hag had reached me and, with an unnatural
leap, was on top of me, the scream going on, an expression on
her foul face now one of lustful delight. I felt her bony fingers
tearing at my pants. She began to kiss me torridly, her breath
in my mouth (her tongue was cold and jagged) like a wind
from an ancient sewer. I felt sick to my stomach again, felt a
trail of vomit down my chin.

At which point, the hideous creature clutched at my
organ—which, somehow, stupidly or controlled by psychic
force (I downright refuse to believe I'd become aroused) had
erected. At which the hag, cackling victoriously, thrust
her skeletal loins onto mine and (well, *use the word!*) raped
me. More than once. Until I wept and begged over and over,
Ruthana, why?!

Then, in a second, all was ended. I could feel again. Nothing but a disabled stomach, total nausea. Severe grating pain
in my genitals. Deep scratches on my chest.

And, for some reason, an enormous rage. Joe Lightfoot
was stupid, he was wrong! His protections—none of which

worked—were laughable. If anything had happened one could laugh at, which it hadn't.

Ruthana? All that? Never! It had not been her. It could not have been. It was someone else. It had to be.

The witch Magda.

☟ ☟ ☟

I raced across the wide lawn to her house, never once considering the possibility that something would be blocking my way or stopping me; I was too incensed for such consideration. I had to see Magda. Not another thought or anxiety crossed my mind.

Reaching the front door, I twisted its knob and shoved the door open. "Magda!" I shouted.

There was no reply, so I charged through the main room, shouting "Magda!" again. Still no response. "Dammit, Magda!" I raged, "Don't try to hide from me!" Why I'd think of such a thing I couldn't tell you. I was prepared for anything, I guess. Rage suffused me. I could hardly see straight. I rushed on, yelling her name repeatedly, even (stupid me) threateningly.

Into her bedroom. No one there. The gargantuan bed did not look menacing or, God knew, inviting. I yelled her name again, in case she was occupied in her private bath. No reply. "God damn it!" I snarled. This was taking too long. My prepared rant—I'd practiced it mutteringly on my long run from the Cottage—was already diminishing. I had to let it out soon. "Magda!" I was virtually screaming it by then.

Into her study. Nothing. I considered, for a wild second, getting out her sickening manuscript and tearing it into pieces.

No time for that, though. I had my fury to unleash. "Magda!" I shouted yet again. My voice cracked. I was losing it. *No*, I thought, enraged. I had things to say to her. *Say?* Not strong enough, by half. Rant. Rave. Explode. That's how I felt. "Magda," I growled, teeth gritting.

I ran into the kitchen. No one. "Well, where the *hell* are you?" I grumbled. I shoved over the voluminous chair, pleased yet guilty at the sound of cracking wood.

My last attempt bore fruit (sour). She was in her vegetable garden, hoeing, a protective smock over her dress. At the sound of the back door slamming—I'd done it on purpose— she looked around in surprise. *"Alex,"* she said. The sound of her voice infuriated me, releasing my rant. (Not bad A.B.)

"Okay!" I started. (Not a notable beginning, but I really wasn't thinking straight.) "God damn it!" (Better.) "You can throw me out because I offended you! You can make me go back to that lousy cottage! You can do all that! But did you have to *torture* me?! Have to attack me like that?! *Look at me!*" I tore open my shirt, showing her the discolored gouges on my chest. I jerked down my pants. "Look at my [can't say it, rhymes with 'sock']! This is what you did to me! I'm covered with these! With *bites*! Are you *happy*?! Have you gotten even with me now?"

She didn't say a word, her face without expression. I waited, but she remained silent. I thought of pulling up my pants, then decided, angrily, to let her look at my battered organ. I left my shirt open, too.

Finally, her dead silence irked me. *Irked?* Come on, Black, you can come up with a better verb than that. Try . . . "made me see red." Fury really does that.

"Come on! *React!*" I ordered, ignoring the cracking sound of my voice. "Talk to me!" I should have said "speak," but my tongue—and brain—was not controlled by grammar. "Talk to me!" I repeated.

She didn't speak. She wept.

That caught me off guard. That I had never anticipated—or expected. Because her weeping was so sudden, so uncontrolled. Her sobs were violent, her cheeks quickly soaked with tears. I had never seen such unrestrained emotion from her, and it shocked me. I stood impaled between being stunned and trying, with decreasing success, to hold on to my anger.

She couldn't speak. Any attempt to do so was swallowed by great sobs that racked her body so severely, she had trouble standing. I could tell that she was trying to speak but constantly failing. All I could do was stand there with my pants down, staring at her obviously brokenhearted state.

"Alex," she managed to say at last. "Alex." Faintly. Brokenly. Just audibly.

Then she managed more, struggling with the effort, unable to control her sobbing.

"How could you?" was all she was able to say between the spasmodic sobs. (Oh, boy. A. Black) And again. "How *could* you?" she asked.

Then she was lost in her weeping, unable to breathe, almost choking with her sobs, moaning—in pain, it sounded like. Embarrassed now (bare assed as well, I feel compelled to rhyme), I began to pull up my trousers. Magda, still weeping uncontrollably, shook her head and waved her right hand at me as though abjuring me to leave my trousers be. Not knowing what she meant, I left them down, well aware of the fact that I must have looked absurd, almost comical. "Magda, I don't think—," I started. She shook her head again, giving me the impression that she didn't want me to say another word.

Finally, she regained her voice, albeit stricken with pain— and, to my amazement—remorse.

"How could you believe that of me?" she asked, she *begged*. "How could you believe I'd do such things? To *you? The father of our child?*"

Chapter Nineteen

Good God. The first two words to emerge from my smitten head. Our *child?* Somehow that seemed to alter everything. Where had fury gone? What rant was remaining? None. I stared at her in stricken muteness.

Then I said—I muttered, "Our *child?*"

"Alex," she said. Was that a smile despite the tears? "We've . . . coupled quite a number of times. Without protection of any kind. Does it surprise you that I finally became with child?" (I believe the word "pregnant" wasn't in common use back then.)

"Well—" My brain was, by now, completely flustered. "You—" No words took shape. Then, suddenly, the retort sprang. "If you knew that you were—carrying my child, how could you attack me that way?"

"Alex," she said, her voice losing strength again. "What makes you think that I . . . *attacked* you?" The word, apparently, much pained her.

"Well, who else could *do* it?" I demanded. "Who else has that kind of power?"

She only gazed at me. As though she knew that the answer was already mine.

I guess I slipped up. I should have pursued the angry questioning. Instead, I asked (naïvely, I suspect), "*They* have such power?"

"And more," said Magda.

Holy Christ, I thought. Now everything was being thrown back in my face.

"But the *exhaustion*," I said, close to protesting now. "The *loss of memory*. The *coldness*. The *horrible voices*. I'd done everything I could to protect me. The primrose pieces around my bed, my pallet. The cast-iron pan. The ashes in the windows. All to stop them. *Nothing worked!* How could it be faeries, Magda?! How *could* it be?!"

"Not *faeries*, Alex," Magda said. "Just one."

Oh God, I thought. She almost had me convinced.

But I forged on. Trying desperately to vindicate Ruthana. "Two nights straight?" I persisted, "That hideous old woman doing *this* to me?!" I pointed forcefully to my beleaguered groin.

Her next words threw me totally.

"Take off your clothes," she said.

I was unable to reply, my mouth hanging open. Then I managed to rage, "I'm in no condition!"

"*Alex*," she cut me off. "I'm not suggesting lovemaking. I want to put some salve on your wounds."

"Oh," I said stupidly. Teenagedly. I simply knew no better at the moment.

Thus, obediently, probably sheepishly, I took off all my clothes, assisted by Magda, and stretched out, naked as a battered jaybird, on the kitchen table while Magda retrieved a small jar from a cabinet and undid the cap. "Now," she said. The way she said it—so businesslike—made me think for a moment or two that the salve-spreading was somehow a dreadful encore to the attacks.

Then as the whitish cream—more than a gelatinous salve—was spread across my chest by Magda's gentle fingers, I felt the pain diminishing noticeably. And when she applied it to my genitals, my know-nothing organ responded—as it usually did—with no discernment whatever regarding what had happened to it. Magda repressed a smile. "I thought you said you were in no condition to—?" she said. I was in no mood to be teased. "It's just a reflex," I mumbled. It sounded absurd.

"Of course," she said. "I know that."

Several seconds of silence as she continued rubbing, very carefully, all the bruises and deep scratches on me, front and back. I have to say that cream certainly did the job.

At last, she said, "That hideous old woman is called The Old Hag, a spirit in English folklore."

"*Magda*," I said, irritable despite my awareness of the fact that I was pretty helpless lying in the altogether on the kitchen table like that. "She was *not* a spirit. *Look* at me! Did a *spirit* do *this*?!" I gestured feebly at my maltreated groin.

Patiently, she answered, "Do you believe that spirits are unable to take on flesh and bone?"

"*Flesh and bone?*" I doubted. "A *spirit*?"

"Yes, Alex. Yes," she said. Then, "Shall I show you books describing it? *Photographs?*"

"Well . . ." Grumpy now. I lapsed into a dissatisfied silence. Then a retort became my countering. "And you're saying that

Ruthana (I didn't hesitate to use her name now) did all that to me?"

Her argument against the point was not expected. Nor well received.

"Consider, Alex. She allowed you to—no, *lured* you to her—even though the little people are extremely loath to permit such a meeting. She conversed with you amiably. Then, when you were convinced that all was well—while she was naked, no less."

That shook me. Had I told her? I couldn't recall. "Of course she was," Magda continued, turning the knife a little more. "She had to be. To allure you. Can't you see that?"

"No," I muttered. Unsubstantiated by conviction.

"I think you do," said Magda. "Anyway, just when you were most comfortable, she told you that her brother—her *awful* brother—was coming. And she staged a flight before her brother—and helped you escape."

"That's right," I explained, lamely. "If she wanted to hurt me, why help me escape from her brother?"

"Who you never saw," Magda stated. "You have no way of knowing if he really exists."

"Well . . ." No retort to that. I *didn't* know. Gilly truly might not exist.

"Oh, God," I murmured. "She seemed so *sweet*, Magda. She said she *loved* me." There, it was out. Magda would have made a good detective, wringing—or finessing—an involuntary confession from the felon in custody.

"I'm sure she did," was all she said.

"I still don't know why she let me go," I told her.

"That *is* peculiar," Magda replied. "I've never heard of that before. Another example of attempted faerie trickery, I suppose. Or she's too young and hasn't refined trickery yet. She may have expected you to return. When you *didn't . . .*" She let that hang.

"And you think she has the power to—," I began.

"I *know* she has the power," Magda said firmly. "You can't underestimate what they can do. Causing 'things' to happen from a distance is the least of them. I'm certain she's old enough for that."

"I was sure—no, I wasn't sure, I *suspected* that it was *you,* Magda," I said.

Her face fell. I can describe it no other way. "If you really believe that, Alex," she started.

"Magda, I'm not sure *what* I believe anymore." That was true enough. My brain was a jumble of possibilities—and confusions.

"If you do believe that I did all these terrible things, you have to leave again," she said.

"And be attacked again?" I said. I was sure she knew I was kidding.

She smiled. "You're done, get off the table," she said.

I sat up. "Actually, that old hag wasn't too bad looking," I said.

"Oh, shut up." Repressing another smile, she whacked me on the bottom.

So there it was. Resolution. At any rate, some kind of resolution. I still found it, bone-deep, difficult to believe that Ruthana had been guilty of those terrifying attacks, but on the other hand (no question why Pisces is labeled the trash bin of the zodiac; my brain was certainly a trash bin of doubts),

Magda had convinced me (almost) that it wasn't her. It was clearly true enough that I had no conception of how powerful the faeries were. If there really was a Gilly, he had accomplished his two pursuits in first-class fashion, scaring the living bejesus out of me on both occasions. I still had vivid memories of the elephant (they couldn't have been real elephants, could they?) charge through the bamboo forest behind me. And Magda actually *saved* me from that! One more golden star for her. Dear God. Was I *perplexed*. In every way. I was a mental wreck. "Determination," try to be my name!

It wasn't.

🐝 🐝 🐝

To make a long story short (corny! A. Black), I remained with Magda. The witch. I shouldn't say that. She was a *wicce*. That's different. At least I always assumed it was. I *should* say Magda, the mother of my impending child. That really bollixed up my brain. Me a daddy? At *eighteen*? What next? A family of twelve? The prospect did me in. If Magda got pregnant *that easy*! How old *was* she? No younger than my mother, surely. Could my mother have had a baby at this age? The idea was appalling. The thought of her coupling with the Captain was enough to turn my stomach. What would he have done, assigned her a certified length of time to give shore leave to his navy-regulated sperm? Jesus Christ, the imaging was too revolting! I already had enough problems on my mind.

So I remained with Magda. In a mixture of trust and mistrust. I believed her, yet I didn't believe her. Everything she said seemed (there's that word again) indisputable. And yet, forever lingering in my psyche was the memory of that sweet-faced

faerie named Ruthana. I knew that she seemed to possess powers (an A. Black combo; acceptable) I had no concept of.

Where was I? Yes, my inability to deny Magda's words,
yet my equal inability to deny the sweetness of Ruthana. So
where did that leave me? On a rocking seesaw. On a wire,
dangling above certainty and its opposite. In truth, I loved
them both.

No, it was a love divided between Magda and my faerie
charmer. One was the love of a son for his mother, albeit
complicated by the fact that we were also lovers.

My love for Ruthana was—let's call it—totally romantic.
With all the flaws that word implies. Blinded vision. Illogical
mentation. Ignorant bliss; the phrase is quite apt. I knew,
when I considered what I still felt about Ruthana that I was
being totally—probably absurdly—unrealistic. But what does
an eighteen-year-old know about true reality?

I had, still, to learn.

All right, then, the love of a son for his mother. His beautiful, voluptuous, passionate mother. It was simple for a dull-
witted teenager to feel love for a gorgeous mom. She treated
me, as well, with all the care of a loving parent. So much so
that, I confess, as weeks rolled by, I thought less of Ruthana
all the time.

For *then*.

Magda cooked for me, baked for me. Absolutely scrump-
tious meals. Delicious cakes. Overwhelming biscuits. Do I
make my point?

She kept me in clean clothes. Took me into Gatford to buy
me new outfits. Once, anyway. The experience was so unpleasant that it pained and aggravated both of us. The looks.

The poorly guarded smirks. The behind-the-hand mutters. Stupid yokels. All very irritating and disturbing. Especially to me. I gathered that Magda was not unfamiliar with such insulting treatment. If she had once been a welcome citizen of Gatford, now she was not. Now she was decidedly unwelcome. Poor Magda. I say that in her behalf—for that period of time. Now . . .

From there on, she kept my clothes as clean and neat as practical. When they began to look their age and fray, she reworked Edward's clothes. Fortunately, he and I were constructed similarly, so any alterations were minimal.

And we conversed. As the weeks turned into one month, then two. We conversed more each day. Magda "opened up," as they say—as much mentally as physically. (Sorry about that.) She told me she was "not legitimate," as they, also, say; the dumbbells. She was the "love child" of Tollef Nielsen— Norwegian-English. She grew up in Central England. Her father was kind to her, her mother otherwise. The absolute opposite of my rearing, I told her. She became intrigued with Wicca when she was in pre-college school. She never went to college. Thrown out of the house (figuratively speaking), she moved off on her own, ending up in Gatford, met Jerry Variel, and married him, gave birth to Edward. I've already told you the rest. Her interest in Wicca rebloomed, providing her need for comfort, which brings you to the present. The present of *then*, not *now*. Does that make sense? Let's hope so.

⚸   ⚸   ⚸

More on our daily conversations.

I described—as best I could—the night attacks on me.

The physical exhaustion. The mental washout. The inability to move. The shadows. The voices. The hag assault.

"And I put out every protection Joe told me to use," I insisted. "The flower buds—what was left of them. The cast-iron skillet. The nail in my pocket. The bottled ashes in the windows and air opening on the second floor. But none of them worked. That's why I—" I broke off, unable to say it.

"Why you thought I did it," Magda finished for me.

"Yes," I admitted.

"Alex," she said, "*darling*. What you don't understand is this: All right, I admit it's curious that your protections didn't help. That's a separate matter. But your description of what you went through was very little [*little?* I thought, reacting angrily] to what you would have experienced from a genuine witch attack. Are you listening?"

"Yes," I said, not convincingly.

"You look as though your mind is elsewhere," she said.

Touché, I thought. Trapped. My mind *was* elsewhere. Caught in a limbo between attention and doubting. What exactly was she saying? "I'm sorry," I muttered.

"What I'm *saying*," she went on (was she sponging up my thoughts now?), "is that, if it *had* been me—and you know now why it could not have been." *I know?* came the thought. Well, yes. I did. The baby. "The attack effects would have been far more severe. You would have been more than immobilized and hearing voices—that's faerie stuff. (*Faerie* stuff? I questioned.) Your abdominal pains—I assume you had them— would have been so intense, they would have made you scream in agony. Your neck would have suffered terrible, painful spasms. Your kidneys would suffer. You would be experiencing an epileptic fit, your legs and arms convulsing helplessly. You would have felt some invisible force pressing down on your chest, you would have become convinced that you were going to die. Your bedroom—or whatever you call it—would have been filled with a hideous stench, so awful that, combined with the weight on your chest, you would have been certain that you were unable to breathe. All that time, you would have heard loud footsteps in your room and yet been unable to see anything, although you would have been sure that something was in the room with you. Then you would have been conscious of some invisible entity leaning over you, whispering terrible obscenities in your ear. Your little faerie protections would be useless."

"Even with a cat?" I asked. Why I felt inclined to josh at that moment, I had no idea.

Magda smiled. A sympathetic smile. I guess she knew better than I did. My joshing was not an attempt to lighten the moment but no more than nervous reaction. "Even with a cat." She allowed my words to contain some acceptable point.

"Do you understand what I just told you?" she asked then.

Did I have a sensible response? "Yes," I said, "except for two things: Can a faerie do all these things? And, if they do have such power, are all the protections Joe told me about of no effect at all?"

"I think that the little people—some of them, anyway— may have far more black magic power than I've given them credit for." Magda said, "This girl—what's her name? [*You know her name!* my mind exploded.] Oh, yes, Ruthana. She must have been extremely drawn to you. No wonder. Faeries are known to be fascinated with human beings. They love to learn all about us. So, when you didn't go back to her . . ."

"But she led me out of the woods," I said, still uncertain about that.

"She must have been so sure of her control over you that she felt she could afford that," Magda said.

"Afford?" I said, pettish now. "Am I a piece of furniture?" Eighteen-year-old logic.

"No, you're a beautiful young man," she said.

"Beautiful?" I snapped, *"Come on."*

And yet I knew I was. Give me my due. Have I even mentioned it till now? No, I've never "utilized" my looks. Well, now I'd be stupid to try. But then? Despite my snapping rejoinder, I knew that Magda was right. And, fully, expected her to embellish the point. Which she did.

"You know you are," she said. Was that an impish smile? It was. "Do you think I would have taken you to my bed if you looked like Mr. Hyde?"

I had to smile at that. But with the utter lack of timing I possessed at that age, I said, "I thought you wanted a son."

Incorrect. Pall spreading. Magda looked disturbed. "Is that what you really think?" she asked.

I knew (instantly; at least I was sensitive enough for that) that I had misspoken. Although I knew that what I had said was, basically, true, I also knew it was misguidedly hurtful. So, once again, I apologized. (I did a lot of that, in those days.) "I'm sorry, Magda," I told her. "I shouldn't have said that."

I didn't wait for her forgiveness. Maybe I assumed it would be forthcoming. "Something else," I went on. "You said black magic. Are you saying that Ruthana was using *black magic* against me?"

She didn't answer at first. Was she still upset about my remark?

I guess she was. "Do you really think I brought you into my house because I wanted a son?"

Yes, I do, my brain responded, devoid of hesitation. Or grace. *I think you wanted another Edward.*

"No," I lied. Hoping, to God, that she took it for the truth. My brain emerged with a mollifying addition. "I know how much you miss Edward. I just wish I *could* replace him."

That did it. Mercifully. Her features softened, and she said, "I *do* miss him. Terribly. But I have never thought of you as a substitute son." Another impish smile. If she had been a man, I would have termed it a wicked grin. "I had no interest in taking my son to bed with me," she said. A few moments of silence before she continued. "Black magic? She must know about it. Obviously she practices it. How else explain those attacks?"

"What *is* it?" I asked. I had a damnable time trying to visualize that angelic-faced creature involved in manipulating dark forces. But Magda was right: How else explain those attacks?

At which point, flashing across my mind—harshly contradicting her denial of any intention of bringing Edward to her bed—was her profane injunction to me while we were coupling. No interest indeed! Yet more confusing inconsistencies in my mind. How was I to deal with them? I simply did not know.

Chapter Twenty

At this point in our conversation, Magda—who seemed to have recouped the stability of her nature—began to explain the nature of black magic. As I surmised (pretentious word, that; well, I probably have become at least semi-pretentious in my old age), black magic was, fundamentally, the manipulation of dark otherworldly forces for some, most likely, devious purpose. The Wicca belief (they *do* utilize black magic, Magda told me) was, not for harmful purposes but good, positive. Otherwise the preparations were pretty much the same, arcane rituals marked by the use of mystical symbols—on their costumes, on the utilized environment—and chants invoking the presence of whatever forces were judged to be desired for the good (or bad) intention.

For instance, in the negative black magic, a feeling of hatred (for whatever reason—jealousy, envy, et al) resulted in an evil elemental (whatever they may be) to be dispatched, hover above, then attack the victim in whatever weak spot the victim might possess. As long as the attack persists—and the Sender must be cautious about that—the victim will suffer

protracted distress if not demise (distress—demise; not bad
A.B.). The Left-Hand Path, it's called.

The drawback is that the attack will evoke no result on
the targeted victim if that person (he or she) hasn't the sort of
character vulnerability to provide enough open flaws in which
the elemental can make itself at home.

The very existence of these evil elementals, Magda pointed
out, engenders the possibility that—without the assistance of
black magic—they can prey on victims for their own malevolent reasons. Such attacks may consist of nightmares (dream
variety), hallucinations, paralysis, grisly manifestations—
blood, slime, and the like—extreme cold, et cetera, et cetera.

"And you think Ruthana has the power to do all these
things?" I asked. In genuine pain.

"I'm convinced that she has," Magda answered.

"Dear God." My eyes were tearing. I really was in pain.

To consider that a sweet-faced angel like her could, will-
fully, consort with evil elementals and do all these terrible
things to me was agonizing.

Magda took me in her arms; she *had* forgiven my remark,
I decided. She kissed me on the cheek. "I know," she told me
softly, "faeries can be very dangerous. I'm a witch (she said it
so casually now), and I have to use as much caution with them
as anyone does. I can summon the powers they have, I know
how to banish them from my home and even to destroy them
if I must. Still . . ."

"You'd *destroy* Ruthana?" I couldn't accept it.

"If I must," she said. Seeing my expression as I drew away
from her, she added, "I won't, of course. Unless it was to protect you. And you're safe as long as you're with me."

I put my arms around her now. I did feel safe in her renewed embrace. The thought that, despite her enchanting manner, Ruthana was a powerful—and menacing—being chilled me. Magda instructed me to lie down and try to physically relax myself. Breathe slowly and evenly, visualizing each inhalation as drawing in a flow of energy from my feet to the top of my head. Imagine that energy gaining in strength as it streamed through my body. Finally, visualize a sphere of white light floating over my head and trust that divine love was protecting me.

While on the subject, to my surprise, she told me that my remark had disturbed her because her loss of Edward still pained her deeply. As a matter of fact, she confessed, she'd tried to "bring him back" through the use of black magic.

Perhaps because her motive was confused, a mixture of positive and negative, the result was dreadful. An image of Edward, a white-faced corpse, his body half gone, the remainder drenched with blood.

"It was the most horrible moment of my life," Magda told me. "A perfect example of the danger of misusing black magic. Don't ever try, Alex. For God's sake, *don't ever try.*"

"I won't," I said. As though I'd even thought of it.

"And please—*please,*" she said, "don't think for a moment that it was ever my intention to replace Edward with you. *It simply isn't true.*"

I had to believe her. Could such pained emotion be feigned? I still wasn't sure.

⚹ ⚹ ⚹

Magda consolidated her position in my life by introducing me to scrying.

When I mentioned Veronica several times, Magda asked me if I wanted to see her.

"She's *alive?*" I asked. Naïvely, of course.

"Somewhere," Magda said. "*Somewhere.* In the spirit world."

"So—" I didn't really understand. "Are we going to have a—*séance?*" I guess I knew the word at the time. Maybe I expressed it in another way. I don't remember.

"No," said Magda with a smile, "we'll use scrying."

Scrying is a method by which hoped-for images may be seen in a mirror. Any kind of mirror is usable, though round hand mirrors work best. Full-size mirrors, Magda informed me, are of use only if the mirror is being used as a doorway into the astral world. (I did not intend such.)

Mirrors, Magda explained, are usually linked to the moon. They are backed with silver, the so-called lunar metal. The glass front is a "lunar substance," frames are best in silver. The round shape resembles the full moon. None of which was of any interest to me. I listened patiently to Magda's descriptions, waiting to hear about my seeing Veronica again. "You *did* love your sister," Magda tested.

"We loved each other very much," I answered, remembering how gentle and kind Veronica was. "Good," said Magda. "That's important."

Magda had purchased her mirror in a Gatford antique shop. It was an old cosmetic mirror, slightly tarnished, with a silver frame. She took it from a cabinet in her study. The first night of the experiment, she put it outside so that the surface would reflect the light of the moon. She then wrapped it in black velvet, black being a lunar color, she said. Did I mention (no, I forgot, old age again) that the back of the mirror was painted black? This was so that the mirror would not reflect anything, distracting the eyes. That way the viewer would be, as it were, gazing into a black pool, making it easier to "see things," as Magda put it. Scrying regulations, I figured. I was sure I'd "see nothing" but I went along with it nonetheless, my yearning to see Veronica outweighing any dubious frame of mind.

The night arrived for my scrying test. In spite of my continuing doubts, I felt uneasy, with no idea of what exactly was going to take place.

Before I started, Magda gave me the handled mirror and told me to hold it carefully, noting whether it brought on any intuitive responses in me. In brief, did the mirror "speak" to me? When Magda said that, I felt inclined to snicker. I held the mirror up to my right ear and pretended to listen. "Not a word," I said.

Magda frowned. "Are you going to take this seriously?" she asked. "If not, we're wasting time."

I winced at that. "I'm sorry," I said. "I really do want to see my sister."

"Very well, then," she said. "Place the mirror on the table. [We were in the kitchen.] Lay it flat and look into it steadily, imagining that you're looking *through* its surface, deep into the darkness. Concentrate your mind on the blackness, focusing your thoughts on the astral world where Veronica is. Stare into the darkness and your thoughts."

I did what Magda told me. Losing track of everything but the blackness in the mirror, the total darkness. Nothing else. Minutes went by. "Keep looking," Magda said quietly. "Stare into the darkness. See nothing but the darkness and your thoughts about Veronica." I sensed, in the back of my mind, that she was hypnotizing me and wondered fleetingly if it was her hypnosis that was going to make me see Veronica. Then, all was lost in the blackness, my need to see Veronica—and Magda's soothing murmur.

I don't know how much time passed before anything happened. Maybe an hour. Maybe two. There was no way to register passing time.

Then, suddenly (and I do mean *suddenly*) the mirror brightened to a light gray, and colors began flashing across its surface. The abrupt transition made me catch my breath.

"What is it?" asked the voice; I'd forgotten who it was.

"Colors," I muttered.

"In clouds?"

"More like moving shadows."

"Moving water?"

"Moving *shadows*," I repeated, getting pettish.

"What colors?"

"Blue. Purple. Green. Pink."

"Which way are they moving?" asked the voice.

"Left to right," I answered.

"Is one of them persisting?"

Persisting? I thought. *Oh, yes. Returning again and again.* I twisted restlessly on the chair.

"Are you uncomfortable?" inquired the voice.

I knew then it was Magda. "Yes," I told her, "nervous."

"Visualize white light around you," she told me.

I tried. It didn't work.

"Color?" Magda insisted.

"*Red,*" I said.

"That's anger," she replied. So patiently, it galled me.

"That's enough," I declared. The mirror went blank in that instant. Magda made a sound of disappointment. "You'd gone so far," she said.

I sat up straight. Without realizing it, I had been bending over, my face inches from the mirror. I looked at Magda, I'm afraid accusingly. "I'm sorry," I said. I wasn't.

Clouds, or moving shadows, moving water, whatever, traveling from left to right signified the approach of spirits, she told me. If only I had stayed with it . . .

That especially I didn't want to hear. Or that the movement of the shadows in the opposite direction—which they were beginning to do when I broke off—meant the withdrawal of spirits.

As for the colors (I barely listened to her as she recounted their meaning) they were yellow, willfulness; orange, indignation; purple, brooding, obsession; and, of course, red, anger. I'm surprised I didn't see a rainbow of those colors. I'd become increasingly rattled and irritable.

As for the clouds—in my case, the shadows—forming on the left meant manifestations; on the right, spiritual insights; rising, revelations; falling, negation; I've already told you about the left to right and vice versa.

While I should have asked questions during observations of the moving shadows, I might have gleaned some desired information before reaching the vision stage. During the questions, the clouds (the shadows) would likely have changed direction. In my case, dropping like lead balloons.

I gave up scrying after one more night's attempt. I'd never see Veronica again, it became obvious. The realization (heartbreaking to me) embittered my persona toward Magda for more than a week. To her everlasting credit, she did not retaliate. I know now that she could have. Easily.

Actually, on my second scrying venture, I thought I did see Veronica. Not her, but an aged, yellowing photograph of her. Which, as I tried to see more distinctly, seemed to alter to an image of (I was stunned by the sight) Ruthana. When that occurred, I gasped and drew up sharply from the blanking mirror. With the abrupt decision, angry now, never to try scrying again. I never told Magda what I thought I saw.

She alienated me further by explaining additional information about scrying. Spirits may engage directly with the scryer. Never attempt to converse with them. Not audibly, at any rate. Thoughts are as "audible" to them as spoken words.

The notion that I might not only have seen Veronica but also communicated with her—in whatever netherworld she now resided—came close to maddening me. Not at myself, of course (I was eighteen, remember), but at Magda. More than that, at life in general. Society. Culture. The world and its hateful citizens. (I've told you more than once: I really wasn't thinking straight.) Magda gave an extra twist to the blade in my heart telling me that evidently I had attained the *first degree*—seeing shadows (aka clouds). Only those in the *fourth degree* would be capable of seeing detailed visions of spirits; and, even those, irregularly. It took a *fifth degree* to summon visions at will; the *sixth degree* enabled the scryer to engage the visions as a participating actor. I felt great about that sarcasm.

※　※　※

As supplemental evidence of my muddled thinking, that night as I lay in bed beside my might-as-well-be-called bride,

I went over and over my cerebral lamentations about the world at large. The world "out there" in all its rotten glory.

Which world was real? The world I was presently in—lying naked beside a witch? Or the world I'd been in from birth up to and including my time in the French trench; now, *that* was reality, horrible reality. The months in the trench. That certainly seemed real enough—the mud, the explosions, the gore, the rats, the endless stench. Wasn't that reality?

It certainly seemed to be in contrast with the gold lump becoming a lump of gray dust. My two experiences in the woods. Ruthana. Magda. The miraculous healing. The God-awful manuscript. The hideous night attacks. Was all that madness *reality*? It certainly seemed to be so at the time.

That lumped-together thinking did nothing for my sleep. Instead, I began to think about the world at large. Still embroiled in war. Thank whatever stars were in my favor (precious few, I imagine) that I had no knowledge of WWII as I now have. If it had even occurred to me that the damned Boche—becoming damned Nazis—were going to rise again after losing WWI—and threaten the world once more—not to mention the ghastly Holocaust—I would have gotten out of bed and hanged myself. Or, at the very least, opened a few veins and quietly bled to death.

I didn't know, thank God. So I was merely miserable, stressed out by my experiences in ye trench. I tried to rationalize it away but with limited (none) success. Maybe Magda could summon up some out-of-this-world forces and heal my stress. I'd be embarrassed to ask. The leg and hip wound—that was visibly acceptable. Stress? Sorry. Doesn't show.

For a while I amused myself—maybe "bemused" would be

more accurate—with memories of the rat wars we enjoyed (we *did* enjoy them, God help us) in the trenches. We took trips to connecting trenches for more rats in the event that our immediate supply ran out. We threw the rats at each other (yes!), laughing like crazy all the time (we *were* crazy), or if we could lay our hands on a pistol, stealing it or confiscating it from the body of a killed officer, we would shoot the rats. Did I already tell you that? I may have. And that the rats exploded "nicely" when struck? Probably did.

Despite my hours of brooding wakefulness, I must, eventually, have slipped off into some kind of REM doze. Because, immediately, I dreamt.

About Ruthana.

It didn't seem to be a dream. It was as though she stood in front of me emblazoned in a dazzling white light. She was crying. Her lips were moving. No sound. I tried to understand what she was saying. Finally I got the words.

"*Please.* Come back to me. *Please.* Come back to me." Again and again. Without sound. As though she couldn't speak aloud. Or was prevented from speaking the words aloud by some invisible barrier.

Created by Magda; it came to me.

Chapter Twenty-one

How long the light (the dream) persisted, I have no idea. All I remembered was Ruthana's exquisite face wet with tears that never stopped flowing. Her glorious tear-glistening eyes directed at me. Her lips trembling as she repeated endlessly: "*Please come back* to me. *Please.* Come back to me."

I woke up with a start.

To hear the rustle of Magda's movement as she awakened. "Are you all right?" she asked in a sleep-thickened voice.

"Yes," I said.

I felt her hot flesh as she pressed against me. "Good," she murmured. I winced as she lay a warm (it felt heavy) arm over me. At one time, when she did that, I would have felt protected. Then, it only disturbed me. Did she know about my dream? I didn't see how she could have. But she had so many powers. About most of which I knew nothing. I waited to see if she mentioned it. If she did, my stress level would have doubled.

She didn't.

I brought up the subject the following morning at breakfast. Not with regard to Ruthana, of course. More having to do with Magda's protection of me—an approach I knew was workable.

"Magda," I began, broaching the question cleverly (I thought, with all the egotism of the standard teenager), "since you live so close to the woods, how do you protect yourself from them? Or do they just leave you alone because—" I broke off, realizing, with dashed egotism conviction, that I'd gone too far.

"Because I'm a witch?" Magda said. Neither kindly nor accusingly. A statement of fact. Which I could, scarcely, deny.

She told me that faeries disliked—were offended and even pained—by sudden noises. Accordingly, she extended (microscopic) threads across her property. She answered my question for me. The obvious question being, How come I didn't bump into those threads? Because, she explained, they are astral threads, invisible to mortal flesh but not to faeries. So when the faeries come in contact with the threads—*bing, bang, boom!* Bells "activate" and—ergo—the little people are dismissed forthwith. Had any of those people tested the threads? Years ago. They'd been dismissed. Forthwith. Doesn't that mean "right away"? I hope so.

Beyond that, the running water in front of her entry acted as a deterrent, diffusing their power. Why, I couldn't tell you, since faeries—notably Ruthana—seemed to relish running water. Maybe only in the woods.

Of course, if the water didn't do the job, the faeries might elect to enter *through* (the door, no) the *walls*. They had that power, being largely astral themselves. (I really did a heap of wondering on that.) The power was stymied by the installation of malefic herb pouches in each window. I hadn't noticed them, although I'd been conscious of an enduring odor in the house—not terribly offensive to me, but definitely ever-present.

Using some form of ritual, Magda had also created what she called a vortex of defensive energy above the house. This so-called cone of power, she explained, when created over the defendant's head (most likely the witch's), gave rise to the myth about the witch's coned hat. Interesting.

All these protections being in effect, it was little wonder that the strange image of Ruthana was unable to speak aloud. It was a miracle that Ruthana was able to appear at all. She must have unusual powers, too, I thought.

None of which assuaged (there I go again) my discomfort at the entire occurrence. I tried to maintain my "general" interest and involvement in the topic of faerie security, but it wasn't easy. When Magda had completed her discourse on the subject, I even tried to make a joke. "Now I know," I said, "why there are no bugs in the garden."

She laughed at my lame attempt to produce humor, and the moment passed. Leaving me hopelessly ensconced (look it up yourself) in my congealed (that, too) depression. How could I go on this way? Torn between my limited acceptance of Magda and my everlasting enchantment with Ruthana. Now I'm back to combos again! Forgive me. This *is* a disturbing section of my account to be immersed in.

☆　☆　☆

My emotional turmoil ended—with a bang—a few days later.

I was out walking on the path; Magda now allowed it, apparently at peace with my behavior toward her. Which surprised me, since I felt that my behavior was, to say the

least, questionable. I, of course, underestimated her activity. I
think, now (God knows I didn't have the wit then), that she
knew, all the time, what was stirring in my eighteen-year-old
brain and acted accordingly. Which meant, I now believe,
lengthen the unseen leash and see what the doggie does. Unkind, I guess. She didn't think of me as a pet (I don't think), but
she knew about Ruthana now and how Ruthana had affected
me. So . . . extend the leash and see what happens.

Which found me strolling unaware along the path.
Uneasily—not because I thought, for a moment, that Magda
was keeping an eye on me. Maybe she wasn't. Maybe I'm over-
estimating her skill at detecting the significance of my behavior. Still, there were the woods themselves. Ruthana was in
there, and up to that moment, I had no idea of (1) how powerful her psychic abilities really were, and (2) was she still, as
she had claimed, in love with me and, because I had unknow-
ingly betrayed her, now in hate with me? You can see that my
emotional turmoil was still very much intact.

At what point in my thought-muddled walk it began, I do
not recall. It probably came on me gradually, step by step. A
sensation of being *drawn* into the woods.

At first, I gave it little credence, thinking—if I was capable
of thinking at all—that the minor physical compulsion was a
psychological effect, not actual.

I was wrong. By the time I tried, once more, to ignore the
compulsion, it was too powerful to ignore. Too impossible to
resist. My body was being drawn inexorably into the woods.
The more I struggled against it, the stronger it became. For
a moment or two, I conjectured (dazedly) that it was being
caused by Magda. But *why?* I argued—thought. Why force me

to encounter Ruthana? Then again, it wasn't that at all. En-counter Ruthana? Why do that? More likely encounter some malevolent faerie who would—?

No! I resisted that with all my might, which was, I tell you, not much at that point. For, while I was conjecturing point-lessly, the drawing went on, unabated. I swear it was as though some invisible entity had me tightly in its grip and was pull-ing me into the woods. Where I, now, was being dragged (but gently) through the grass and around the bushes and tree trunks.

At that point, I gave up resisting. The drawing was too careful. If Magda was behind it, would it be so? I didn't think it. It had to be Ruthana. But why? To punish me? Or to reaf-firm her love? I could not wash from my brain the memory of her in the white light, weeping, begging me to back to her.

The answer came in short order. Standing in a clearing ahead of me, Ruthana was waiting, arms outstretched to em-brace me.

Then we were holding each other—her with passionate ardor, me with half-uncertain caution.

The other half was grateful joy.

"I'm sorry I did this to you," she murmured. "I just had to see you."

"*I'm* sorry I didn't come back," I murmured back. "I couldn't." It was a lie, I knew. But I couldn't tell her the truth. That re-turning was not available to me because of the attacks on me.

"It's all right," she said. "You're back now, that's all that matters."

I had to know. The question was festering in my mind.

The opportunity to ask was delayed as Ruthana drew back

from her embrace and took me by the hand. Led me through the woods to near the waterfall where I had first seen her. I noticed then—how strange that it didn't seem consequential to notice it immediately—that she was nude. As she had been in the beginning. Never in my life had nudity seemed so innocent.

We reached the rock on which we'd sat originally, and she seated me on it, then instantly perched her warmth on my lap and, without a word, kissed me. So lingeringly that my manhood (the only aspect of it I possessed at my age) rose to the occasion.

Did it bother Ruthana? She laughed softly. (Dare I describe it as a giggle; it was close to that.) "You're ready to love," she said with a childlike smile. Then she gazed at me intently. "Alex," she said, "I love you so. If you want to love, I won't stop you."

Physically, I wanted to—very much. But my brain intervened. "Ruthana," I said.

"Yes, my dearest darling," she replied. *Oh, God,* I thought. How could I ask now?

But I had to. "Did you . . . attack me?"

She looked genuinely confused. "Attack you?" she asked.

I girded my mental loins and told her about the attacks. Leaving no detail undescribed. As I did, I saw her expression alter from confusion to horror—to, finally, defensive pain.

"Did you really think I did that to you?" she asked, her tone one of gentle protest. "Do you really believe I would ever do that to you?"

She was crying, then. Sobbing as though heartbroken. And I was convinced, at that moment, that Magda *had* initiated the attacks. And lied to me, almost convincing me that Ruthana, not she, was responsible.

I tried to kiss away Ruthana's flowing tears. "Don't cry," I said, (My love for her returned in force.) "I didn't want to believe it. I tried to, but I couldn't. Magda—"

"*Magda*," she broke in. It was the first time I heard anything but softness in her voice. She sounded angrily contemptuous now. "That terrible witch. How could she do those awful things to you? Then make you believe *I* was the one who did them? Do you still believe it?"

"No, my darling," I assured her. It was surprising how simple it was to express my feeling toward her. "I love you very much."

The crying ceased. I drew a handkerchief from my shirt pocket (wincing as I pictured Magda washing, then ironing it) and dabbed, as carefully as I could, at Ruthana's lustrous eyes. She was smiling again, my words had reassured her. Magda never seemed that immediately appeased. "Thank you, Alex," Ruthana whispered. "Thank you. I love you, too. But you know that."

She said she failed to understand how Magda could have acted (reacted, I thought) that way. Didn't she realize that such attacks were unwarranted? (My word, not Ruthana's.) I said I didn't understand either. There was a lot I didn't understand about Magda. "That's because she's a witch," Ruthana told me. "No one understands what witches think."

"That's for sure," I said. I wasn't sure at all.

I shifted my arms. It was difficult to clasp her because of her size. She sensed it immediately. "What is it?" she asked.

"Nothing," I lied. I didn't want to hurt her feelings.

"I know what it is," she said. "Wait."

Jumping (I mean *jumping*) off my lap. She darted (I mean *darted*) behind a tree. I wondered what she was doing. Did she have to go to the bathroom? I thought impolitely.

It wasn't that. In a few moments—less than half a minute, I'll guess—she reappeared.

Full size.

I know my mouth fell open. So did my brain. How did this miracle occur?

She ran (*ran* now, not darted) back to me and plunked herself on my lap. I think I said, "Oof!" at the extra weight. Ruthana laughed delightedly. I drew in an obvious breath. Which delighted her even more. She kissed me on the cheek. If there is such a thing as a happy kiss, that was it.

"How did you *do* that?" I asked. Still a mite breathless.

"We can all do that," she said.

"For how long?" I asked, my voice a trifle wheezy.

"As long as we want," she said, as though the answer were perfectly clear. "My brother did it—I mean my stepbrother."

"He did," I said, confirming information to myself.

"Yes," she replied.

"For how long?" I asked. I wanted to know. I didn't like the idea of her shifting without control.

Now her expression darkened. Had I asked the wrong thing?

"Until he died," she answered quietly.

"Oh, I'm sorry," I said. But, still more curious, added, "Why did he do it? Change size, I mean?"

Ruthana sighed deeply. "So he could go to war," she told me.

A glimmer of light in the unknowing shadows of my brain.

"He wanted to defend our country," she said. "We told him that the Middle Kingdom was our country, but he wouldn't listen."

A glimmer above a glimmer. Like Gilly, it appeared she had the same distaste (I can't describe it as the same hatred) for the human race.

I cut to the chase, as they say. "Was his name Harold?" I asked.

"No," she answered, "Haral."

"Oh," I said. Curiosity unrelieved.

"He changed it to Harold," she said. Then, "Why do you ask?"

"I knew him," I said. "I was in the trenches with him."

When I said that, her eyes lit up. I swear to God that's what they did. For that matter, her entire face lit up. No better way to describe it. "You *did!?*" she said. Exultantly. No better way to describe that either.

I told her everything I could remember. How friendly Harold had been. How informative on military matters. How he taught me British slang.

"What's that?" Ruthana asked. Brightly curious.

I told her, remembering as many Brit words as I could. "Beer and skittles"—not easy. "Bob's your uncle"—that's it. "Pigs might fly!"—yeah, sure, sarcastically. That one evoked a peal of delighted laughter from Ruthana. But, finally, she said, "He must have been joking with you—and himself—because we never talk like that. It's funny, though. Harold was always funny." That darkening expression again. "Except when he deserted our country for England."

"Yes." Lacking further knowledge, I had to agree with her.

That sigh again. Incredibly deep. "Were you—" She hesitated, then went on. "—with him when he—died?"

I avoided any gory detail, describing only the charm of his smile and his final words to me, *"When you go to Gatford . . ."*

"I'm so glad he said that," I told her (from the heart). "I'm so grateful that I came to Gatford. And met you."

"Oh, *Alex*," she murmured, kissed me tenderly on the lips. "I'm so grateful that you came, too. To me." She looked worried then. "You don't still think I did those awful things, do you? I swear, on my life, that I would never do a thing to hurt you." Another kiss. I hugged her tightly. So much so that she murmured, *"Ooh."*

"I'm sorry," I apologized, "I just want to hold you close."

"Alex, Alex." A rain of kisses. On my lips, my chin, my cheeks, my eyes, my forehead. Well, everywhere available for kisses. I enjoyed each one.

I asked her then about the gold lump. Told her how it had become a pile of gray dust.

"You didn't get it in your eyes, did you?" she asked. It seemed an odd question.

"No," I said, "why?"

"It could have blinded you," she told me. "Even killed you if you'd breathed it in."

I remembered Mr. Brean's abrupt demise and wondered it that was the cause. No answer to that. I'd have to accept Ruthana's word on it.

"The gold," I said, "where did it come from?"

"Us," she answered simply. "We can do that. My stepfather did it and sent it to Haral—Harold, as you called him."

"And it turned into dust?"

"It had to when a human took it," she said.

"I'm human," I said. "It didn't turn into dust when I had it."

A strange response to that. "You're not completely human, then," she said. Again, simply. Nothing portentous.

The simplicity of her reply staggered me.

"Did Haral—Harold—give it to you?" she asked.

"In a way," I answered, going on to describe the magical circumstance of the gold lump appearing in my duffel bag. My god, but life was magical those days!

"Well. That explains it, then," Ruthana said. "He wanted you to have it. That protected it from—" She failed to come up with the word.

"Dissolution?" I suggested.

She laughed. "If I knew what that means," she said.

"Another word for turning into dust," I told her.

"Oh." She smiled. "You're so smart, Alex."

"No, I'm not," I said. "I just read [pronouncing it as a rhyme with 'red'] a lot."

"You must see our books," she said.

"I'm dying to," I told her.

"*Dying?*" she said. Much concerned.

"Just an expression," I said. Seeing the look of concern remaining, I added, "A way of speaking." Her look continued, then abated as she noted the comforting tone of my voice.

"Oh," she said. "You worried me. To say 'dying.' I don't like to think of that. You dying? It would end my life."

"*Oh, Ruthana,*" I could hardly speak, I was so in love with her. I'd thought Veronica was sweet. Compared to Ruthana, she was one of Dracula's wives. The comparison struck me later; I didn't read the novel until Arthur Black was under way.

We kissed and kissed. Do I sound romantically absurd? Can't help it. That's the way it happened. Endless kisses. Only the sound of our endless osculation. Other than the birds and breeze in the trees. Plus the distant splashing of the waterfall. Too bad I couldn't say "the birds and the bees in the trees." A. Black would have enjoyed a chuckle at that. But Alexander White was bereft of critical acumen. Eighteen years old, criminally (perhaps a bit too accusatory an adjective) naïve, A. White lost in a dream world of love. Only his organ showed any sign of reality recognition. (Good combo there.) Recognition exaggerated as Ruthana helped me off with my clothes.

Ruthana, accustomed to living twenty-four hours a day in this dream world, knew what was occurring in my nether regions. She smiled at me with innocent pleasure. "You want to love," she observed. Not too difficult an observation, since my organ was halfway to the moon.

"I do," I said. Throatily.

"I'm yours to love," she murmured. Then, with a quick kiss on my lips, said, "But first."

First? I thought. *What first?* Did I need to wash myself? I had no rubberized protection with me. The last of those was still in France. What then?

Ruthana stood, smiling impishly at the turgid state of my groin. Then, to my surprise, told me, "I want you to meet Gilly."

Oh, God, I thought. My organ—up till that moment as hard as a ramrod, quickly lost rigidity, much to Ruthana's amusement. "I'm sorry," she said with another smile. "We can restore it when needed." I hadn't realized her sense of humor was droll.

"Okay," I said. Regretfully now. "But why do I need to meet Gilly?"

"If you're to stay," she said.

"Stay?" I reacted. Without thinking.

"Don't you want to?" she asked, concerned again. "Don't you want to live with me?"

The thought excited and alarmed me at the same time. "Yes, of course, I do," I told her. And meant it. "But I'm not . . ."

"One of us?" she said, not asking; telling.

"Yes," I said. (My penis was completely flaccid by now.) "I thought I could before. When you said I wasn't completely human."

"You're not," she told me.

"But you said when Harold—Haral—gave the gold lump to me, that was why it didn't turn into dust."

"That's right," she said.

"Well, then." I didn't get it, but I didn't want to argue with her.

"Don't worry," she said.

"But I do," I went on. "I want to stay with you, very much. But I don't see how."

"We can change you," she said.

Now I was really set back on my brain heels. *Change* me? What on earth did that mean?

"We'll talk about it later," she said. Another quick kiss. She said then, "I'll send for Gilly."

Send for him? "You know where he is?" I asked.

"I'll *send* for him," she said, as though case closed. It didn't matter where he was. She'd *send* for him. Another scrap of evidence. Ruthana had powers. Change me. Send for Gilly. Period. *Whoa.*

She turned and looked into the distant woods. I saw no particular alteration in her face. No squinted eyes, no tightened lips, no lines or ridges on her brow. Just . . . looking into the woods. Without me noticing any physical tensing, "sending" for her brother. Correction. Stepbrother. I wondered, for several seconds, whether she had any family of her own.

It didn't take long. I was primed for an elephant charge through a bamboo forest. Not a sound. He didn't even approach us from a distance. Abruptly, he was there. Had he just materialized in the air? I couldn't tell. It happened too fast. He might have—as Ruthana did—darted up to us from the woods. On the other hand, he might just have materialized in front of us. Magic was becoming matter-of-fact to me. By then, I could believe—and accept—anything at all.

What did Gilly look like? Well, he was solid, not, as Magda had suggested, imaginary. Dressed in green, Ruthana's height. Nowhere as attractive as Ruthana. She was stunningly beautiful. He was—how shall I put it?—acceptably masculine. Black-haired (very thick) and black-eyed, his features regular though undistinguished. It was his expression that set him apart.

Mean.

Clearly, he had no regard for me—unless it was hatred. (His expression chilled me.) He seemed ready to pounce on me at a moment's notice, prepared to throttle me fatally.

But instead, he glared at Ruthana. Eyed her up and down. *Incestually?* I thought, tensing. I couldn't very well box him, naked. But no, it was with disgust, contempt. Because I was naked? No doubt. Why hadn't Ruthana had me dress first?

Gilly's first words. "Changed yourself for *this?*"

"I want you to leave him alone," she said. No plea. An order.

Was that a faerie snicker? It sounded more a snort. *"Leave him alone?"* he said. Utterly disdainful—even arrogant.

"Leave him alone," she said. Her tone was firm and un-afraid.

An eye duel then. If flames had been exchanged between them, I would not have been surprised. It was a tournament between equal enemies, or were they equal? No. Because Gilly backed off, lowering his glowering gaze. No doubt of it. He was, at least, unable to contest Ruthana. At most, afraid of her. And she loved *me?* This powerhouse faerie? Unbelievable. Yet I had to believe it.

"Now I want you to shake his hand," Ruthana said. A calm, but definite, command.

"I will not," Gilly said. No, snarled. If he had shape-shifted to a wolf, I swear I would not have been taken back. Terrified but not surprised.

"Then *go,*" Ruthana said, "and the gods protect you if you ever hurt him."

Gilly looked at her with hatred. "Just stay out of my way," he told her. "Or *you* die."

With that, he was gone. Dematerialized. I knew it now. Could Ruthana do the same? I felt sure she could. And the prospect of staying with her malevolent stepbrother lurking in the background, I must say, unnerved me.

Ruthana saw my obvious distress and came over, put her

arms around me. And, in an instant, powerhouse Ruthana had been revived as my loving angel. Only for a moment did I question my sanity in trusting her so completely. Then Mr. Manhood reasserted his (uncontrollable) upstanding presence.

Before the obvious occurred, though, a smidgen of rationality remained with me, and I said to Ruthana, "Will you tell me something?"

"Of course, my love," she said. I felt grateful that she didn't call me "darling," as Magda had.

"You spoke about—changing me," I said. "How?"

"In size only," she answered. "I have to, Alex. I don't like being human. I'm not used to it. It makes me unhappy."

"So you'll make me smaller," I said.

"Yes, we can," she said. "But only if you're willing."

"Oh, I would be," I said. Then—cautiously—"Would it hurt?"

She laughed. "A little bit," she said.

I think I winced. "What *would* I feel like?" I asked.

Another childlike laugh. "Smaller," she said.

Oh, boy, I thought. *Smaller.* To remain with Ruthana, I'd have to resemble one of the little people.

In brief, become a faerie.

Chapter Twenty-two

It happened then. The inevitable. Ruthana sat on my lap. I slipped inside her easily. I wondered briefly if that meant she wasn't a virgin. I didn't care. I knew that her mind, with re-gard to me, was virginal. Don't understand why I knew it. I just did. This was the first time she had had sex this way. With total love. She told me so later.

Her movement was slight. Her breathing quickened—but to such a small degree, that I could barely notice it. Also minimal, the sounds of passion she made were scarcely audible. I was struck by the difference between Magda's gasping, hissing, and moaning and Ruthana's delicate arousal. My initial inclination had been to thrust and with-draw determinedly—as I did with Magda. Ruthana's tranquil approach subdued me, and I realized that animal-like huffing and puffing were unnecessary. We were making love, not lust.

It ended quickly. Virtually motionless, we climaxed together—the only moment I heard an audible *"Oh!"* from her. Not to mention my pathetic groaning. Ruthana, smiling, kissed me tenderly. I had never known such simple ecstasy. No carnality. No lecherousness.

Heaven.

☆ ☆ ☆

In several hours, my heaven turned to hell.

It happened this way.

"I have to go back," I told Ruthana.

Her expression, up until then blissfully secure, tightened into a mask of fear and disappointment. "Alex, *why?*" she asked.

"I have to say good-bye to her," I answered.

The disappointment was obliterated by sheer dread. "But it isn't *safe*," she said.

"Is it safe here?" I asked.

"Yes, it is," she answered. "We can protect you."

"Gilly, too?" My question was labeled: *Distrust.*

"Not him," she said. "He'll leave you alone. *I'll* protect you. So will Garal," she added quickly. (Garal—Haral—was there a connection?) A look of pleading tensed her face. "Please, Alex. Don't go back. *It isn't safe.*"

I put my arms around her. "You thought I meant to leave you," I said. I kissed her gently.

"I did," she said. "But now, I'm frightened. She's a terrible woman, Alex. A dangerous witch."

"Well, first of all, I'll never leave you. *Never,*" I told her.

"Thank you, love," she said. "I'd die if you did. But now—"

I stopped her with another kiss. "I have to say good-bye to her, Ruthana. I'm not sure she attacked me." I put a finger across her lips to stop her protest. "I don't mean I think you did it. I know you didn't. Maybe (the notion sprang across my mind) Gilly did. Doesn't he have the same power as you?" I asked.

"No," she answered. "Not as much. If he did, he would have attacked everyone in Gatford, he hates them so much. But none of us is capable of such attacks. We wouldn't even know how to do them. So it couldn't have been Gilly. Alex, I'm telling you it was the witch. They were witch attacks."

I was affected twofold. On one side, I was duly impressed by Ruthana. She had never spoken to me at such length. On the second side, I was discouraged that my "inspiration" regarding Gilly was null and void. So it *had* to be Magda. And here I was planning to go back to her. Momentarily, an image of a fly returning to a spider's web flitted disconcertingly across my mental eye. I resisted it. I had to return to Magda, bid her a grateful farewell. Dangerous or not, I had to take decent leave of her. She was carrying my child, after all. I felt bad about leaving Magda with the baby, but how could I possibly stay with someone who had used black magic to attack me? I had to end things with Magda. Ruthana didn't understand. I had to explain.

"Ruthana, let me tell you why I have to go back," I said. *"To say good-bye,"* I added quickly, seeing the expression of alarm on her face once more. "She's been very good to me. She *healed* me, for heaven's sake! I had a terrible wound on my right hip and leg; I got it in the trench in France, a shell explosion. Part of me was torn apart; you never saw it, thank God. And she *healed* it! Maybe she used a witch's ritual to do it, but she *did* it, I was completely healed. I'll always owe her for that."

"But," she started.

"Let me finish," I said. "Magda has been very kind to me ·
for the past few months. She treated me as though she was my
mother. [*Don't ask me if I slept with her!* my brain pleaded.] She
cooked for me, took care of my clothes. We talked. We took
long walks together. It was all very pleasant. I never felt in
danger. Not for a moment." I avoided any mention of the
manuscript.

"I'm making it sound as though I plan to stay with her," I
reassured her, "that isn't it at all. It's just that—very likely—
she has no idea what happened to me. I went for a walk and
disappeared. She's probably upset by that. So *please.* Don't
think, for a second, that I want to leave you. I don't. Not at
all. I want to spend the rest of my life with you." I managed a
smile. "I'll even get small for you."

My attempted jollity failed to reach her. And I knew I had
to tell her. It was wrong for me to keep it from her. Absolutely
wrong. "Ruthana," I started. She gazed at me worriedly, as
though she knew I was just about to tell her something awful.

Which I was. "Magda is—" I couldn't say the word. "—with
child."

She stared at me. Speechless.

"I know I should have told you before," I said. "I was
afraid to."

"Why?" she asked. So guilessly, I wondered if I'd heard her
tone correctly.

"*Why?*" I asked. It sounded more like a demand, although
I didn't wish it to.

"You think that we didn't all assume that you and she
were—?" Now she couldn't seem to say the word.

"*There was no love involved,*" I said. "No, that isn't true,"

I amended, determined that she hear the truth now. "I won't take back everything I said about her. There *was* love at first. Magda gave me love. I *believed* her." That was true as well. "Later . . . it was *different*. I became afraid of her."

I took her hands in mine. "She had a son who died in the war. She wanted me to replace him." I gritted my teeth. "In *every way*," I said. "Which I did, God help me. I *did*." I drew in a feeble, gasping breath . . . "If you can't forgive me, I'll understand. I will. I swear I will."

She didn't answer. Instead, she walked away from me! I was astounded. Had I failed the entire explanation? I stood, aghast. Was my return to Magda to be permanent? All sorts of dire possibilities crossed my mind. Magda would never forgive me. She'd know exactly what happened. I'd rue the day. In spades.

Not so. To my amazement, there was Ruthana in front of me again. She was holding a small vial in her hand. She held it out.

"What is it?" I asked.

"Protection," she said, "if you must go."

She went on to explain that the vial contained a powder. Shockingly, I discovered, it was the powder that had probably blinded and killed Mr. Brean.

"*I don't want to kill her, Ruthana.*" I drew the line. "I just want to say good-bye to her."

"I don't *want* you to kill her," Ruthana said. "I don't like killing. But you have to protect yourself. In case—" She hesitated. "—she goes after you," she finished.

"Ruthana, I don't think she'll 'go after' me," I said. "She loves me." Seeing that expression again, I added, "Well, she said she did. I don't know."

Silence then. She continued holding the vial. Reluctantly, I took it, slipping it into my jacket pocket. (I forgot to mention we were dressed by then. We'd remained comfortably nude for—I estimate—more than an hour.)

"I'll take you out of the woods," she said.

I shivered. Was she accepting my departure too readily?

I should have known better. Moving close, she wrapped her arms around me, holding tight. "Remember what I said," she whispered. "If you don't come back, I'll die." I knew she meant it. It was a frightening admonition. Not a warning or a threat. A statement of her love. I had to respect it.

One more fervent kiss, and then we started through the woods, hand in hand. In a short while, unopposed in any way, we reached the path. It was far from the spot where I'd entered the woods. My god, did it all take place *today*? It seemed much longer.

We held each other for at least a minute. We kissed. "Be careful, my love," Ruthana said, an audible break in her voice. "Use the powder if you have to." It sounded as though she meant *when* you have to. I put aside that possibility and kissed her one last time. "I *will* come back," I assured her. "It's going to be all right."

Little did I know.

I left her and walked out onto the path. As I started toward Magda's house, I looked back at the woods. Ruthana was gone. Had she walked away—or vanished as Gilly had? Whatever way she'd disappeared, the sight was unnerving. Did she think—was she convinced—that I'd never return? No way of knowing. But the very possibility was distressing to me. I just realized that the word "distressing" contains the word "stress." Which is why—no vast discovery—the word implies the presence of stress. Bravo, A. Black! Candidate for the Nobel Prize in Literature! Not.

Where was I? Back on the path, returning to my witch's house. Hansel and Gretel rolled into one. Why can't I take this more seriously? I was feeling pretty damn serious walking back along that path. I really did have no idea how Magda would treat me when I told her I was leaving. She's been so— yes, it's the proper word—*sweet* to me the past few months.

But *now? This?*

I was almost to the path that led to Magda's house when I heard the call. *"Alex!"* Shrill. Overwhelmed.

Magda came rushing up to me. Her face flushed and wet with tears. I knew instantly that my departure was not to be the easiest task in the world.

"My god, my darling, where did you go?" she asked, sounding breathless. "I've been out of my mind!"

Oh, dear, I thought. Simplistic reaction. But I couldn't allow terror to invade my system. If I did, I'd never get back to Ruthana.

"I'm sorry," I said. It was difficult to speak coherently. So—as I usually did—I lied. "I've been walking," I told her.

Stupid lie. "For *hours?*" she asked. She didn't sound distrustful, only flabbergasted.

"It's a long path," I continued lying. I hoped it was long.

"I know," she agreed. She embraced me torridly, and I was—pointlessly, no doubt—aware of how different her capacious breasts were from Ruthana's. "My god, you frightened me," she said. "I thought the faeries had gotten you." Now that really dismayed me. The faeries *had* gotten me. One of them, at any rate. How was I going to get back to that one now?

"No," I lied thrice—I was getting deeper and deeper, into the quicksand of prevarication. (I advise you to avoid it; remain on the solid, smooth ground of truth.) How would I get out of it? For a moment, I considered using the powder right away, blinding Magda and retreating into the woods.

I couldn't do it. I renounced the impulse. It would defeat my intention, destroy my purpose. Which was an honest one. Even now, I appreciate that. Hurling the powder into Magda's face at this point—when she had been so kind to me—would be, at best, contemptible. I would never forget such a moment of cowardly surrender. I was more in debt to Magda than that.

So, instead, I tried to console her as we walked up the path and across the lawn to her house. We went inside and sat on the sofa. I held her in my arms, her voluptuous warmth affecting you-know-who. (I keep telling you I was only eighteen, not a whit mature!) Only when I compelled my distracted brain to rein in did Mr. Johnson (I believe that's what they call him now—I have not the slightest know-how why) manage to allay his automatic traverse toward inflexibility.

He dropped like a stone when Magda told me, quietly, "You've been lying to me."

"What?" I muttered. The numbskull I was.

"You heard," she said.

"I didn't lie," I lied. Poor, pathetic me. How was I ever going to get back to Ruthana?

"You did," said Magda. Firmly. "You've been in the woods again. With that faerie girl."

That's right, I was, I thought. I couldn't say it. I was really being cowardly now. It shamed me. "No," I lied yet again. *Why are you lying?* I condemned my tongue—trying to elude the fact that my brain was responsible. I *had* to change directions. "Yes," I forced myself to say. "You're right. I was. That's why—"

I was halted in midsentence as Magda pulled away from me—I should say "jerked"—and looked at me intently—I should say "glared."

"You lying bastard," she called me.

Her abrupt change in demeanor, her use of profanity, shocked me.

"Magda, I apologize," I started, "for—"

Once again, I broke off. This time blocked by her sudden rant. (I should say "infuriated rant.")

"You had to go back to that little woodsy bitch, *didn't* you?" she accused me. "Had to fuck the faerie way! Was it nice?! Did you come inside her?!"

That was too much; temper replaced shame. "Magda, that's enough!" I cried. "She's completely innocent."

"Innocent, is she?!" Magda cried back. "Luring you into the woods to let you fuck her!"

"Stop it!" I yelled. "She didn't do that!! She *loves* me!" I made the final incriminating statement then: "And *I love her!*"

Dead silence from Magda. Her face gone bloodless, she looked at me with a murderous expression. Her voice sounded thick as she said, "You'll be sorry you said that."

"*Why?*" I demanded, unaware of the depth of her rage. "I love you, too. It's just—"

"Don't tell me that, you lying prick," said Magda, her

language shocking me again. "I know you don't. I'm only Magda to you. Your *witch whore.*"

Somehow, I sensed that she was right. That *was* how I felt about her.

"I was your mother," Magda said. "And you loved fucking your mother."

"No," was all I got out, chokingly, before she ranted on.

"You wonder if Edward fucked me! Yes, of course he did! That's why he enlisted! Isn't that why you enlisted, you little shit?! Because you loved fucking your mother?! And felt guilty for doing it?!"

"*No!*" I raged. "You're *wrong!*"

She ignored me. Kept on ranting; it appalled me, all the vileness in her brain. "Your mother was a whore!" she screamed. "She loved sucking your cock, didn't she?! *Didn't she?! Sonny?!*"

"I think you're horrible," I said. "I think you're sick. I feel sorry for the baby."

"Oh, *do* you?!" she demanded. "Don't bother, there is no baby."

I don't remember, but I think my mouth fell open. "*What?*" I said, my voice barely audible.

She heard it, though. "*There is no baby,* Alex. I got rid of it."

Dear God. It was all I could think, my brain suddenly gorged with the ghastly memory of Self Aborting an Unwanted Chimera. I tried to rid myself of the memory, but the bloody image clouded my awareness.

"You did *that?*" I asked; *very* weakly.

"*Yes, I did, darling,*" she said with a terrible smile. "I buried our daughter—what there was of her—in the garden. You want me to dig her up?"

"How could you do such a thing?" I muttered.

"You want me to *describe* it?" she asked. The terrible smile again.

"*No,*" I said.

"You thought I wanted your baby," she persisted. "*I didn't.* I wanted Edward's baby. But he was dead, so I had yours instead. But I wanted a son who could be my lover. And the baby was a girl, and I didn't want a girl. So I ripped her out and buried the pieces! *Shall I go on?!*"

I felt as though my head were caught in an ice-cold vise. I could barely breathe. Her rant had frozen me. All I could do was shake my head. At least I thought I shook my head. Maybe I didn't.

Magda bared her teeth. "You still want me to be your mama, don't you?" she said. She yanked open her dress, pulled up her now swollen breasts, and thrust them out to me. "All right, suck Mama's tits," she snarled. "Nurse on Mama's tits again."

I had to fight off my ungovernable loins. I did, though, so horrified was I by her insane behavior. "*Get away from me,*" I told her.

She would not relent. Pushing against me, she tried to push her breasts in my face. "Drink Mama's milk!" she commanded. To my astonishment, a milklike liquid began squirting from her rigid nipples. It couldn't be natural! It had to be something Magda was doing. I confess, I almost succumbed.

It was near too much for a fallible teenager. How I managed

it was a tribute to my love for Ruthana and secondarily, most secondarily, my sense of rightness.

Which is when the notion suddenly occurred. I'd say inspired me, but it was hardly an inspiration, more a foolhardy defense. "Is this a *witch* thing?" I asked harshly, trying to push her away. "Did it come from your manuscript?"

Magda went rigid, the flow from her breasts abruptly ceasing. She looked at me the way Medea must have looked at her children—hate and love combined. *"You've been in my library,"* she said. The way she said it raised a coating of ice on my bones. Now I was truly afraid. I had enraged a witch who hated me, most likely wanted me dead. "I'm sorry." I tried, "I didn't mean—"

I had no conclusion for my lamebrained excuse. There was none. I knew it. And God knew Magda did as well. I wondered (only half-alert now) what she meant to do as she pulled away from me and stood. She didn't close her dress. She pulled it up across her head and tossed it aside. Now she was naked. I struggled to my feet and moved with laborious stiffness toward the front door.

"No, you don't," said Magda. "Mama doesn't want you to go." She could hardly speak (it was more a growl), but her intent was clear. She pushed up to her feet and staggered to the end of the bookcase. Reaching to its side, she pulled back a sword; it looked more like a machete. She walked toward me. *"Your head is mine,"* she mumbled thickly; her throat sounded clogged. I kept moving clumsily toward the door.

With a startling, terrifying cry, Magda began running. I glanced back quickly. She was brandishing the sword, clearly intent on decapitation. I noticed her lolling breasts as they bounced up and down. No arousal. I was too afraid. My god, was I afraid! *"You can't get away!"* Magda shouted, her voice now frighteningly loud.

The powder!

I whirled and plunged, as best I could, a hand into my jacket pocket. To my horror, I almost dropped the vial, juggling it between both hands before I got a grip on it. Magda was almost on me. I struggled with the vial, trying to open it. Magda reached me, took a savage swipe with the sword. Whatever instinct saved me, I don't know. I ducked beneath the slashing blade. Magda stumbled, off balance from her frenzied attempt to behead me. I opened the vial and threw the gray powder at her. It caught her full in the face.

She screamed in pain, and I saw that much of the powder had struck her eyes. She staggered to one side, dropping the sword and reaching up, misdirectedly, for her suddenly blinded eyes. "You bastard!" she cried, *"You fucking bastard!"*

I didn't wait for more. I moved infirmly for the door and left her thrashing through the room, unable to see, eyes running with uncontrolled tears; her lurching body colliding with furniture, snarling as she flung over smaller pieces.

I opened the front door and left, running without stopping until I reached the path.

Ruthana was waiting for me.

I clung to her with desperate need. "Thank God," I said. I repeated it so many times—unable to think, only overswept with gratitude—that I lost count. I was safe. That's all I knew. *I was safe.*

Wrong again.

III

Chapter Twenty-three

The first thing my faerie friends did was make me small.

I know that sounds far-fetched. Actually, it sounds like an Arthur Black contrivance. But I assure you it took place. Anyway, if you buy my account up till now—witchcraft, Middle Kingdom faeries?—you shouldn't have any trouble swallowing my losing a little stature.

God knows I had more than any trouble swallowing the drink they gave me to get smaller. I threw up half of it. And a *little* stature, did I say? Six feet two inches to three-one? *Yow.* That's shrinking!

But I did it. I had to. I couldn't stay with Ruthana otherwise. I know she'd assumed full human size, but that was only temporary; she couldn't manage it permanently. She only did it for—well, you remember what. (I'm blushing inside.) Furthermore, I could not remain human size either. It was not acceptable, not permitted. I had to get small. I know it sounds ridiculous, but it was a fact. Stay full size? Impossible. I'd be ousted from Middle Kingdom. And that was unacceptable to me. I loved Ruthana too much. Much too much.

So I endured three weeks of—what shall I call it?—

diminution. Not pleasant. Not pleasant at all. Remember what I told you about a witch's becoming invisible? The flesh slowly contracting, the skeletal bones gradually losing density, the organs dissolving? I experienced something akin to that. I could actually *feel* my body getting smaller. The more I drank of that dreadful stuff, the faster it happened; most of it in the third week. I spent one night in sheer agony. Ruthana tried to comfort me. In vain; she'd understated—I guess she knew it would hurt but didn't want to frighten me.

There was nothing she could do. The process was under way, and there was no way to reverse it while it was taking place. How *simple* the process was for them. Boom! Size changed. Just like that. Not for me. If I hadn't loved Ruthana so much, I would have asked them (pleaded with them) to put me out of my misery—skeleton slowly shrinking (pretty good triplet there), flesh slowly drawing in, even my eyes (my eyes, for Chrissake!) getting smaller. All in a solitary room who knew where? On a simple cot. Suffering.

Finally (another week of it, and I would have—well, not made it, put it that way), it was finished, I was faerie size. It still sounds stupid (another triplet!). But—regardless—it *did* happen. Ruthana and I were the same size; from now on my name was Alexi. We "loved" to celebrate the occasion. I thought that while we were "doing it" that the process could have—in my diseased imagination—gone on uninterruptedly until I was a firefly—a size they claimed they could assume. Six-two to an insect! Disturbing image. It delayed my climax.

Not too long, though.

※ ※ ※

Our wedding was a small affair. No hordes of applauding guests. No orchestra playing Mendelssohn. No dance. No sit-down dinner—chicken or fish.

Just Ruthana and me.

Together in a paradisical (if that's not a word, it should be) glade in the woods. Next to a sweetly (that *is* the appropriate word) bubbling stream, surrounded by birch trees (sacred to the faerie folk) and flowers of such brilliant hues that I hesitate to describe them. (A. Black has his limitations.) Let's just say that the colors were heavenly and let it go at that.

Our ceremony was equally small. I don't mean small; there was no element to it that was "small" in any way. I mean it didn't take hours; it was over in several minutes.

Ruthana was wearing a pale blue gossamer gown, virtually transparent. I have never, in this life—and, perhaps, in my next—seen such beauty. Golden-haired, angelic face, exquisite body—you see now why I used the words "paradisical" (real or not) and "heavenly." There are no other words possible.

Of course, there were some guidelines to our marriage. I was not to ask Ruthana about her life before she met me. I was not to strike her. Ever. I must not look at her at certain times. (I think we know what that means; even faerie females must abide by the moon.)

Since none of these rules were difficult for me to follow, our wedding was permitted. In our case, without a full Middle Kingdom brouhaha, but permitted nonetheless.

It could not have been better. Ruthana and me in this wonderful setting. Drinking a delicious potion, Ruthana whispering an ancient love spell.

You for me
And I for thee
and for none else
Your face to mine
and your head turned away
from all others

You like that? I do. A lot.

We "loved" that night. Over and over. Mr. and Mrs. Alexander (Alexi) "Shrimp" (except in relative terms, of course).

I was at home. Sweet home. Beautiful home—Gatford woods. Safe home.

※   ※   ※

Well, not exactly. There was still Gilly to contend with. The first time he saw me, newly sized, he said (nastily as always), "You think you're one of us now, don't you? You're *not*. You're still a Human Being. (That's the way he expressed it, as though the words were capitalized. And dirty.)

This is what happened the first time he attacked me. Grade A attack first crack out of the bag; that was Gilly. Good ol' Gilly.

Ruthana and I were walking together, hand in hand. She never left my side. When I slept at night, she had some sort of protective force watching over me. Either that or she did something to Gilly that made him sleep, that used to infuriate him. As though he needed additional fury to bolster his already overflowing supply. Ruthana even waited for me—patiently, discreetly (to a fault) when I emptied my bladder and/or bowels. God, she was patient! I didn't like the idea that she had to keep a constant lookout for her crazy brother-in-law, but there it was. The price I had to pay for living with Ruthana. And was glad (limitedly) to pay.

As I said, we were walking in the woods, holding hands. Summer still abided, the tree foliage breathtaking with different shades of green, the ground strewn with fallen leaves of the same colors. They crackled underneath our feet as we walked. Ruthana was barefooted; I was wearing a pair of shoes taken from Gilly's voluminous collection. (That didn't please him much either, let me tell you.)

As we walked, I was asking Ruthana a question that had plagued me since our first meeting in, as I recall, June. If she had control over Gilly, why did she make me flee from Gilly in the first place?

Her answer was immediate—and sweet. She knew, she said, that she had fallen in love with me but was so confused by the emotion (a first for her—I never asked her further about that) that she wasn't able to think clearly and could only, on impulse, get me away from Gilly and out of the woods. Before we parted, all she could think of saying was that she loved me. I accepted her answer completely.

So much so that I asked for a second one. The raucous party I heard that night in my cottage. Was it real or imagination? Oh, it was probably real, she answered simply. Middle Kingdom parties often do get noisy, and the celebrants make little effort to suppress their gaiety. "Did they keep you awake?"

she asked me sympathetically. I kissed her and said it wasn't that bad, I just wondered what it was.

I told her then that since form-enlarging was only a temporary ability for faeries, I couldn't help but be amused by the image of how the "trench boys" must have reacted to the sight of Harold shrinking to faerie dimensions when he died. Ruthana smiled at that, but explained that Harold could not—on his own, away from his true home—have managed to retain human size. He had to be assisted.

"How did he do it, then?" I asked.

"The way you did," she said.

"*That much pain?*" I asked, astounded.

"The other way around, of course," she answered.

"Did—?" I hesitated to ask. But did. "Being in the army meant that much to him?" I asked.

"England meant that much to him," she answered.

"Did Gilly—?" I started, couldn't finish.

"Gilly hates human beings; as you know," she said, "England is human beings."

"Yes, I understand," I said, remembering that I joined the army not out of love for the United States but of hatred for you know who. I should stop calling him that. He was Captain Bradford Smith White, USN. Still is, I suppose. No, he couldn't (God forbid) be alive. The United States Navy—and the world—must be rid of him by now. If not he'd be—let's see—at least 109 by now, a wrinkled old prune of a man, still mean as hell, bitching in a naval retirement home somewhere on the East Coast. Ghastly image. Can I never be rid of his deletenous self?

Having been, involuntarily, plunged back into family,

I—without thinking—inquired about Ruthana's family. Her real, her blood family.

Her answer was hesitant, even guarded. In the Middle Kingdom, there are no families in the customary sense, she told me. The entire body of them is their family. Their unity comes from a relationship not of blood but of community, of environment. Ruthana *did* have a blood father, but he was killed in an accident, and Garal's (in a sense) family "adopted" her and raised her. So, in truth, to call Garal her stepfather and Gilly her stepbrother (or brother-in-law) isn't accurate. More than that I can't say. I never did understand it. It was too involved for me. All I chose to believe was that Ruthana lived in a woods enclosure with Garal, with Eana (her stepmother?), and Gilly. And another brother I never met, he'd left the group. And Harold, of course, mustn't forget about Harold. (Haral.)

I started all this by telling you it was about Gilly's first attack on me. Mea culpa, folks. Senility again. Or some such animal. On the other hand, how could I have written this entire account if my brain were immersed in senile waters? I couldn't have. So there.

As we walked, it seemed to feel that I was being watched. It was not the first time I had known the discomforting sensation. Whenever I mentioned it to Ruthana, she told me—calmly, as always—that it might be Gilly, but more than likely was my imagination since, except for once, an owl flitting from tree to tree, obviously following us, she'd never felt that Gilly was tracking me.

"Oh, there's that damned owl again," I said as I noticed it sitting in a tree to my left. "It's not Gilly?"

"Perhaps it is," Ruthana answered. "He's no danger, though."

"I'm getting very tired wondering if he's following me," I said. Complainingly, of course. Of course, of course. I use that phrase a lot now. I'm getting tired of it. Not as tired as I was of Gilly's animosity; but A. Black tired, writer tired. Hate an overused phrase albeit appropriate.

Her fingers tightened on mine. "Don't be afraid, my love," she reassured me. "I'll always be with you."

"I know," I said, "I know. I just wonder, now and then, if I should be here at all."

"*Alexi, don't say that.*" Already there were tears in her eyes, trickling down her cheeks.

"Oh, don't cry," I begged. "I wouldn't leave you for the world."

"Why do you say it, then?" she pleaded. "You don't think you should be with me?"

"Not *you*," I said. "I'll always be with you. If I have to kidnap you back to . . ."

"The *Human World?*" she said. She sounded horrified.

"No, no," I said. "I'd never do that." My illogic was a trap now. How could I disengage myself from its piercing teeth?

What happened next caught me totally by surprise.

"Look!" she said, pointing across a stream we went walking by.

I turned to her, wondering why she was pointing.

"I said *look!*" she commanded, grabbing the back of my neck (my god, her fingers were strong!) and turning my head forcibly toward—what?

Whatever it was was just beginning to form—a dragon-like creature with a head like a cobra, scrawny arms it used to hold itself upright. It had a red roosterlike comb on its head, and two small flames emerged from its mouth as it breathed.

"My god, what *is* it?" I asked. My breath was having difficulty emerging at all.

"A *Basilisk*," Ruthana said quietly. So quietly, it made my blood run cold. A. Black had, often, been accused—or praised—for writing that. But A. Black never saw a real basilisk.

I did. And a chilling sight it was. Its skin—if that's what it was—gray and mottled, looking less like skin than like ruffled tree bark. Its eyes—aye, there's the rub, as Hamlet said.

"*Don't look at its eyes,*" Ruthana said. Again quietly, blood-chillingly.

"*Why?*" I asked. Like a stupid child.

"*Just don't,*" she said. Every word verbally italicized.

I didn't. She said something else. About the basilisk's deadly venom. I listened in frozen silence.

"You're not looking at its eyes, are you?" she asked, implored.

"No, I'm not," I told her. "It's not going to attack us, is it?"

"No, I'll see to it," she said.

With that, she threw up both hands and cried out words I cannot possibly remember, part Latin, part French, part—well, it sounded like gibberish to me.

Whatever it was, the cobra-headed dragon faded, then disappeared. The entire incident (nightmare) took only minutes, ten at most.

"Thank God," I muttered.

"Or *me*," she said. For an instant, I had a look at her (how shall I put it?) faerie ego.

"You told me not to look at its eyes," I said.

"I did," she replied.

"Why?"

"They're deadly," she said. "One look can kill you."

I started to respond, but she continued speaking. "Most important. You looked at it first."

"First?" I asked. Fully confused now.

"While it was *forming*," she said.

"Is that why you grabbed my neck?" I asked.

"Yes," she said, "I had to make you see it before it could see you."

"And if I hadn't?" I said.

"You would have died," she told me. Once more quietly. I absolutely shuddered.

"Oh, *Alexi*," she said. "I've frightened you. Forgive me."

I tried to smile. To grin, actually—but that was out of my league. "You have strong hands," I said. I wanted it to be some kind of jest. I failed. Suddenly, Ruthana was all apology and sorrow, crying—almost uncontrollably, it seemed. I held her in my arms, thinking momentarily how snugly she fitted into my embrace now that I was three-one not six-two. "Don't cry," I told her. "You saved my life. Again."

"Is it all so bad?" she asked brokenly.

"No, ma'am," I said, bad-joking-headed again. "I live for danger. I am Alexander the Great. I mean Alexi."

She knew it was a poor joke but responded with kind indulgence. "Thank you—Alexander," she said. "I mean Alexi."

Then was all serious again. "Isn't there danger in *your* world?" she asked, clearly in need of further reassurance.

Again with the lousy, however well-intentioned, humor. "Oh, sure. But only wars, not basilieks." I even got the word wrong. Eighteen, (almost nineteen) what can I say?

"Does it really make you unhappy being here?" she asked. Soulfully (the perfect word).

"No, not at all," I said. "As long as I'm with you, wherever I am is heaven." *A bit much, Alexi,* I told myself. But true.

Sort of true, I thought.

Chapter Twenty-four

So that was it. Ruthana seemed to be convinced of my sincerity. I hoped she really was. I couldn't be sure after what I'd said to her.

My next—what shall I call it?—adventure came the following week. You recall that I mentioned three rules a man must agree to in order to marry. I'd never (even *thought* to do so; that's a lie) asked her about her life before she met me. God knows I never struck her. I would rather have lost an arm than strike that angel. That left the third requirement—to not look at her at certain times. Where did they get that one, from the Bible?

Anyway, "that certain time" came around. I was to avoid her. What about Gilly, then? Ruthana foresaw that as well, bless her angelic heart. She asked Garal to keep an eye on me while she was sequestered with "her problem." Despite reluctance—Gilly *was* his son, after all—Garal agreed.

And I experienced one of the most inspiring days of my life. One of them, did I say? *The* most inspiring day of my life.

It began gradually. After meeting Garal (I'll describe him later), he and I went fishing. At first, I wondered why he looked into the pond carefully, as though searching for something. What? An available fish? I couldn't tell. Later on, I learned—a ghastly way—the answer.

But, for then, it signified good fishing—and delicious dinner—so we sat on the edge of the pool (a pond), our bamboo poles extended and leaning over the water, cords (I don't know what else to call them, or what they were made of or how they were made—I sure know a lot, don't I?) dangling, dipped below the surface (dangling, dipped, not bad) of the placid water, waiting patiently for some fish to offer up its life to faerie sustenance. Life in all its aspects being so real to the faeries, I wonder if that includes sentient fish. Now, I'm wandering. Sorry, again.

The long and short of it was that I asked Garal where the name "faerie" came from. I found out (later) that Garal was a teacher—a much-informed scholar of the Middle Kingdom. And *Beyond*. (I'll get to that presently.)

The word "faerie"? It's derived, by some, from Homeric sources (whatever they may be), what the centaurs were called. Later, Knights of the Crusade encountered Paynim warriors whose language possessed no letter *P*. Consequently, their word *peri* ("little folk," one assumes) was pronounced *feri*.

Beyond that, lacking (I would say) further recollection, the word became, in France, *faee* or *fee*; in Italy, *fata*; the root, in Latin, *fatum*. Got that? I didn't.

Later on, the word became plural, and in France, the verb *faer* (meaning "to enchant") became the noun *faerie*. The word became worldwide. Thus its presence in Northern England. Remembering that the derivation of the word had to do with an actual phenomenon, not an imaginary one. The beings of Middle Kingdom *exist*. I can't emphasize that enough. They exist. I was there.

They *still* exist.

☆ ☆ ☆

I thought Garal was finished. He was not. He was just getting warmed up. I remember, with pleasure, his warm smile and mellifluous (good word; means "euphonic," "musical") voice as he went on with his discourse. He saw that I was fascinated. Otherwise, he would have lapsed into friendly silence, I'm sure. As a matter of fact, he said, at one pause, then another, "Have I told you too much?" Or, "Am I becoming tedious, Alexi?" Each time, I assured him that it all intrigued me. It did.

Now he spoke about the types of faeries. I won't go into all of them; there are too darn many. Just the key ones. Garal, for instance, and his family were Elemental Faeries. This meant that they resembled human beings and procreated similarly. They were (are) capable of many faerie tricks. I call them tricks, but they are not "tricks" per se; they're abilities. Such as appearing and disappearing at will. Shape-shifting—into animals, plants, trees. (I find the second two hard to swallow, although there are extensive faerie archives regarding same.) They can assume human size (temporarily) and move with astounding speed; I saw that with Ruthana. Invisibility? I've already mentioned appearing and disappearing at will. Isn't that enough? Besides, it's too damned reminiscent of Magda's manuscript. Ugh!

Next step in Garal's discourse: the History of Faeriedom; I should say, Middle Kingdom. Also, excuse me for capitalizing "History." I flunked History in college. Maybe you did, too. Oh, well. Never mind.

The Elemental Faeries come in four categories—Earth, Air, Water, and Fire. Well, let that go, it's much too complicated. Almost twenty different types under each category! Forget it.

The Middle Kingdom—or Faerieland—Garal went on to say, is a locale within our world yet not. How's that for an enigmatic explanation? The realm has many names. I'll give you just a few of them. The Inner-Plain. The Ethereal World. A Parallel Universe. Enough? Okay, how about Land of the Dead? Ghost Dwelling? That's too much. Scratch it.

The inhabitants of these worlds have been known as Angels (I buy that one), Demons (not so much), Imaginary Beings (not at all!), Ghosts (nope), and Faeries.

No culture in the world does not accept the existence of these elusive beings who live somewhere between our world and that alternate one. Faeries are a universal phenomenon. Every country has them in residence. The most popular of these is what is called The Little People. Or the Wee Folk, the Good Folk, the Blessed Ones. (*Daoine Maithe.*) How come I remember that?

Faeries have existed as long as humans. And have been the subject of folklore since time began.

Faeries are sentient beings with feelings like our own. They have individual personalities. Some are helpful, some mischievous, some dangerous. (Amen to that.) Fundamentally, though, they are sensitive and deserve respect. (Not that I will ever respect my memory of God-awful Gilly.) They really loathe human injustice. (Who doesn't?)

They can shape-shift for only a limited period of time. (I told you that, I was thinking of Gilly and the Basilisk. Indicative that he chose that hideous shape to shift to.)

A gift from faeries—gold, silver, jewels—is illusory and will revert when the enchantment ends. Mr. Brean found that out the hard way.

More? Why not? Some disparate facts about the residents of Middle Kingdom.

First of all, if you happen to visit Faerieland, you'll be hard-put to depart. Especially if you leave the "guided" path—by which I presume, the path the faeries lead you on. And they *will* tempt you to return. I can verify that.

Faeries can elect to manifest themselves in the mortal world, but must take on smaller forms to compensate for lost energy. So watch out for that ant when strolling through the woods! (Just kidding.)

Sharp noises hurt their ears: bells ringing, hands clapping, and such. Didn't Magda tell me that? Didn't Joe?

They are fascinated (and repelled) by human beings and appear in shape-shifted forms to us, particularly as domestic animals. *So be kind to your web-footed friends.* (Isn't that how the song goes?) *For that duck may be somebody's mother.*

Some believe that faeries are androgynous and have no discernible gender. I can definitely shoot that one down. Ruthana androgynous? *Please!*

What I do believe about faeries is that they are unique. They can be mean or kind. Courtly or coarse. They feel anger, joy, and sadness. They function as elementals in Nature but think for themselves.

Above all, they require respect. They hate it if they are belittled, ridiculed, or slandered. Mankind, of course, cannot endure anyone different in appearance or beliefs. True or false? You know my choice.

Impressed by my knowledge? Don't be. This part is based on research, a writer named Edaion McCoy. For my part, I can only verify what he says. Most of it, anyway.

Our treatment of Nature—which they revere and nurture—infuriates them. Resulting in many pranks. I understand that. And appreciate it. I'm a nature buff myself.

There are some faeries who hate all living creatures, even their own kind. (Guess who *that* was.)

There are some faeries to avoid, just as there are some people to avoid. Yet you don't reject the entire human race because of those few rejectable individuals. Equally so, don't turn your back on those few faerie bad apples. Get it? I did.

"Am I becoming tedious, Alexi?" Garal asked at that point.

I told him no, but he chose to give me a break. With a very nice experience.

"Have you done scrying?" he asked.

I told him about attempting it (uselessly) in Magda's house.

"Oh, yes, the witch," he said. So casually that I had no further doubts regarding Magda. There was simply no way to disbelieve Garal.

※　※　※

It isn't necessary, I discovered, to stare into a mirror to scry. Any body of water will do—a lake, a pond, a pool, a *puddle*.

Since faeries could not look into mirrors (I never found out why), they prefer to gaze into still water. It worked better, anyway. It certainly did for me. I found out later that, while unaware of it, Ruthana was enhancing my psychic ability. Which I had none of until she instilled it.

Garal took our fishing lines from the pond and laid them aside. We had caught no fish. I don't think Garal had any intention of catching any. (I found out later that he wasn't crazy about the taste of fish, anyway.) He had us pretending to fish (I took it for real) so we could converse in peace. Which turned out to be a teacher-student exchange: the teacher lecturing, the student listening.

He had me lie on my chest and stomach and gaze intently into the water. I was amazed at how quickly those clouds (pink) appeared, how soon they were moving left to right. "This is incredible," I said. He shushed me. "Yes, sir," I murmured. The obedient student.

Then, in no time, it seemed (and was) as if, instead of scudding pink clouds, I was looking at a landscape very much like the one we were in. I bought a television set in 1970, and this was like that, clearly pictured. (Even with a soundtrack!)

From a distant grove of trees—all summerlike, no autumn-tinted leaves—a figure came walking toward me. He looked familiar. He waved. *My god!*

Harold.

No wound. No uniform. Dressed as Garal was, beige trousers, green jacket. He looked very happy.

"'Ello, chum!" he greeted me. "I'd shake your mitt, but we're in different places."

"You're alive," was all I could think to say.

"If you say so," he replied, with that familiar, beguiling smile. "In different places, though. I'm in kind of a Dreamland. You—" He looked around. "Good Lord, what are you doing *there*? Oh, my uncle's toe, is that Garal I see?! Hey, Dad! *What's going on?*"

I explained, as well as I could, my presence in the Middle Kingdom. He looked astounded, mouth ajar. *"You and Ruthana?"* he asked, completely floored by that. "What about Gilly? Isn't he a hornet's nest?"

"He sure is," I said. "He tried to kill me the other day."

"G'wan," he said. Then, "Well, I'm not surprised. He and I were not exactly comrades." For some reason, that amused me. I could never, under any circumstances, visualize Harold and Gilly as chums. One was sweet, the other toxic. Brothers? Impossible to imagine.

I asked Harold how he'd come to join the army—after attaining human size, of course.

"Well, I'll tell you," he explained. "I thought, for some reason, that it would be noble to fight for Blighty. Little did I know what it would be like. Oh, by the way, I took on a Cockney accent to fit in. If I'd known you long enough, I would have told you who—what—I really was. Well, maybe not, we little folks are damned secretive—as I'm sure you've discovered. Ruthana *is* a sweetheart, isn't she?"

"I adore her," I told him.

"Good," he said. "The girl deserves to be adored. If I hadn't been her brother—" He let that one go.

Changing the subject, I asked him a pair of questions. Had he lost any size when he—died? I had trouble using the word. And what about the lump of gold?

No, he remained human size until he reached what he referred to as Dreamland. (Summerland?) And Garal sent him the gold. "He had it in for me at first—when I told him I'd made up my mind to enlist. But he forgave me—he's a good soul." When he said that, I heard a grunt of pleasure behind me and realized that Garal had been looking across my shoulder at the scrying images. I didn't turn around, for fear of losing the image, but I smiled and knew that Harold was aware of why I was smiling.

When I told him about Mr. Brean, Harold didn't look surprised. "Greedy bugger," he said. "He might have known better. He *was* from Gatford." The last of his words, I didn't understand.

"But it stayed gold for me," I said.

"Of course," said Harold (Haral). "You were my chum. Still are. Don't plan on joining me too soon, though. You still have a while to go." That was nice to hear. I don't know why he said it, but he was certainly right. Assuming eighty-two is a while to go. Not exactly biblical, but enough for me.

There was not much more to say. I tried to talk about our time in the trenches, but I could tell that he was not too interested in that anymore. I can see why now. Afterlife is more, far more interesting. I'll confirm that one day. Stick around. Maybe I'll do another book from that side. Through a medium, I guess. I doubt spirits use pen and paper as I do. Maybe possession. There's a notion.

Well, onward. Harold and I conversed awhile longer—it was as though we were chatting face-to-face. Mostly, he wanted to know what my reaction was to Faerieland. What did I really think of it? "Wonderful," I said. *"Gorgeous."* He laughed at that.

He was sorry to hear about the pain I endured losing size. We shared a laugh about that mutual experience—the crunching of the skeleton, the shriveling sensation in the flesh. No fun, we agreed. Him in reverse, of course.

Then, to my immediate dismay—later I was okay about it—he was saying good-bye. "See you someday, chum"—and the scrying picture faded; I was staring at water again.

Someday, Harold. It's a date.

Chapter Twenty-five

The second—and third—attack on me occurred as follows. Sounds formal, doesn't it? I'll utilize A. Black vernacular. *Soon after, Ruthana's crazed brother took another crack at slaughtering young Alex.* You see what kind of excess Black was prone to use—permanently staining world literature with overkill.

The attacks, then.

No. First, I meant to tell you that my afternoon with Garal was the most inspiring day of my life. I forgot. I'd better tell you now. How could I have been (here's another combo) dumbly derelict in my writer's duty? Once again, forgive me.

Did I tell you what Garal looked like? *Who* he looked like, I mean.

Don't laugh now. Unless you really want to.

Judge Hardy.

That's right. Andy Hardy's father in the Mickey Rooney film series. Handsome, gray hair, wise, and patient. Lewis Stone was the actor's name. The only difference between Mr. Stone and Garal was height. Garal was three and a half feet tall. I'm sure Lewis Stone was taller than that. And he didn't wear a Munchkin-like green jacket like Garal.

While we were ambling through the woods—did I mention how ideal the weather was that day, warm but with a cool, refreshing breeze? There I go again, sidetracking. Well, I'm eighty-two, almost eighty-three! *Excuuuse* me!

Where was I? Yes, Garal and I ambling through the woods. (Did I mention the weather? Ha-ha. Joke.) I asked him about the relationship between the faeries and the citizens of Gatford. He told me that, at one time, centuries ago, the relationship had been extremely cordial. Well, maybe that's exaggerating. Very nice, though. The Gatford citizens treated Faerieland with respect. They did favors for each other. The Gatford citizens left milk (always fresh) and bread for the faeries. Reciprocation consisted of such things as helping trees and plants grow bountifully, locating runaway pets and cattle (faeries *love* animals; well, most of them do), and other friendly acts. Gatford, at that time, was Gateford—a gateway between the worlds.

Then, for some reason, the causes obscured in history, war "broke out" between the worlds. I put quotation marks around the words "broke out" because the commencement of any war always entails a breakage of some kind. Intelligence. Awareness. Humanity. All breaking simultaneously.

The war lasted close to a hundred years and involved some nasty—and brutal—exchanges between human beings and faeries. During that period, the ugly bridge I mentioned some time ago was built to harm any little people who tried to cross it. The ugly cathedral-like structure on the opposite side of the stream was constructed for ritual magic to be performed to further harm the faeries. Dear God, what "human" beings will conceive of to assail their "enemies"!

The war never really ended. Gateford became Gatford,

and hostilities submerged. Gatfordites no longer respected Middle Kingdom. They feared it and used caution regarding it. They hunted in the woods, occasionally "bagging" a faerie; Gilly's real father. I never did believe that he was blood-related to Garal.

Now for the inspiring part.

"You know, Alexi," Garal said, "we speak of human beings and faeries. Yet both races—if we call them that—are flesh and bone. In reality—true reality—we are neither. We are mind, soul, spirit."

I waited for more. There had to be more.

There was.

"You know, Alexi," he went on, "the body is surrounded by an invisible formfitting series of layers. These are fields of energy, each one more vital than the one below. The bottom layer is what has been called the *aura*. These layers continue to exist following bodily death. The body, you see, is only a mechanism, an organ the mind uses during physical life. Are you with me?"

"I'm with you," I told him. "Incredulous, but with you."

He smiled. "There you go," he said. "*Now.*"

He continued. To say that, just as the Earth has an atmosphere in which humans—and faeries—have their being, so does the aura provide a life-giving atmosphere for the body. During physical life, this aura interacts with the spiritual world.

"In other words," Garal said, "the spirit of our higher self—the outer layers—interacts with the Earth world."

"Are you saying," I asked, "that these layers—these fields of energy—are in *contact* with the spirit world?"

"Exactly," he said, "using the material body as the basis."

"The body as a mechanism."

"The brain as an organ, yes."

"Okay," I said, "I'm with it so far."

He smiled again. "Good," he said. "Continuing, then."

This other existence of ours—our spiritual existence—is our soul. That continues after so-called death. This is our real self. This is Reality.

Sleep, in fact, Garal told me, is a reflection of death. I no longer give credence to the word. We do not *die*. We *pass on*. Sleep has been—aptly—called the "twin brother" of death. While our physical body sleeps, our spiritual body remains awake. The body we use after we pass on.

I know this is heavy stuff. I barely assimilated it when Garal was instructing me. I hope you do.

"Some people, of course, die without dying," he said. "Pass on but return. Humans call it 'near death.' A fitting description. They see a portion of Afterlife—what we refer to as 'the Existence Following'—and, presently, return, or are drawn back against their will, to physical life. They never forget the experience. It affects the remainder of their life." The great human psychologist Carl Jung (I was startled—but shouldn't have been—that Garal knew about him) said that his near-death experience marked a "major" turning point in his work.

"Just remember this," Garal went on. "When we die (that now unacceptable word), we only pass on from one world to another." This from Emanuel Swedenborg, a famous Earth theologian. Whose existence I was surprised that Garal knew about. I should have known better.

His description of Afterlife—what he, personally,

envisioned—was remarkably similar to the exquisite environment (good combo there) of Faerieland. I hope, by now, that
the word "faerie" no longer makes you either grin or grimace.
Believe me. They *exist*. So does their exquisite world.

I told you it was an inspiring afternoon for me. If I have
failed to convey the thrill and wonderment I felt at Garal's
words, forgive me. The woods. The weather. The breeze.
Garal's presence by my side. His words. It was all, to me, mesmerizing. If not to you, blame it on Arthur Black. I told you
he was a deficient author. Or did I? Well, he is.

Chapter Twenty-six

The next attack was unexpected. Just as bad. Just as awful.

Ruthana and I were walking. After a while, she became a little weary. Her extra weight, you see. I forgot to tell you that a little time after I became an official little guy—though never according to Gilly—our "loving" produced the beginnings of a child in her lovely body. I believe they could decrease or extend their period of gestation at will. Ruthana's choice was six to seven months. Accordingly, that afternoon, after we had walked awhile, she felt the need to rest.

Notice how undramatically—even casually—I mentioned Ruthana's pregnancy? (I still don't like that word.) As opposed to my reaction when Magda announced that she was carrying "our child"? Her announcement knocked my socks off (as someone said). I really didn't want a child. To my discredit, I should have taken steps to prevent its conception. But then it might have happened anyway. Magda wanted it. That I firmly believe. She did nothing to prevent it.

And I was the surrogate father—in lieu of Edward. Anyway, I was shocked at her announcement. Or should I say "pronouncement"? Any way you look at it, her body was not conceiving a love child. God knows how she really felt about that baby. Toward the end not much, that was for sure. The memory of its (imagined) enforced "birth" will remain with me forever. That damned manuscript.

With Ruthana, the entire parentage experience was heavenly. She seemed to relish the gestation more each day. She would pat her stomach gently and speak to the baby endearingly—as though she had no doubt whatever that the baby could hear every loving word. Which, for all I knew, the baby did—enjoying the sweet verbal caressings—as any baby would.

My point is this—in case I have failed (and probably have) to convey it. Magda carried a plan; Ruthana a baby conceived in love. Big difference there.

At any rate, Ruthana needed a rest.

One more addendum. Two. Number one—we were resting in a meadow. It was early November, but the day, despite the date (pretty good triplet there, sorry) was not chilly at all. Summer persistent through fall, resisting winter. What winter? False autumn? Late summer? There's another expression for it, but I forget it. Anyway I, later, learned that there was no quartet of seasons in Faerieland, only spring and summer.

I do remember that Ruthana seemed a little sad that day. I didn't know why. She was usually so redolent with cheer that her dispirit disturbed (I won't say it) me. While we were resting, her lying down, her golden-haired head in my lap, I asked her what was bothering her.

"It's the eleventh day of the eleventh month," she answered.

Or was it an answer? Two questions popped into my brain.

Was the baby eleven months old? What happened to the six to seven months' choice? And two, were the two elevens part of some faerie ritual I knew nothing about?

Both questions redundant, as it turned out.

"The war is over," she said. "Germany surrendered."

"Well . . . isn't that good?" I asked, pleased to hear it.

She didn't reply at first.

"Ruthana?"

Her voice broke as she answered, "Not for Haral."

Oh. I felt guilt. And shame. I should have known.

"I'm sorry," I said, "I should have known."

She smiled (bravely, I thought), picked up my hand, and kissed its back. "I understand." She paused. "You knew him, though. You were there when he—died."

"I was there when he lived, too," I told her, trying to cheer her. "He was my good friend." I hoped he was.

"I know he was," she said. "It's been a comfort knowing that. I miss him so."

Still trying to cheer her, I told her what else I could remember about Harold. How we met, the splashing of mud, how we sat together during bombardments, how he guided me to Gatford, even providing me with the wherewithal to live there.

"He must have known that I'd meet you," I said. "He was our Cupid."

She smiled again, apparently at peace now, and closed her eyes.

I watched her as she slept. Dear Lord, she was beautiful. Assuming there is a god and He is also god to the Middle Kingdom as to ours, He had created a masterpiece of grace and elegance in Ruthana's appearance. Everything about her presentment was, beyond question, perfection. Oh, I do run on. You get my message, though. I was in total and enduring love with a flawless angel. Nuff puff for one book.

No, not enough. I have not completed the portraiture of my beauteous faerie. Her eyes. An eerie blue green; yes, that undeniable combination. The blue of stirring water, the green of placid. Lustrous, searching eyes. I always felt that she was seeing far more than I was. That, in gazing at me, she was looking straight into my soul. How wonderful—yet, as I have indicated, eerie.

Her skin. The color of rich cream with a translucent coating of rose pink. Her nose. Designed by the greatest Renaissance artists, ideal in every aspect. Her lips. My God, how perfect. How yearning to be kissed—which I did proliferately. Soft and warm and yielding. (Lord, even ancient Arthur Black is trembling in remembrance!) Her body. Well, let's skip that. I'm not as old as the Red Sea, you know; the tide could rise.

Well, to the attack.

It began in such a subtle manner that, at first, I didn't pay attention to it. I heard what seemed to be a slight wind overhead. To me, it registered as an autumn breeze. Stupid me. An autumn breeze indeed. It "blew" two or three times before I took notice of it as something to be conscious of. A recurring breeze. Which became, in consequent moments, a recurring wind. A rushing sound. Like the noise made, possibly—

—by wings.

Only after numerous repetitions of the sound did I become engaged. Not alarmed yet. Merely involved in the persistent—I must admit now, *haunting*—sound. Gradually I became—very slowly—cognizant of an anxious sensation. What was it? Clearly, a bird. But how big? And why, I began to wonder, was it constantly passing over us? Over. Over. Again and again. As though—the notion chilled me—*searching.*

"Ruthana?" I murmured. I hated to wake her. She was sleeping so serenely. But I felt, somehow, that it was, probably, needed.

She stirred, making a tiny sound that, under other circumstances, would have (what's the phrase?) "turned me on." As if I was ever turned off in her presence.

I nudged her again. "Ruthana." The sound—the rushing sound—the (now no doubt) wing sound—was closer overhead. "*Ruthana,*" I said, more urgently.

She opened her eyes. Those wonderful blue green eyes. Staring into mine.

"What's that noise?" I began to ask.

Before I could get the words out, she sat up and stood with astonishing quickness (considering the size of her baby-expanding stomach), a look of tensed apprehension on her face. "Up!" she cried—commanded, actually. She grabbed me by the arm and yanked me to my feet. "Run!" she gasped. And started racing me toward the distant woods.

"*What is it?*" I asked, just able to breathe.

"*Griffin,*" she answered.

At which a bloodcurdling screech swept down from above. A great form dove down on us—me, in particular—I screamed at what felt like claws tearing at my back. They made me suddenly fall. I twisted over with a cry of pain. What I saw was enough to kill me with the sight. Today, it would put an end to me. At eighteen, I had embedded in my psyche, will to survive. So I was horrified, not wrenched from life.

It was part lion, part eagle: its head and white-feathered wings those of an eagle; its body that of a lion except for its tail, which was that of a giant snake. It was the lion's claws that had ripped at my back. I thought I heard thunder rolling in the sky.

The eagle's eyes were human. They seemed to regard me with rage, albeit they were milky and lacking a pupil.

"*Come!*" I heard Ruthana's voice command me. Her hand was clutching mine, pulling me up. The griffin's wings thrashed at the ground as I began to run again. Scramble, actually. Bolt for the nearing woods, leaning forward as I scampered for my life, prevented by Ruthana from a face-forward tumbling onto the ground. I felt blood dribbling down my back, a throbbing ache. Behind me, I heard that awful screech again, the driving thrust of its wings as the griffin leaped into the air, pursuing us. How could Gilly shift himself to such a nightmare creature? I wondered for an instant. Then self-preservation took over, and once more, I attempted to run erect. In vain. I would definitely have lost it were it not for Ruthana's supporting hand and arm.

Again the violent crash on my back. I cried out, stricken. The pain was excruciating. I was sure I was being ripped apart. I jerked around once more, a scream of dread escaping me. The griffin's eagle face was directly above mine, milky eyes staring. Its grisly screech enveloped me. I knew, in that moment, I was done for.

Then, a miracle. At least, it seemed a miracle to me. With

a sudden move, the lion's weight was off my back. I heard the thrashing buffet of its wings. I turned to see.

Ruthana stood with a hazel wand in her right hand, pointing it toward the griffin. (It was much like the wand Magda had used in healing my wound.) From its end, blue flame was projecting.

"Quickly!" she cried; her voice sounded hoarse. *"Into the woods!"*

I lurched to my feet and ran almost blindly toward the trees, trying to ignore the dreadful stabbing pain in my back. Behind and above, the griffin shrieked—in rage, it seemed—and I could hear the sound of its hurtling ascent as it continued chasing me. I sensed Ruthana running near me. Panting now. I'd never heard that sound before.

Finally, the trees were around us and Ruthana jarred to a halt, gasping, out of breath, another sound I'd never heard from her.

"It can't get through the trees," she managed to say.

But it could. And did.

At any rate, it tried, shattering its massive weight through the foliage, snapping off limbs and branches in its crazed attack. One of its wings was torn away. It shrieked with pain.

"I don't understand," Ruthana said in a trembling child-like voice. *"This is wrong."* The sound of dread in her voice was my most frightening moment of the entire assault. Terror-stricken, I was frozen to the ground as the huge creature smashed down within a foot of me. I saw the root ends of its lost wing spurting blood.

I looked at Ruthana. She was staring at the fallen griffin,

openmouthed, an expression of petrified disbelief on her face. I looked down at the griffin. What I saw then drove a cloud of blackness over me. I toppled over, losing consciousness. "Alexi!" I heard Ruthana's cry of alarm before I was enveloped in night.

What I saw was not dissimilar to the illustration in Magda's hideous manuscript detailing the process of shape-shifting. In this case, what I saw was the bony structure of the white-feathered wing transforming gradually to the structure of a broken, blood-oozing arm. The lion's body slowly altering to that of a shattered human form. The eagle head becoming, second by second, a human head, the eyes still milky, the face still taut with teeth-bared hatred.

What I saw was Magda, dead.

Chapter Twenty-seven

"At first I thought it was Gilly," she told me, "but when the griffin followed us into the woods, I knew it couldn't be. He'd know the woods would stop him. *She* didn't."

"Or maybe she just didn't care," I answered. "Maybe—no, not maybe—she hated me so much, she was determined to kill me. And it killed her. My *god*, how she must have hated me."

"Witches are like that," Ruthana said. "You're well rid of her." She declared it in a matter-of-fact way. And that was it. Magda was out of my life.

I was (sort of) in Garal's home. (Don't ask me to explain that; I never could.) I'd been there since the griffin attack, carried by Garal and—I, later, learned to my surprise—Gilly. He was in awe of his stepfather and obeyed him implicitly. Ruthana wanted to help, but Garal forbade her lest she endanger the welfare of the child.

So, when I "came to" (as so many A. Black protagonists do), I was in Garal and Eana's residence, my back—I, also, later, learned—in semi-shreds. They gave me something to drink, which immediately allayed the severe pain. Then, over a period of weeks, they worked on my back, their healing magic fully as efficacious (another dandy elitism) as Magda's—or whoever—or whatever—she'd requested help from. In a short while, the back was taken care of. Lovingly ministered by Ruthana, Garal, and Eana, the torn-up flesh was restored. I never looked—or asked to look—at the griffin's destruction. I preferred not to see it. It was, doubtless, hair-raising.

During my recovery period, who else but good ol' Gilly came to visit. Not to wish me well, of course, but to express his amusement that I, much less Ruthana, believed the griffin to be his shape-shifted responsibility. "You think I'm stupid?" he asked.

"No, I don't think you're stupid," I said. "I think you're a God damn vicious son of a bitch." I was feeling sassy. Also safe in Garal's house.

My words only evinced a smile from his goddam, vicious lips. "Get well," he said, patting me on the shoulder. "So I can kill you."

"*Good luck*," I snapped. But I was far from feeling (three!) snappy.

I was scared.

✕   ✕   ✕

Later, I spoke to Ruthana about it.

Wasn't there some way to prevent Gilly from attempting to murder me? Were there no preventive laws in Middle Kingdom?

She only reiterated the only law in Middle Kingdom. Life was sacrosanct, untouchable. Gilly could be punished for a life-threatening action, no more. *After* the action, that is.

"Punished *how?*" I asked. "What if he kills me?"

Ruthana smiled at that. A sad smile, naturally. "He can be put away," she said.

"Not executed?" I asked.

"Oh, no," she said. "All life is precious."

"What about *mine?*" I persisted. "Less than precious?"

"It is to me, Alexi," she said quietly. "If you die, I die. Like Gilly's mother did after his father was killed."

"Oh, *Ruthana,*" I could hardly speak. She lay beside me— carefully—and I held her as tightly as I could. "I love you, Alexi," she whispered. "You are my life."

"Oh, God." I squeezed her until my back stung from the effort.

"*Careful,*" she murmured. "Don't hurt yourself."

"I won't," I promised.

She kissed me lovingly. "I'll watch over you," she said. "Gilly will never harm you."

"He'll try, though, won't he?" I asked.

Her answer was simple—and chilling to my bones.

"Yes, he will," she said.

※　※　※

And so it was. Big-time. If I'd hoped—and I did—that he would take a break from his quest to obliterate me, I was doomed to disappointment. (This is sounding more like an A. Black tome all the time. *Midnight Middle Kingdom Massacre?* No, too long. *Midnight Gilly Kill?* No; forget it.)

I was in danger, though. Constantly. Let me enumerate what that bastard (sorry) did to undo me.

1. Somehow (I never found out how—another faerie mystery)—he managed to modify the paths on which Ruthana and I customarily strolled. At first, it created no worse than a slightly confusing alteration in our route—pleasant in any direction. I think Ruthana knew what Gilly had done. There was a smile of faint amusement on her lips. Then, at a specific moment in our walk—maybe fifteen to twenty minutes into it, she took hold of my arm abruptly—she was on my right—and halted me. "*Wait*," she said. I watched curiously as she edged forward, pressing her foot down. Did I mention the ground was covered by leaves? In front of her was a pile of them. "Oh, yes," she said, as though understanding. She tapped her foot down sharply, and the leaves collapsed. They had been obscuring an open hole. "An old well," Ruthana said. "Not used anymore."

I drew in a shaking breath. "Good ol' Gilly," I said. It occurred to me then that, if Ruthana hadn't sensed the trap Gilly had set, she might also have fallen into the well. Clearly, Gilly knew it, too. She was his sister, carrying a child. If she'd been killed, a primal faerie rule would have been violated.

Later that day, Ruthana—and Garal—took Gilly to task for his infringement of Middle Kingdom law. I wasn't privy to their reprimand, but as I gathered from Ruthana's later account, they had raked him over the coals. I doubt if their castigation did more than aggravate my dear stepbrother (I guess that's what he was considered to be), but at least it got me a week's respite before—

2. Ruthana and I were sitting in a lovely glade when the tall figure of a man emerged from the woods in front of us. He

was completely naked, his body glowing with a bizarre yellow green light. "My god, what's that?" I asked. Ruthana was un-flustered. "Ignore him," she said. At that, the glowing man glared (glowing—glared; not bad) at me, raised his fisted hand threateningly, and vanished. "What in God's name *was* that?" I asked, more strongly. "Gilly, of course," she said, "trying to frighten you." I exhaled—hard. "Well, he succeeded," I said. She was amused. She laughed. (Which didn't please me.) "He'll do worse," she told me.

3. And so he did. He felled a tree behind me. It missed Ruthana, who—in her usual quick way—pushed me out of the tree's rushing descent. Obviously, I knew then (or suspected, anyway) that Gilly made no further attempt to include his sister in his homicidal plots. I was, at once, both pleased and displeased at the realization. Pleased that his devious plans did not entail harming Ruthana. Displeased because she might, inadvertently, be injured or killed while protecting me.

On top of that, I felt damn provoked at Gilly's invulnerabil-ity. Maybe it was a leftover attitude from my human being days—but it still seemed to me (no, *more* than seemed) that ei-ther Gilly should be tossed in the clink permanently or I should be armed with a pistol to use at his next attack. About that time, the fantasy of pumping a slug into brother(-in-law's) nasty brain was pleasing indeed. Because of or partially due to—

4. Gilly tried to steal my shadow. How this is done is also way beyond me. But he pulled it off—for a few minutes—before Ruthana undid it. And let me tell you, the disappearance of one's shadow is incredibly dismaying. Try to visualize it. No,

you couldn't possibly. Take my word for it. It makes you physically sick, nauseated. It's so against natural law. It's also fatal if it lasts. Which, thank heaven, did not happen to my vanished shadow. Where Gilly put it only God knows. Ruthana got it back, however. Saving me from what she said would be a horrible death. One more escape from Gilly. As in—

5. Gilly appearing suddenly, pointing a hazel wand at me. From the wand end, blue flame shooting. Blocked and inverted by Ruthana's wand. Since the griffin attack, she kept it on her person at all times. (Where—once more—I have no idea whatever.)

6. Oh, why go on? Except to tell you of the attack that almost worked.

Ruthana and I were sitting beside a shallow pool, feet dangling in the water. She was getting large now. Maybe it decreased, somewhat, her perspicuity (big word, that; it means, I think, her clarity of awareness). Sports writers would have observed: "She was not on top of her game." She sat smiling to herself; she did that a lot toward the end of the gestation. She kicked her feet slowly and idly in the pool. I was in a dream state myself. Soon our baby would be born. I did not miss human existence at all. I was with my precious angel.

All was well.

I should have known better. I thought it was our kicking feet that leisurely stirred the water. I was wrong. I should have warned Ruthana sooner. I didn't. I stared into the rippling water as though hypnotized. Something was beneath its surface, rising. A fish? An uprooted plant? An optical illusion?

A *hand*! Surging up from the water's surface! Green, scaly, long nailed, clamping itself around my ankle! I was so shocked, I couldn't make a sound, my voice paralyzed by mindless terror.

Then something even worse. A huge round *thing* popped up, the body of the hand. It, too, was scaled, purple in color. It had a gigantic mouth and huge eyes staring at me, gleefully it seemed.

My strangled whimper would likely, all on its own, have been enough to arouse Ruthana. As it was, she became aware before I made a sound because, in an instant, moving with the incredible speed I'd seen so many times, her right hand seemed to shoot out and grab the hand, yanking it from my ankle.

To my horror, I saw the green hand clutch at her wrist and begin to pull her down. Ruthana's face was gripped by fright. "Alexi!" she cried. Off-balanced by the weight of her stomach, she began to fall forward toward the pool. I remember crying, "No!" and grabbing at her arms. The huge eyes of the creature opened wider. As did the gigantic mouth. I saw its teeth, greenish yellow, ready to clamp on Ruthana's arm. I pulled at her as hard as I could. "Gilly, *no!*" I screamed. "*Your sister!*"

To this day, I have no way of knowing if I had anything to do with the attack ending so suddenly. I only know that, in an instant, the ugly hand released Ruthana, and its gross purple body vanished beneath the flailing water—which, abruptly, became still again.

※　※　※

My meeting with Garal, Ruthana, and Gilly was a somber affair. Garal had ordered it immediately following the attack at the pool. Why he allowed me to attend, I don't know. No matter my sanctioned approval in the Middle Kingdom, I was, nonetheless, an "outsider," a human being given limited access to the Kingdom. I could never be considered a full-fledged faerie. (I should be impressed with that triplet, but recollection of the meeting and its grim nature prevents me from enjoying the three-word combo.) I suppose it was my relationship with Ruthana that made the difference. Of course it was.

"Well, what do you have to say?" was the opening statement of the meeting. From—needless to say?—Garal.

"*Say?*" countered a sullen Gilly.

Garal waited, his features carved from stone. I saw a betraying swallow on Gilly's throat. Garal clearly held sway over him. Not only was he Gilly's "father," he was also the accepted leader of the clan.

"What do you *want* me to say?" he finally asked. He tried to make it sound like a demand but couldn't quite bring it off.

Garal cut to the bone. *"That you tried to kill your sister,"* he said.

I knew the word "blanch." I'd never seen it, though. At Garal's words, Gilly's face lost color, very quickly. He was frightened. *Him.* The faerie thug who had terrorized me since my entry into Middle Kingdom. The little black-haired brute whose one goal was to kill me. It was his turn to be frightened. *Him.* I gloried in the moment.

"I didn't mean to," was all he managed to say.

"Yet you tried to drag her down into the shellycoat's maw," said Garal. Accusingly now.

Condemningly.

"Father, he's a Human Being!" (Still the capitalized pronunciation.) Gilly tried a switch in his defense. "They killed my real father. Made my mother die! Am I supposed to forget that? Forgive Alexi because he's our size now? He's still a Human Being. *I will not forgive him!*"

Garal's voice was cold. I felt a numbing gratitude that his anger was not directed at me.

"*I'm speaking of your sister,*" he said. "I forced myself to overlook your attempts on Alexi's life because I knew Ruthana would protect him, *I* would protect him. But the attack on your sister is unforgivable!" I had never heard him raise his voice. It was a daunting sound.

"I didn't *mean* it!" Gilly shouted. It was not a daunting sound. It quavered. Something else I'd never heard, especially from Gilly.

"*That's not the point!*" said Garal. "You *did* it. That is the end of it. You are going to the Cairn."

Did I say "blanch" before? I swear to God that all the blood rushed out of Gilly's face; his skin grew wax white. "No," he whimpered. "*No.*"

"*Now,*" said Garal. "This instant."

Another sound I never heard—or even thought of hearing. Gilly crying. Sobbing. A pitiful sight. I actually felt sorry for him. *Him!*

Garal led him away. Then both of them vanished in that inexplicable faerie way. I sat in wordless withdrawal. Ruthana was crying, too. Softly. Miserably. I put an arm across her shoulders. Imagination? Or did she twitch as though resisting my comfort? I felt emotionally adrift.

Not helped when Garal returned, appearing next to me in that sudden faerie manner—zip! Like that.

He put his hand on my knee—and, abruptly, I experienced an unpleasant twinge of memory, the movement bringing back an image of the Captain, although, God knows, he'd never placed a hand on me. It was just something in the moment that dredged up a recollection of Lecture Time.

Which it was. "Alexi," Garal said, "you know that this is not a common happening. It has *never* occurred in my family."

"I'm sorry," was all I could say. My inner voice, naturally, jumped up with *What do you expect from me? Regret? The bastard tried to kill me over and over! If he hadn't made a mistake and gone after Ruthana, would you* ever *have punished him?! Probably not! Maybe after he finally did me in! What good would it do me then?!*

None of which I vocalized. I sat in chastened muteness as his reproving went on. It *was* reproval, never doubt. I was still an outsider. I had (in all innocence, God damn it!) caused a rule to be broken, and I must be careful never to breach that standard again. I kept glancing at Ruthana as her father (stepfather; oh, who the hell knows?) spoke. Looking for an expression of sympathy. At least understanding—for me, I didn't see it. She agreed with every quiet injunction Garal made. My alienation from Middle Kingdom was called up again. Magnified. I would be reminded of it at a later time. In a different way, but even more radically.

At least, however, I was rid of Gilly.

For a while.

Chapter Twenty-eight

Arthur Black (at least the kernel of his black-hearted fetus) slithered into the world during that period. No longer attacked on an almost daily basis by his beloved (step)brother, he had time to plant the seed of his dire existence.

Alexander White wrote a novel. *MIDNIGHT.* An innocent commencement of the soon-to-assault-the-reading-public *MIDNIGHT* parade. I say "innocent" because, initially, it was. I meant it to be a love story, a story of moral retribution. Of course, with my background—and with the recollection of the alarming incidents in my life with Ruthana—there were any numbers of scare-stuff in the story. (There I go again— *scare-stuff in the story;* Arthur Black in genesis.)

These were the lone elements which the publisher (it *was* published, years later, reviewed, and sold rather well) later— even later (better never)—brought to unnatural birth the author known as Arthur Black (*born in London, son of a distinguished military colonel, three times decorated veteran of the Great War, graduate, with a master's degree, of Oxford University where he majored in Literature and Philosophy*).

Hell, I never even got out of high school!

♉ ♉ ♉

I must say that my new family was damn gracious about my novel—except for Gilly, I'm sure; although I doubt he was told about it.

It was a nice piece of work. As I said, a love story. Inspired (needless to say, he said) by Ruthana.

What the story was (is) about is a young man (me, of course) who travels to the woods of Canada. I was going to have him travel to the woods of Northern England but decided otherwise, lest I offend my brethren. I call them that; it's how I truly felt about them.

At any rate, my young protagonist hied himself to the Canadian forest to bag an elk. Ruthana didn't like it that his motive was to hunt but consequent pages ameliorated that.

One afternoon, the young man (named Roger) is attacked by a large wolf. He shoots it, then discovers, to his shock, that when he approaches the dead body, it is in fact, the bloody corpse of an old man. (Note the early spawning of A. Black grisliness.) He is totally stunned by this. Equally so when he is surrounded by a group of angry Forest People (as I called them). They are enraged by what he's done. Among them is a lovely young maiden named Aleesha. The old man was her grandfather.

To make a long story short (a capacity I totally lack), Aleesha spares Roger's life by explaining to the other Forest People (as I called them—I said that already, didn't I?) that her grandfather was showing unfortunate signs of mental decline and was shape-shifting devoid of discretion. I forget, exactly, how she explained it. Roger was—reluctantly by some, especially Aleesha's brother (guess where that came from)—exonerated and, with limitations, accepted by the Forest People—who were human-sized, not small—this tickled the faeries considerably.

So time went by. I will not divulge all the details of my masterpiece (joke) but say only that Roger and Aleesha fell in love, and he came, more and more, to embrace the Forest People way of life, taught their various skills. (The faeries loved this section; I was requested to read it aloud on many an occasion. I became quite popular for a time. To my [by then] nineteen-year-old delight.)

How the novel progressed and concluded, I will keep a secret. If it has a happy or a tragic ending, I will not tell you. (It *was* a sort of A. Black send-off tale remember, so I leave that up to you.)

༝ ༝ ༝

I will not forget the afternoon Ruthana took me by the hand and walked me through the woods. Life in those days was idyllic in every way, so I thought little about where she was taking me. I simply enjoyed the stroll. Spring was in the offing. Sound poetic? I was in a poetic mood. In a short while I would celebrate my first year in Gatford. In even less time, I would become a happy father, the mother my beloved Ruthana.

So imagine my surprise when she led me toward the path. For several long minutes (they certainly seemed long to me), I thought she was putting me out of the woods, out of her life. Was my presence so disturbing to her? It wouldn't be that difficult to understand. I had disrupted her existence in many ways. I was, despite my diminished stature, still a human being—or, as Gilly had it, a Human Being. She was carrying a baby put inside her by a race unknown to her. My proximity generated a situation in which Gilly's vengeful hatred of humans was so completely exaggerated that it made him miscalculate and endanger his own sister's life; a definite dereliction (I won't say it!) in the Middle Kingdom. Because of this he was imprisoned in the Cairn. I'd simply done too much harm.

The more I thought about it, the more convinced I became that she was expelling me from Faerieland; perhaps on Garal's order.

"You're putting me out, aren't you?" I said.

"What?" She hadn't heard. I repeated the question—more a despairing statement.

"Putting you out?" she said. She sounded confused.

I blurted out my list of anxieties.

"*Oh, Alexi!*" she murmured, stopping in her tracks.

"Isn't it true?" I asked, also stopping. "Haven't I ruined your life?"

"*Alexi. My love. Ruined it? You've made my life heaven!*"

"Then . . . why—?" I started.

"*Putting you out?*" she sounded painfully incredulous now. "I would never do that."

"Then why . . . the *path?*" I asked.

I'd removed my hand while enumerating my doubts. She took it back now. Firmly. "Come," she said.

We walked to the path. There, she stopped and pointed. I looked. Magda's house.

Burning.

※ ※ ※

For a while—how long I don't remember—I was speechless. Then, at last, I was able to speak. Not coherently. "How?" was all my brain was able to produce.

"We don't know," Ruthana said. "We think that the people of Gatford did it."

"Why?" Another ill-produced word from my unhinged brain. The intense relief of hearing that Ruthana was not getting rid of me magnified by the unnerving sight of Magda's house on fire created a word void in my head. "*Why?*" I said again, blotting out her answer. Which was, "Because she's a witch."

"I know but—*is*, Ruthana? She's dead, isn't she?" I felt cold asking it.

Colder yet at Ruthana's answer. "Part of her."

"*Part?*" I couldn't recognize my voice, it sounded hollow, hoarse.

"Her second body is still alive," she said.

Again that voice sounded unrecognizable to me. "*Second body?*"

"Didn't Garal tell you?" she asked.

"*No,*" I said. Then, "*I don't remember.*"

She recounted to me (I guess Garal had said something like it) that we have several bodies, one of them physical.

"That was the body you saw in the woods," she told me. "The body she shifted to the griffin body. The body that was killed."

"Then . . . her—second body? . . ." I was totally mixed up.

"Is her—did Garal name it?—*astral* body? Spirit body? It's still alive. There has to be a second death."

"Second death," I muttered. Caught between confusion and the deep blue sea.

Ruthana nodded. "Then the rest of her can move on." Her expression darkened. "I would hate to see where, she's done so much evil."

"So much *good,* too," I found myself protesting. "I was with her for months. She healed my wound. She was very kind to me."

"Are you sorry you left her?" Ruthana asked. She meant it.

"I didn't leave her, she chased me out."

"And tried to kill you, Alexi."

I sighed. I felt rotten. "I know," I said. "My home is with you."

"Oh, *Alexi,*" she said. She was in my arms again. Her soft lips on mine. "I *love* you," she whispered. "Don't ever think you ruined my life. Don't *ever* think that."

"I won't," I promised. "Thinking it made me sick."

She kissed me tenderly. "You never have to think it again," she said.

We stood in silence for a while, looking at the fiery blaze of Magda's house.

"I suppose there's no way to put it out," I thought aloud.

"None," she said. "We can't do it. And the people of Gatford won't do it. We believe they started it, of course."

I said no more. I did wonder why the faeries could do nothing. I didn't ask. Ruthana read my thought. "She tried to harm us any way she could," she told me. "We're not sad to see it burn."

I noticed, at that moment, that we were not alone. All through the trees, I saw a host of Middle Kingdomites, all standing quietly, watching. A few of them—the younger ones—were smiling, even grinning at the leaping flames. Most of them, however, to their credit, observed the (by now) conflagration in grave muteness. There was no way of knowing what terrible hostilities had existed between them and Magda. (I knew nothing about it from her.) Memories of dreadful events I'd experienced gave me some idea; but details? No. I actually lost track of the fire, turning my head to look at the different faeries.

I had never seen them in such numbers before. They were a fascinating sight. Every age, every appearance, all short in height, of course, all dressed in clothes of various color. All—do I dare express it so?—*cute*. Well, they were. Dwellers of Middle Kingdom. Secretive to a fault. Fast moving. Innocent yet capable of alarming mischief. Lovers—and nurturers—of Nature. A (virtually) unknown race of legendary people, little people. It was hard for me to believe I was one of them. Of course, I wasn't.

I had to tear away my rude inspection of them. I managed it somehow, returning to the burning house. It was, now, a holocaust. (An original definition of the ghastly crime we, later, were witness to.)

"There's no way . . . Magda—as she is now—can put it out?" I asked.

"None," said Ruthana. "She is not part of this world now. I mean not in this . . . what is the word my father uses? Diminishin?"

"Dimension?" I suggested.

"Yes." She nodded. "Magda is still in the house but in a different—demenishen."

I didn't correct her. All I could accost in my brain was an image of Magda in the house, unable to do anything but watch the belongings of her life consumed by fire. The furniture, the books, her bed, for God's sake! The painting of Edward! Even in another dimension, it had to be a wrenching experience for her to watch helplessly as these priceless possessions burned.

You wonder, perhaps, why, so easily, I accepted the concept that, her physical body dead, Magda still existed. Listen, folks. After all I'd seen in 1918, I would have bought the Brooklyn Bridge for twenty cents. Little green men from Mars? Probably. Rocket ships to—what?—the moon? Why not? For Jesus' sake I'd lived with *faeries* for six months! A *witch* for three! What was left to disbelieve?

⚔ ⚔ ⚔

So the house of Magda Variel was burned to the ground. Well, almost. Some of it remained, blackened, charred. And any sign of the Gatford Voluntary Fire Department? My ass. I hated to think of Joe gloating over the consumption of the witch's house. He probably did, though. Hadn't he alerted me to her witchdom? Hadn't he told me how to cope with her? No, that was with the faeries; he was obsessed with them, too.

Well, he had brought me bread and milk and fixed the roof of Discomfort Cottage—give the man pluses for that. And he was a product of his time and place, God bless his superstitious bones. Oh, Christ. I'm getting tolerant in my waning years. Or is it feeble-minded? Anyway, Joe's superstitions proved to be true. Magda *was* a witch. The woods *did* swarm with faeries. I should write him a letter. *Dear Joe, you were fucking right.* (There, I've used the super-naughty word. And I'm not even apologizing for it.)

I have become conscious of the fact that I am killing pages to delay what is becoming those dread words (worse, I think than the "bad" one).

The End.

But it's not, you see. Almost but not completely.

Chapter Twenty-nine

The birth of Garana took place on February 29, 1919. It was a painless and harmonious delivery. They always are in Faerieland. Or so I was told. Why not? Was there any stress to deal with? Not at all. Except for human beings with guns.

I will attempt now (probably without success) to describe the celebration that took place in honor of Garana's entry into Little People Land. I suppose I might have shown resentment that my daughter wasn't named Alexana or something like that. I assumed that despite every emotional attachment I felt for Middle Kingdom, I was still, fundamentally, a human being, and my child's name reflected that albeit subtly. Actually, I did feel disturbed by it but had to understand. Ruthana picked up my distress and tried to comfort me. Garana was still my blood daughter, she said. Nothing could change that.

Yes—the celebration. I *did* recall that my marriage to Ruthana was unattended by my Faerieland brethren. Because it was a polyglot wedding, faerie with human being—or mortal as we are sometimes called. But aren't faeries mortal? Aren't they corporeal as much as human beings? I guess not. They are partly (how much I never knew) also incorporeal? Astral?

Ruthana seemed bodily enough when we were loving. Oh, who knows? I've been sidetracked again. Arthur Black would put me in a home for askew authors.

Well, I must, as best I can describe the natal day celebration. I said I would, and by God, I will. I might go off center periodically, but I do manage to get back on target. Eventually.

You know that faeries love to dance. No, you don't. I never told you. Well, they do. A lot. As much as possible. And what better excuse than the birth of a Middle Kingdom citizen?

The music? Fiddles. Panpipes. Pennywhistles. One delicious melody after another. Did you know that many so-called folk songs were derived from faerie songs? For instance "The Londonderry Air." That was one of them. Of course, there is a melancholy feeling to that one. There was nothing but joy and energy to the dancing music that day. All to the throbbing, mesmerizing beat of tiny drums, the rhythmic cadence of feet as they battered lightly at the ground. Whirling, jumping faerie figures, dressed in vividly colored costumes adorned with flowers, sparkling with jewels of every shade. Voices singing jubilantly, peals of buoyant laughter. These were happy people. No matter their size. They were surfeited with merriment. As was I, watching on the sidelines, enchanted by the sights and sounds of their delight. I have never, since, experienced such total exultation.

Which made the sudden silence an oppressive heaviness on my ears. I had to shake my head to clear it of the gaiety of musical clamor I had been relishing. I looked around in curious wonder. Everyone had stopped their excited jigging. They were starting to move near the edge of the immense glade we were in. *Why?* I thought. What could have caused them to, abruptly, terminate their beloved dance? Then I saw. The figure of a man emerging from the woods.

Gilly.

I thought (I hoped) that the gathering faeries were going to attack Gilly, showing angry disapproval of his unforgivable behavior.

I was fated to disappointment on that one.

Embraces were rampant, handshakes plentiful. They were glad to see him. He had, I suppose, discharged his punishment in the Cairn and was now being welcomed back once more, a full-fledged member of the clan.

Garal was beside me then. I wanted Ruthana, but she was still resting. "He's passed his time in the Cairn," Garal told me.

"Now what?" I asked. Tremulously, I'm sure.

"He'll be all right now," Garal said. Not to comfort me, I felt. More to put me in place.

"I hope so," I said.

"I'll bring him over," Garal replied.

Before I could protest, *No, don't!* he was gone. I watched as he entered the group. Respectfully, they parted from their leader, and he moved to confront Gilly—who was smiling broadly from his friends' enthusiastic greetings.

Seeing Garal, he lost the smile, although its replacement was an expression of pleased respect. Garal gave him a welcoming hug, and Gilly smiled. They spoke briefly, Gilly nodding at whatever his father said, Garal now nodded as well, looking at his son with guarded assurance. He took Gilly by the arm and began to escort him from the clustering group. I felt myself begin to tense. Gilly had given me so much unwarranted angst. I was (justifiably, I thought) terrified of him. What was he going to do now? Especially, after spending—what was it?—six months in the Cairn. The ugliness of which was only imaginable to me.

But now—incredibly!—he was smiling at me. Had he forgiven me? Reformed? Wonder of wonders, as he approached, he broadened his smile. He extended his right hand to shake mine. I felt a wash of tremendous relief. He *had* forgiven me! Well, at least, accepted me.

"I'm back, Alexi," he said. His tone was warm. His handshake firm.

And tightening.

"Time," he said.

"*Gilly*," Garal warned him.

Too late. Gilly's left hand—in the pocket of his jacket—jerked out. He was clutching something in it.

"Gilly!" cried his father.

Just as Gilly hurled the gray powder in my face. In my eyes. Pain!

Blindness.

Chapter Thirty

Let me tell you what I've read about blindness.

The human eye—I'm talking about mine, I don't know if faerie eyes are different—is cradled in a socket known as an orbit. The eyelids protect it from dirt and bright light. Obviously not from poisonous gray powder—but I'll get to that. The white of the eye is called the *sclera*, its tissue opening the *cornea*. Behind the cornea is the *pupil*. Surrounding the pupil is the *iris*, the color of the eye. Behind that is the *lens* controlling the focus of the vision. Lining the back wall of the eyeball is the *retina*.

With me so far? I'm almost done.

At the center of the retina is the *macula*, providing central vision and fine details. Finally, the *optic nerve*, connecting the eye and brain. Why am I telling you this? Not sure. Still trying to understand what Gilly did to me. Something rotten to the eyes. That much I know.

I won't go into common vision aliments. You know them as well as I do: nearsightedness, farsightedness, astigmatism, presbyopia. (The last still a mystery to me.) None of them apply. Nor do vision problems caused by age. I was nineteen years old, for Christ's sake! My visual acuity was sharp as a tack. Until, of course . . .

Eye trauma? Getting closer now. Foreign objects? I'd classify that damned gray powder as a foreign object, sure. A *lot* of foreign objects. Symptoms? Sudden pain in the eye. Sudden decrease in vision. I'll say. Red eyes? Probably. I couldn't tell you. All I can recall of the griffin's (Magda's) eyes was a milky whiteness. I imagine that's what my eyes looked like. Those foreign objects obviously damaged my cornea and lens, probably more.

Chemical burns? No doubt. Direct contact? Of course. Eyeballs seared. Serious damage to the *conjunctiva* (the membrane that lines the eye) and the cornea, and more—in my case. Macular degeneration? A walk in the park. I was blind. Got that? *Blind.*

※　※　※

Things I know about blindness. Remember, I was *there.*

My first reaction? As indicated. *Pain.* My god, what pain! No wonder Magda screamed. I screamed. And not for ice cream. For relief. Which didn't come. I couldn't help screaming. My eyeballs were on fire. Imagine the sensation of holding your finger over a flaming burner. I mean holding it. Holding it. And *holding* it. Until you're sure your finger is going to ignite. As though the pain center in your brain is gonging EMERGENCY!! Add to that a fiery scorching in my face and in my throat. A hot, I mean *hot!*—swelling there. A conviction that I couldn't breathe. An expectation that, each time I *did* breathe, dragon fire would escape my lips.

More. A rush of hallucinations clogging my brain. Gilly's

face zooming in and out of vision, laughing with insane delight.
Black and white. Like a cheap, silent movie. Ruthana running
toward me, then away from me. Garal trying to push my head
under burning pond water. Magda thrusting a burning wand in
my face, expression maniacal. Her clothes catching fire. Her
tearing off her clothes. Her nipples shooting fire at me. Wild
laughter. Hers. Everyone's. Faeries dancing, burning, laughing.
The griffin attacking me, Magda's head on it, laughing at me.
A flaming owl in my face, screeching deafeningly. None of this
in sequence, mind you. An admixture of demented images and
noises. All made doubly, (triply, quadruply,) horrific by the burning pain in my eyes. And the *blindness*.

What I know about blindness.

1. It's scary as hell. Especially when you're only nineteen years
old and take 100 percent vision for granted.

2. Space—and time—lose all significance.

3. Calling it darkness is not accurate. *Total* darkness would be
a blessing. You still see (at least I did) occasional flashes of
light, some gray clouds. (Presaging nothing but further blindness, however.)

4. Not only is it terrifying, it's humiliating and frustrating as
well. Vacillating between both extremes. Complete visual
frustration, then blank, utter horror.

5. Headaches. (For me, anyway.) Nausea. Insomnia. God, how
I would have loved to chop up Gilly!

6. A few (very few) positives. You hear a lot more keenly. Un-distracted by sight, you sense a limitless environment around you. Not that these positives made the difference for me. At nineteen? Phooey! I say. *Phooey!*

7. The worst of all. In the beginning, I comforted myself by reliving my past. Not that I had a hell of a lot of it at nine-teen. But there were certainly some interesting highpoints in the past year plus.

The problem was that visual—even auditory—memories began to fade after a while. Even my dreams began a slow—and maddening!—deterioration. I suppose it was because my eyesight had been virtually (or actually) destroyed. So what I couldn't see in wakefulness, I couldn't see in sleep. Poor me. A nineteen-year-old is not exactly a fountainhead of philo-sophical insight. Mostly, I was pissed off. And unhappy, of course. Ruthana did her all to assuage my unhappiness. She really did. It helped. Somewhat.

Where was Gilly? Back in the Cairn. He did a dreadful thing. His sentence was lengthy, I was told. I wanted to hear he'd been convicted to a hangman's rope, a headsman's axe. No such luck. Such punishment was verboten in Faerieland. Too bad. I'd have done it myself. Hanged him or beheaded him or both. No such luck times two. I tried not to convey this dark ambition to Ruthana. She probably knew anyway. She *was* telepathic. So was I, the realization gradually dawned on me.

I, also, realized that, without making any kind of issue over it, Ruthana had increased my—how do I put it without sounding like a dope?—creative ability. My frustration was immense. I was filled with ideas. I yearned to write them down. Pour out endless novels—no such possibility when blind. What, dictate to Ruthana? Out of the question. My frustration—inflamed by my creative surge—increased my frustration exponentially. Ruthana assured me that I *would* write again, no doubt of it. Sure, I said, nodding my blind head. Not believing a word of it. But I guess she knew.

The fading—visual and mental—of my memories. I gave up trying to summon any vestige of recollection about my boyhood—the Captain, my mother, Veronica. Those recollections went fast. The best I could do, at first, was "seeing" my experiences in the trench, my meeting with—and later despair at his "death"—Harold. My trek to Gatford. In the beginning of my struggling remembrances, I was even able to visualize (quite well) the cottages I saw, even managing a chuckle at my recollection of so-called Comfort Cottage.

I should have bypassed my early days there. Joe. His cautioning. My first experience in the woods. By the time I came to Magda, my insights were already paling. I had to grit my brain-teeth in order to recapture those moments—my first visit to her remarkable house. Another chuckle recalling her remarkable bed—and the remarkable gymnastics that had taken place there. Magda's healing of my wound. The Good days. Then the darker ones. (I was almost glad to "see" *them* fade away.) The arguments. Expulsion from her house. Reconciliation. More good (as well as lustful) hours. Peace. At a price, naturally.

Then my meeting with Ruthana. Did she—in my blindness—know what I remembered? She must have—for the visual details suddenly became vivid. As though she was literally projecting them into my mind. She probably—wonderfully—was.

Because the following images were blurred again. Indistinct. My discovery (a coward's word for "theft") of Magda's hideous manuscript. All moments jumbled then. Only the final scene unmistakable. Magda's assault on me. My use of the powder. How did Ruthana foresee that need? My flight from Magda's blind rage. Return to the Middle Kingdom—and Ruthana.

From there, my memories were clear. (Ruthana *must* have been responsible for that.) My decrease in size. That pain seemed negligible now. My happy days with Ruthana. My afternoon with Garal and my education regarding true Reality. Not that the knowledge was very helpful with my eyes so totally out of commission.

Or were they? Such was the final stage of my blindness.

It took months. Had to. Week upon week of what? I couldn't tell you. I didn't know then and I don't know now.

Their healing process.

It was truly good of them. Wouldn't it have been more convenient—easier certainly—to leave me a blind, mortally wasted human being, stuck in their habitat? Surely. But they *were* good. Kind. Thoughtful. And they restored my sight.

Easier to say than to explain. How *did* they do it?

Granted, the powder seemed to be their own concoction. I learned during that healing time, so they knew what the ingredients were. Or *are*—I'm going on the assumption that the powder is still being produced, although it's difficult for me to know why. The faeries seem an unlikely people to utilize such toxic dust. There was, at least to me and, presumably, Ruthana, a valid reason to use it against Magda. I would have lost my head if I hadn't. That meant a good deal to me. Nineteen, you recall. My head still had some use to me.

Anyway, the ingredients. English ivy. Foxglove (a source of digitalis). Jimson weed. Holly leaves. Amanita (mushrooms). I urge you not to try the recipe at home. The amounts are essential. You'd never get them right. Thank God.

What did they do to heal me?

Procedures while I was awake—conscious, that is.

Put some kind of stinging wash in my eyes. The stinging was not so severe as the one I felt when Gilly first threw that damnable powder in my eyes. For days on end, I couldn't erase the memory of the griffin's (Magda's) milk-white sclera, pupil, and iris. As though they had been marinated in liquefied dough. Gradually, that image left me. Fortunately, being sightless, there was no way to witness my reflection. No mirrors, anyway; I'd have had to see it in a pond or something. I knew what it was, though. And was sharply reminded of it each time they (Garal, I presume, maybe Ruthana; I don't think there were any Middle Kingdom physicians, though I wouldn't bet on it) worked on me.

Anyway . . . the eyewash helped. A little. Very little. On occasion, I had a momentary view of gray (always gray) light in my eyes. Not that I could see anything. No, no. Good ol' Gilly had done an A-1 job on that. The wee bastard.

What else? Massages. To my temples and forehead. I knew that was being done by Ruthana. Her touch was unmistakable. Gentle—loving. And, of course, accompanied by her sweet voice. Telling me to never lose faith. My eyesight would return. She promised me. Sometimes I fell asleep while her fingers were massaging me. What I didn't know until later was that her mother sometimes relieved her when she tired—or had to breast-feed our daughter. On those occasions, I might awake—and never realize that Eana now massaged me, her touch, too, so gentle, so loving. Only when I spoke to her and she replied did I realize who it was. If I indicated any alarm at Ruthana's absence, her mother quickly reassured me.

Massages, then. And some kind of creamy salve (also stinging) applied directly to my eyeballs. And, often, cool, damp cloths laid across my eyes for—I guesstimate—an hour at a time. Mostly Ruthana would remain with me during those periods. I came to—almost—enjoy them. They were so quietly peaceful. During them, Ruthana would sing to me in her soft, angelic voice. I have, at times, attempted to transcribe a few of the melodies she sang, but the effort is a waste. The notes alone do not contain more than a hint of the magic conveyed by Ruthana's voice. Long ago, I gave up the attempt.

What else? The eye washes. The massages, the creamy salve—or salves, there may have been more than one kind. The cool damp cloths. The singing. For all I knew, that may have been part (an important part) of the healing process.

Anything more? Yes, I'm forgetting the drinks. The potions, I guess you'd call them. They were tasty; they were awful. Several varieties. I came to know the difference between them. Some were sweet and fruit-flavored, reminiscent of orange juice, apple juice, creamy milk. Others . . . yuck! Like drinking battery fluid! They *had* to be helpful, I told myself. Something tasting that ghastly had to be curative. Or why bother? Garal laughed when I told him that. His laughter, on that occasion, was not of any comfort, or pleasure. But I went along with the vile beverage, more concerned with sight repair than taste bud catering.

So that was when I was conscious. I can only surmise (wildly, I admit) what they did when I was either asleep or— very possibly—drugged. I know, by guess (and by gosh), that there were lapses of time I could not account for. So I assume that, during those lapses, I was, as they say, "knocked out." Probably one—or all—of those drinks rendered me unconscious.

What they did to me when I was "out," I couldn't say for certain.

I can guess, though.

They removed my eyes.

Why I say that, don't ask for proof. Only the vaguest of memories attest to it.

You've probably seen (I hope you *haven't*, it's a loathsome sight) photographs of eyeballs pulled out (either accidentally or deliberately) from their orbits—or, if you prefer, their sockets— and hanging down over cheeks, dangling by the optic nerve. It *has* been done, how often medically, I couldn't say. I'm sure it's occurred a thousand times in war, gouged out by blades, no doubt torn away completely. Sure. Good ol' mankind.

Well (even guessing that this actually took place), I'm sure that my faerie healer (most likely Garal, I doubt if Ruthana could have stomached it) used extreme care in removing my eyeballs from their orbits. How, I can't imagine. (I'd rather not imagine) Why? I can't imagine that either, but my guess has a bit more coherence.

To wash them. Dip them in some therapeutic medicine. If, as I understood it, the cells of my eyeballs were clogged with poison, eyewashes could have only a limited effect. A more direct and penetrating soak or "scrub" was called for.

How long my eyeballs were absent from my head, again I have no idea. I do recall one dream I had in which my eyeballs tumbled from their sockets and were grabbed up by a laughing shellycoat. Maybe that took place while Garal—or someone—was immersing my dislocated eyeball into whatever healing balm was on the schedule that day. Maybe not. It was a frightening dream, though. Jesus God, the whole experience was frightening; let me tell you! *Stay out of the damn woods!* No, I don't mean that. If you (males) have the good fortune to accost a Ruthana, you'll be blessed forever. The very sight of her—

Which was what mine was, at least three-quarters of a year following the Gilly attack. *Bing!* Like that. A shade suddenly raised before my eyes. Ruthana's darling face in front of me.

"I can *see!*" I cried. It might have been the most ecstatic moment of my life.

"*Oh, my love!*" she said, her voice close to strangled. I did not react to that. I held her close, my face pressed into her golden, fragrant hair. I believed her sobs were those of joy and gratitude.

I was wrong.

When I drew back to gaze once more at her exquisite face, I saw, for the first time, her expression of anguish, her cheeks soaked with flowing tears.

I misunderstood. "Do I look so bad?" I asked, convinced that I did.

"Oh, Alexi, no, *no*." she said, her words thickened by despair. She threw her arms around my neck and kissed me fervently. Her lips were wet with tears.

Now she drew back, quickly, a look of dread on her face. "*Oh, love,*" she murmured.

"What?" I asked. Her dread had entered my heart by now. "*What is it?*"

She could barely speak. She almost gasped the words.

Which were, "*You have to leave.*"

Chapter Thirty-one

I stood riveted to the spot. And she was gone. *Bing!* Like that again, in the faerie way. Why she left like that I didn't understand until later. She couldn't face what was about to happen. Her gone in an instant, Garal in front of me the next instant. At one time, their incredible ability to vanish or appear in a split second would have startled me. Now I only wondered why.

"I have to *leave?*" I asked

Garal nodded. "Yes."

"*Why?*" I asked, almost demanded. "What have I done?"

His smile was melancholy. "Nothing," he said.

"Then *why?*" I demanded now.

"Because of what you are," he said.

"A *human being?*" I said angrily. "It's Gilly, isn't it?"

"Part of it," he told me.

I didn't get it. "Can't you leave him in the Cairn?" I asked impatiently. I knew they couldn't but I had to ask.

"That isn't possible," Garal said. Dear God, his tone was very patient. I knew I was in for it.

"*Why not?*" I asked again, demanding. "Would it completely

disrupt your lifestyle? Is it better to let him keep trying to kill me?"

"No," he said quietly. Then, "That isn't it either."

"*Why not?*" I said. I knew that I was being argumentative. But I didn't want to lose Ruthana. "Garal," I went on, protesting, "why did you let me stay here in the first place? You must have known that Gilly hated me."

He was silent.

"*Well?*" I said. I knew my voice was strident now.

"We shouldn't have," he said. "It was a mistake."

"A *mistake?*" Now my voice was shrill. I knew I was losing. "*Why?!*"

"*You weren't meant to live in here,*" he said.

His voice and words made me tremble. "Why did you admit me, then?" My voice trembled as well. *Admit?* I remember thinking. What kind of word is that? It sounded stupid.

"Because of my daughter," he said.

"*Ruthana?*" I asked. Feeling immediately dumb. He knew her name. She was his daughter, for Chrissake! Hadn't he just said so?

He did not respond to my gaffe. All he said was, "Yes." Quietly. Still patiently. I think I would have preferred it if he lashed out. I should have known better. That was not Garal's way. He was the soul of containment.

"*You did it because of her?*" I asked, completely stressed by now.

"Of course," he said. "She is our princess."

I must have sounded dense. "She's a *princess?*" I asked.

"I don't mean royally," he explained. "I know she is your

princess though. And to Ruthana, you are her prince. Her love for you is boundless. So great that we allowed her pleas to let you in to be accepted. We made a mistake."

He sounded so doleful now that my defensive anger faded. "Why was it a mistake, Garal?" I asked. *I* actually sounded patient now.

He hesitated. Then said, "Since your sight returned, have you looked at yourself?"

"I beg your pardon," I said. A foolish thing to say—but I was so perplexed by his comment that I couldn't come up with anything better.

He wasted no further words. "You're *growing*," he said. "The diminishing was only temporary. In a while, you'll be a full-size human being—again. We didn't know that would happen."

"Can't you—diminish me again?" I asked. It was an honest inquiry. I meant it.

"We wouldn't dare to try," he said. "It would be too dangerous. Don't you recall the pain?"

"*Yes. I do,*" I told him. I *had* noticed an increase in the size of my hands and feet, a biting throb in my body. But I'd endure it all again. I couldn't bear to lose Ruthana. I told him so.

He only shook his head.

"Garal, I'll *do* it!" I cried. "Don't make me lose Ruthana!"

"Alex," he said. His use of my human name made me shudder. "You don't understand. It was all a mistake. You were never meant to be one of us."

His tone was so final, I had no response. Except one very weak, "Why?"

"Because it's not your world," he said. "No mortal can exist here for long. They'd become unhappy."

"*No*," I protested, "*I wouldn't*. I've been very happy here."

"It wouldn't last," Garal told me. "Do you think you are the first human being to stop here and want to stay?"

I must say that stunned me. I had no idea. "Did they . . . choose to diminish?" This was all unnerving news to me.

"Some," he said. "Some died trying. You *do* remember the pain."

"*None of them stayed?*" I asked. Already my human self was cutting in.

"They couldn't," said Garal. "Those who survived the diminishment could not survive their loss of spirit. If they remained, that spirit withered and died."

"*Oh, God*," was all I could say. I knew that he was telling me the truth. It was devastating to me.

Then I said, "Will I lose it all if I leave?"

He shook his head. His smile was kind. "No," he said. "Whatever is important to you will always remain with you."

❄ ❄ ❄

My farewell to Ruthana was a strange one—an ambivalent one.

At its most disturbing was Ruthana's desolation. At the other extreme, my mounting resentment that I was being ousted from Faerieland. *Why?* The question remained to plague me. It couldn't be because of Gilly. They knew about his hatred of me when they diminished me. Why do it then if his hostility wasn't an issue? Yet they did. Wasn't it possible that Ruthana could teach me all her powers so I could defend my-

self from Gilly's assaults? For that matter, after enough attacks had failed (I omitted more blinding powder from the
estimate), wouldn't he just give up? Get to know me? Discover that I wasn't such a bad person after all and become
my friend? That last possibility was the most improbable—
but I was really desperate for an out. I was willing to consider
any solution.

As for the rest? That, after a while, my spirit would wither
and die? The more I examined that scenario, the more far-
fetched it seemed. I was supposed to accept that as the main
reason to exit the Middle Kingdom? I simply couldn't believe
it. Continuous examination of the idea seemed to reveal it,
more and more, as threadbare and unacceptable.

So what did that leave me with?

My angelic love in total desolation. Clearly, she believed
what Garal had told me. Every word of it. *Every blessed word.*
How could I contend with that, much less obstruct it? It was
her life's conviction. Maybe it was even true. I didn't possess
the armament to subdue it. I'd only frighten her if I tried. I
didn't believe it. I didn't want to. She did. That was the gist of
it. It was part and parcel of her culture. Period. Amen. Selah.
Damn it!

So all I could do was hold her in my arms, kiss her on her
hair, her cheeks, her lips. She could not stop crying. "Weeping" is more the word. Mourning and grieving. Sobbing. Eyes
brimming with endless tears, cheeks remaining soaked with
them, no matter how often I patted them with my handkerchief; which, at length, grew soggy. I had to wring it out more
than once. Poor Ruthana. She was inconsolable. Ravaged by
sorrow.

Finally, I had to speak, though.

"Are you *sure?*" I asked.

Which only evoked a fresh torrent of tears, another moan of despair.

"I guess you are," I said.

For some reason, that brought on a smile. Coupled with her pained expression, it was reduced to a grimace. "Yes, Alex," she said.

Why does she so easily address me by my world name? I wondered. I let it go.

And yet I couldn't. Not completely. "Did you always know this?" I asked. *This?* I thought. What part of it?

She seemed to know. I'd forgotten she was telepathic. "Yes," she said.

"And yet—" I hesitated. I was slipping into exception speaking now.

I did it, anyway. Forgive me, Lord. She was so desolate. She deserved better.

But did I give it to her? I did not. Why? I was desolate myself. I was on the verge of losing the love of my life. Get it, folks? Nineteen. Not too smart. Hurting. Reacting, like the kid I still was.

"You knew it when they—diminished me?" I asked.

She drew in a long shuddering breath. "I wouldn't let myself believe it."

Wouldn't believe it, eh? The sharp-tongued lawyer in my brain contested her. I felt justification and guilt combined. Especially when Ruthana sobbed again and clung to me more tightly.

I understand. I wanted to say it. To comfort her. But my teenage brain (Jeez, I wasn't even twenty yet!) rebelled. *It isn't fair!* I wanted to say that. But, at least, I had enough control, enough sympathy. I didn't say it.

"It isn't Gilly, then," I did say; to calm her, I thought.

It was labor for her to speak. I noticed how red and inflamed her eyes were, poor sweet thing.

"No," she said. "I could have managed him."

Still, that assurance in herself where her brother was concerned. I didn't count her reply. *What about the shellycoat?* I could have said. *What about the powder in my eyes?* I said nothing. Why bother anyway?

I was losing direction, I realized. I was about to give up the only woman (*was* she a woman? a girl? an astral being?) I had ever loved. Or (I now know) would ever love. I tightened my grip on her and sobbed myself; I confess, it startled me. "I *love* you, Ruthana. I *adore* you."

"Oh, Alexi!" she cried. God bless her, she called me by the name I'd taken in her land. "I love you so! *I'll die when you leave!*"

"*Don't say that,*" I pleaded. "*I need to remember you soaring through the trees. Invisible. Enchanted. Bathing your exquisite body in the waterfall unseen, and laughing in the woods, causing leaves to rustle. Dancing in the glades, a vision of innocence and playfulness.* Don't take all that away from me!" (Where did those words *come* from?)

"Oh, Alexi, never, never! I *promise* you!" We had our last passionate kiss. Then she spoke aloud to me, a final blessing by someone she called the White Lady. I have never forgotten it.

What has not worked will now succeed.
Those who cause you distress will change or vanish from
*   your life.*
Doors of opportunity will open unexpectedly.
What you believe will prosper.
Your mind will be free.
New ideas will come to you.
You will be kind and generous to others.
You will be truthful in all things.

Smiling now, her tears controlled, Ruthana reached into a pocket and took out something. Which she laid in the palm of my right hand.

The most enormous emerald I have ever seen. Maybe not as big as Harold's gold lump, but *big*. I have never shown it to an expert, God knows never thought of selling it. You know why.

"I'll keep it always," I told her. "I've had enough gray dust in my life."

She laughed, then looked serious. "I *want* you to keep it always. To remember me by."

"I will," I promised her. A promise I have always kept.

I was already dressed in human clothes Eana had altered to fit me. Despite my growth I was still a good deal short of six feet two inches—although I was sure I'd regain that height. My bones and flesh were still in the achy act (oh dear, combo) of restructuring. Soon I'd be back to the world. Which, at the moment, I had scant desire to rejoin.

Anyway, Ruthana walked me through the woods (still bright with summer green), her hand in mine. Strange but, now, she seemed to me more of the different race she was—all variant, all powerful, totally mysterious. I glanced at her once. I preferred to look ahead and, believe it or not, although she still was my beautiful Ruthana, something in her expression differed from what I had grown accustomed to. She was closer to being an exotic, faraway creature who had—it now struck me as miraculous—told me that she loved me.

I looked at the woods. I felt a pang of regret that I had said good-bye (I guess she was aware of my presence) to my daughter. For my entire life, I have conjectured what she looked like as she aged. However gradually, I could not imagine. Ruthana? If she was fortunate. My genes surely held her back, poor child. I was handsome, yes, but after all, I was a human being and what could a faerie progeny expect from that?

※ ※ ※

When we reached the path, I saw that we were directly opposite Magda's burned-out house. The Gatford citizens—a pox on them—had never bothered to repair it. I wonder, now (circa 1982), if they ever did.

Maybe they couldn't. Maybe they'd tried and been dissuaded. "Don't go in there—if you're tempted to," Ruthana told me. "*She's still there.*"

That gave me the shudders. I used that imaginary scene in one of my novels. *MIDNIGHT WITCH*, as I recall.

Ruthana kissed me gently. "Remember me," she murmured.

"Good God, do you think I won't?" I said. With my usual teenage conceit.

She smiled, understanding. She still had that ability, I recognized. "No, I don't," she said. "I know you will."

"I always will," I swore. "Oh, God, I'm going to miss you, Ruthana!"

She kissed me again, more ardently now. Then she smiled. I saw tears rising in her eyes. "I'm going to vanish now," she said.

And so she did. One second there, one second not. My Ruthana. Disappearing in the woods.

Not in my heart.

Chapter Thirty-two

I suspect this will be the final chapter of my book. It pains me to say it. Why? Because I've spent so many pleasant hours telling you my story. I hate to see it end. However—

To continue.

I returned to the States six months after my twentieth birthday—which I celebrated by tossing my cookies in the North Atlantic. I'd been doing it all week—the crossing marked by endless tidal waves. I call them that. They were probably just big waves. I have a tendency to exaggerate—or have you noticed? But not the story itself. I swear to God it's true. Well, believe it or not.

I'd say I returned to the United States, but as we know, they're hardly united. Massachusetts—Texas? Sure. Practically twins. West Virginia—California? Joined at the hip. You get the point.

For some insane reason, I took a trip to Brooklyn to see the old homestead. Not that I intended to ring the doorbell. The thought of being confronted by *him* was not to be considered. I don't think he was there, anyway. I should have known when I saw, parked at the curb, an automobile that was probably driven by a sentient being. Not the funereal, hearselike limo *he* usually chauffeured. Sitting straight up, that "Get out of my way, I am Captain Bradford White, USN" look on his iron-bound face.

No, *he* wasn't there. Thank God for that. What if, by accident, he'd stepped out, seen me, and without a moment's hesitation, began to lambaste me for my failings? I would have had to kill him or, at least, taken advantage of my newfound faerie power (not utilized yet) to reduce him to a pulp. Just kidding. I've never had that much power. It would have been nice, though.

I couldn't stay in Brooklyn. The remotest possibility that the Captain and I might cross paths was enough to send me scuttling for the subway. I took a train to Lower Manhattan, where I rented a small (translation: "cheap") apartment. I purchased a portable typewriter and paper, contacted a publisher, and asked if he'd like to see my novel. He said yes and, making a long story short (for once), it got published. *MIDNIGHT* sold well enough, and he said would I place a bit more emphasis on the "scary" stuff in the second novel? That was amenable to me. After losing Ruthana and vomiting my way across the Atlantic, I was in little mood to take on a tale of romance.

So I wrote *MIDNIGHT DARKNESS*. The publisher like the repetition of the word "midnight," so I suggested a series of Gothic novels using that word. He agreed and asked if I minded the pen name Arthur Black. I didn't. In my frame of mind, he could have called me Daniel Death. (I even suggested that, which amused him no end.) So Arthur Black entered the world. Happy Birthday, Mr. Black! Long may you engrave! Which he did. Twenty-seven of the damn atrocities.

One nice thing happened while I was occupied in my boiling pot. I had (almost) become accustomed to having nightmares about my days (and nights) in the trenches. I would have thought any nightmares would have to do with the monsters I'd faced in Faerieland. Not so. No nightmares at all, as a matter of fact. Only lovely dreams about Ruthana, the two of us walking in the lovely woods, hand in hand, talking. Embracing. Making love softly. Wonderful dreams. I came to the assumption that Ruthana was responsible for the cessation of the awful trench dreams, commencement of the lovely ones. Why not? She had the power. I knew she did.

Then the dreams stopped altogether.

☒   ☒   ☒

It was June of 1921. I was walking on Sixth Avenue. I'd sold my third MIDNIGHT novel. I was acquiring a modest reputation as a writer (not an *author*, God knew) of "dependable" material. There was talk (okay with me) of extending my contract to include five more MIDNIGHT novels. I'd even later allowed myself the luxury of permitting my basic social crankiness to enter *MIDNIGHT MONSTERS*, said monster being the offspring of the Hiroshima blast. I pride (*pride?* come on) myself that I was one of the first writers to create these atomic offshoots. As my Professor Morlock expressed it, "How sad to have released the inner power of the atom only to kill." But now I'm pontificating. Sorry.

Where was I? Walking on Sixth Avenue. Brooding over Ruthana. I did that all the time. The loss had so embittered me that it colored my every approach to life. Frankly, I was surprised that the emerald hadn't turned back to dust. That I couldn't understand. It comforted me (a little) that I still re-tained this symbol of my feeling for Ruthana. I often sat at night, staring at it, really expecting it to recede to its original state, making it known that Ruthana was lost to me forever.

It never did. That seemed a mystery to me. But I accepted it. It was all I had. That glittering jewel of perfect green, un-changing, beautiful, reassuring.

I almost missed the window—it was in an antique shop. I'd been there several times. Then I saw *it* and I turned back sud-denly, staring at—a figure. Eight inches high. Immaculately sculpted. I couldn't take my eyes off it. Had he (no, that was absurd) posed for it? Impossible, I thought. And yet it was *him.* I would have sworn to it.

Garal.

I stared at the figure intently, endlessly. That kind, won-derful face. Deep with knowledge, warm with understanding. How could the artist manage that?

I had to know.

Entering the shop, I accosted the clerk—who turned out to be the owner of the shop. I never got his name.

"That figure," I started.

"Figure?" He smiled at me.

"In the window," I said. *Of the faerie,* I almost added, then didn't. "The—old man."

"Oh, yes. Garal," said the owner.

Something like an electric shock spasmed through me. "Garal," I repeated numbly.

"Yes," said the man. "Would you like to take a look at him?"

I could only nod. I wondered if he could see the stricken

expression I was sure was on my face. If he did, he said noth-ing about it. He walked to the front window, picked up the figure, and carried it back. I almost cried aloud at him for holding Garal by the head. But I controlled my reaction. He'd think me even stranger than I felt he already did.

He set the figure down, and I pretended to examine it, an appraising potential buyer. I even heard myself murmur, "Hmm." As though considering purchase. I tried to ignore the heavy pulsing of my heart. Close to pounding, in fact.

I began to speak, but several separate questions emerged in a jumble of nervous sounds. I pretended to be amused by my verbal medley, took a deep breath, and inquired (attempt-edly casual). "The name? Where did it come from?"

"No idea," said the man. "That's been its name as long as I can remember."

"You don't know where it came from?" I said.

"The man who sold it to me, I guess," replied the man.

"Was he . . . English?" I asked.

"Think he was."

"I see." Nodding. Feigning not to be deeply involved as I was. Had the artist lived with the clan? Had he left as I did? Had he sculpted an image of Garal? Too many unanswerable questions. Certainly in a Sixth Avenue antique shop.

I was unable to pursue the matter further. I paid for the figure ($250, a good chunk of my money—although I would have put out a thousand if it had come to that). Heart still pounding, I took a taxicab back to my apartment (another expense I had never dared to venture). I wanted to get home. There was something I had to do.

※ ※ ※

There was a cast-iron frying pan in my kitchenette. I'd never touched it. It reminded me too much of the terrible night in Comfort Cottage when I was—misguidedly—trying to protect myself from attack by Ruthana. Now I had to touch it. Had to almost fill it with water. Seeing the figure of Garal gave me the idea—I thought the inspiration—of contacting Ruthana by scrying.

I carried the partially full pan into the main room and set it down in a patch of shadows. Then, lying on my chest beside it, I concentrated on the motionless water. It had worked so immediately when I'd contacted Haral. If it was true that Ruthana had bestowed some manner of psychic awareness on me, wouldn't it be as immediate now?

Immediate it was. A flash of clouds across the surface of the water. Red. Flaming scarlet. Then what looked like mist. Or smoke. And the sound of distant screaming. Why was Ruthana screaming?

Suddenly, a ghostlike phantom came hurtling at me. Shrieking with rage. Demented, murderous rage. How could Ruthana—?

In an instant, I knew it wasn't her.

Magda's twisted maniacal face filled the water surface. Teeth bared, a scream of insane hatred flooding from her mouth. Dear God, how she hated me!

With a cry of dread, I overturned the frying pan. Water splashed across the wood floor, the screaming stopped. "I should have known," I kept repeating in a feeble voice. To this day, I can invoke a sense of sickened dread in myself, remembering those hideous moments. Guilt as well. How much I'd hurt Magda, I never could decide. I tried a lot.

※ ※ ※

It was not until the next afternoon that I did what I should have done in the first place.

I pulled down all the shades, making the parlor relatively dim. I was going to burn a candle I'd purchased in a psychic shop, then decided against it. Either I had some powers of my own, or this attempt was doomed to failure. But I would not succumb to Magda-style *wicce*. I would perform this rite with simple honesty.

Garal's figure was set in the middle of the floor. I sat, cross-legged, facing it.

"Garal," I said. I didn't chant it. This was without occult guile. I spoke to him directly, as though he literally existed in the figure. Garal. My mentor. My teacher. My dear friend. "Please come to me," I asked. "I need to talk with you."

Silence in my parlor. Except, of course, for the occasional rumble of a passing elevated train.

"Please come to me, Garal," I said. I was absolutely certain that he would.

I don't know if the figure suddenly expanded to become him (I'd lost track of the figure), but whatever happened, there he was, just as abruptly as he'd appeared in the woods of Northern England.

"Yes, Alex," he said. As casually as though his appearance were a matter-of-fact occurrence.

The pounding of my heart had lessened. I was with my teacher again. His smile filled me with tranquillity. And yet I had to know. "Ruthana," I said. "Is she all right?"

His expression grew disheartened. "Ruthana left us in April," he said.

I couldn't speak. The room grew dark around me. *Left* us? Then I spoke. I had to know for certain.

"*Died?*" I asked. Was that my voice? Surely not. It was so thin, so weak, so shaky. "*Passed on?*"

"Yes, Alex," he said.

Then no more, regarding me in silence. April, it occurred to me, was when the lovely dreams had ended. It *was* her, then.

"Why?" I finally said.

"Her heart broke," Garal answered.

"*No,*" I sobbed. "She told me—"

"That she'd be all right?" said Garal.

"*Yes.*" I was trying not to cry but felt tears streaming down my cheeks.

"She wanted you to leave without regret," Garal said. "She loved you that much."

"*And I loved her,*" I told him, my voice broken to the point of inaudibility.

"I know you did," said Garal. "It was a faultless love." He said nothing more, watching my helpless weeping sympathetically.

"And my daughter?" I asked.

"She is well," Garal told me.

I stiffened then, reactive anger in my still-immature brain. "I suppose Gilly's glad I lost Ruthana," I said.

"Gilly is gone," Garal told me.

"*Good,*" I said. "I hope a hunter shot him."

"He did," said Garal. "Gilly shifted to the body of a wolf and chased the hunter too far."

"*Good,*" I said again. At least there was that small satisfaction. (inadequate combo). It did nothing to alleviate my heartache about Ruthana's death, but it helped.

Garal vanished then. A smile. A blessing. And he was gone.

I could easily understand how a heart could break. For days, I felt that mine was on the verge of severing. I thought I felt the split occurring. I prayed for it to happen all the way. So I could—possibly—be reunited with Ruthana. I *wanted* my heart to break. Very much.

⚶ ⚶ ⚶

It didn't, though. Damn sturdy organ. It remained intact.

So there's my story. I hope you liked it. Believed it, anyway. It *did* happen. All of it. Exactly as I described it. Please believe me when I say it *really happened.*

Well, a few more details. In 1936, I moved to Los Angeles. By then, five more of my MIDNIGHT series had seen print, one of them selling to the movies. I settled into a beach apartment, wrote two more MIDNIGHT books, and started drinking. After a year of that foolishness, I attended an AA meeting, which helped.

I never married. Why bother? Ruthana was my only love.

Anything else? Yes. One telling detail. I still have the emerald. I keep it in a safety box. No one knows anything about it.

Remarkably enough, the emerald looks unaffected by time.

It still glows with an unearthly shimmer. I guess it always will. It signifies, to me, that Ruthana still loves me. And is waiting for me.

Somewhere.

Editorial Note

The author known as Arthur Black (born Alexander White) died in his sleep on May 20, 1985. The following verse was found in his belongings:

AT THAT MAGIC TIME
IN THAT MAGIC PLACE
I MET THE ONE TRUE LOVE
OF MY ENTIRE LIFE
MY FAERIE PRINCESS
RUTHANA

Bibliography

Andrews, Ted. *Enchantment of the Faerie Realm.* St. Paul: Llewellyn Publications, 1993.

Cavendish, Richard, ed. *Man, Myth & Magic*, Vols. 1, 2, 14, 23. New York: Marshall Cavendish, 1970.

Dick, Stewart. *The Cottage Homes of England.* London: Crescent, 1909.

Ettinger, Albert M., and A. Churchill. *A Doughboy with the Fighting Sixty-ninth: A Remembrance of World War I.* Shippensburg, Pennsylvania: White Mane Publishing Company, 1992.

Finley, Guy. *The Intimate Enemy.* St. Paul: Llewellyn Publications, 1997.

Greeves, Lydia. *The Perfect English Country Cottage.* New York: Thames and Hudson, 1995.

MacManus, D. A. *The Middle Kingdom.* London: Max Parrish, 1959.

McCoy, Edain. *A Witch's Guide to Faery Folk.* St. Paul: Llewellyn Publications, 1994.

Matheson, Richard. *The Path: Metaphysics for the '90s.* Santa Barbara: Capra Press, 1993.

Mynne, Hugh. *The Faerie Way.* St. Paul: Llewellyn Publications, 1996.

National Geographic. New York: National Geographic Society, January 2008.

Randolph, Keith. *The Truth About Psychic Self-Defense.* St. Paul: Llewellyn Publications, 1995.

Schur, Norman W. *British English, A to Zed.* New York: Facts on File, HarperCollins, 1987, 1991.

Slesin, Suzanne, and Cliff Stafford. *English Style.* New York: Clarkson N. Potter, 1984.

Stepanich, Kisma K. *Faery Wicca: Theory & Magick, A Book of Shadows & Light.* St. Paul: Llewellyn Publications, 1994.

This Fabulous Century: Sixty Years of American Life. New York: Time-Life Books, 1969.

Tyson, Donald. *Soul Flight: Astral Projection & the Magical Universe.* Woodbury, Minnesota: Llewellyn Worldwide, 2007.

Waters, Colin. *Sexual Hauntings Through the Ages.* New York: Dorset Press, 1994.

Winter, J. M. *The Experience of World War I.* New York: Oxford University Press, 1989.